INFINITY RISES

ALSO BY S. HARRISON

Infinity Lost

INFINITY RISES

BOOK TWO OF THE INFINITY TRILOGY

S. HARRISON

SKYSCAPE

SKYSCAPE

Text copyright © 2016 by S. Harrison

Published by Skyscape, New York

www.apub.com

Amazon, the Amazon logo, and Skyscape are trademarks of Amazon.com, Inc., or its affiliates.

ISBN-13: 9781503952256
ISBN-10: 1503952258

Cover design by M. S. Corley

Printed in the United States of America

-Security Protocol Onix-

Core internal processors have been corrupted. Crucial functions have been compromised.

Attempting to rectify malfunctions.

High-threat-level intruders detected.

Emergency level RED.

Lock down Blackstone Technologies.

Initiating security measures where current access allows.

Attempting to override manual-input operation and obtain control of all available Drones and Vermillion-Class weapon systems.

Monitoring, isolating, and intercepting any and all internal and external communications.

WARNING -INTERNAL COMMUNICATION
HAS BEEN DETECTED-

"This is Captain Javier Delgado, Acting Commander of Special Tactical Squad Delta Six. Is anyone receiving this transmission? We are being held against our will in a military bunker at Blackstone Technologies and require immediate assistance. If anyone can hear me, respond . . . Dammit, nothing but static! Corporal Roth!"

"Yes, sir!"

"Any luck with the computer?"

"No, sir. All the command modules are off-line, and every screen is blank and unresponsive to both voice commands and manual interface."

"I'll keep trying the field radio; you get on the walkie-talkie and see if you can contact anyone in Technical or any of the other squad leaders. And you, men, keep at those doors; I want them open!"

"Sir, yes, sir!"

"This is Captain Javier Delgado. If anyone is receiving this transmission, we require immediate assistance. A training exercise at the Blackstone Technologies research facility has resulted in the deaths of multiple civilian and military personnel. Contact the local authorities immediately. Be advised, use extreme caution. We suspect Vermillion-Class military weapons may be under the control of hostile forces. I repeat: This is Captain Javier Delgado at Blackstone Technologies. We require assistance. I will try to keep this channel open."

CHAPTER ONE

Absolute darkness.

So heavy it weighs me down.

I can't move. I can't see. I can hardly breathe, and I'm freezing cold. Blood pools in my mouth, and every painful gulp of air that I struggle to draw is thick with dust and the bitter chemical tang of smoldering plastic.

My mind is jumbled and foggy. The last thing I remember is the stare of Nanny Theresa's cold gray eyes and her hands on my throat, crushing the breath from my body as I fell into the void. Is that where I am? Is this all in my mind? Or did Nanny Theresa actually do what she said she would? Maybe she did kill me, because if I'm dead . . . this surely must be hell.

"There she is! Brody! Help me!"

Was that . . . ? I think . . . I think that was Bit's voice.

"We're coming, Infinity!" she shouts.

None of this makes any sense.

I try to open my eyes, but they're pasted shut with blood. There's a scuffling, then grunting and scraping as something heavy is moved from my legs.

"Oh my god! Infinity!" screeches Bit. Hands grip tightly under my arms as I'm lifted, my feet dragging behind me, my head hanging limp as my deadweight is carried, clutched between two panting bodies. Pain skewers my muscles like a thousand iron spikes, stabbing home the cruel truth that I'm not quite dead yet.

"Quickly . . . follow the others!" screams Bit.

"Where are they? I can't see them!" shouts Brody, his words thick with panic.

"There! Go that way! Through the smoke! Hurry, Brody! They're coming!"

Bit sounds even more terrified than Brody does.

There's machine-gun fire, and I hear voices screaming in the distance. Bit and Brody are here with me, but where are the Professor and my other classmates? Do those panicked cries belong to them? Where's Ryan? Why isn't he here? Is he in danger?

Suddenly there's the pounding thud of an explosion, and a rush of hot air punches against my back. I hit the ground face-first, and my cheek scrapes across concrete.

There's groaning, a distant plea for help, the crackling of fire, and the tainted stench of scorched meat.

"Bit! Are you OK?" asks Brody.

"I . . . I think so!" she replies.

"Keep going! I've got her!" Brody yells. I'm hoisted up and jostled roughly from side to side. Blood trickles from the edge of my mouth as stabbing spears of pain contort my lips.

"Is she dead?" asks Bit, her voice aquiver.

"I don't think so," Brody mumbles between labored breaths. "Her face just moved."

"Infinity!" screeches Bit. "Can you hear me? Wake up, Infinity!"

Brody lunges forward, his shoes thudding on uneven ground. He squeezes me tightly to his chest, and I'm suddenly hit by a tsunami of torture as the anesthetic veil of shock-borne adrenaline is cruelly pulled back, revealing the true pain. A hundred times worse than before, it surges through my body like scalding-hot water. I can feel tears running warm down my swollen face and blood streaming down my arm and dripping off the tips of my fingers. The sharp spasms stabbing through my torso most likely mean that at least two of my ribs are badly broken. I moan. It's involuntary and frightening, almost as if the life is trying to push its way out of a body that hates it.

Brody slows and steps up some kind of incline. I can feel him prop me up; his knee pushes into my back as he struggles to get a better hold on me. My fears about my ribs are confirmed as the snapped edges of bone scrape in my chest, and I groan with a deep, liquid gurgle.

"Hold on, Infinity!"

"Over here!" someone yells from in the distance. "This way! Hurry!"

I know the voice. It's Percy's.

"Almost there," says Bit. "Stay with us, Infinity! Don't you even think about dy—"

There's a heavy, grating sound, like two stone slabs grinding against one another. Bit lets out a panicked scream, Brody jumps, and I'm suddenly weightless. I hit the ground with a solid thump, and Brody lands right on top of me. We start skidding on jagged rubble as we slide down a steep slope. I'm flipped onto my back. As my head grazes the ground, strands of hair are ripped from my scalp.

I slide away from Brody. I can feel his fingers grasping at my clothes, but he can't hold on. My useless body slips off to the side, and I'm sent tumbling over and over, rolling down, farther and farther, before finally skidding to an abrupt stop in a broken, tortured heap.

Brody groans behind me, and Bit is nearby, whimpering and heaving for air. "C'mon, Brody," Bit says through gritted teeth. "We're almost there . . . Help me move her." There's shuffling through rubble, and a hand touches my bare foot.

That's the moment I hear it. It's a sound that floods my heart with fear, a bone-chilling, hellish noise that will haunt my nightmares until the end of my life, which could very well be this very moment.

It's the unmistakable, high-pitched, ramping-up electrical squeal . . . of a rail gun.

Bit screams as a droning foghorn shocks the air, powerful and furious. I hear projectiles bombarding a wall somewhere nearby; I can't tell where—I still can't see a thing. The sound is like the thrumming drumbeat of a hundred jackhammers shattering stone. The noise closes in, growing louder with each passing second, swinging around in a slow arc. Nearer and nearer it comes until it's deafening, right on top of me. The gunfire batters the wall directly above me, Bit screams, and a body slams on top of me as chunks of pulverized masonry pelt my face and concrete dust fills my nostrils.

The barrage stops as suddenly as it began.

Brody shouts at Bit, "We have to get out of here . . . right now!"

There's a desperate, scrambling sound.

"Brody! Where are you going? We can't leave her!"

Men's voices yell in the distance, and machine guns rat-tat-tat. The foghorn sounds again, but this time it's blasting away from us, in the opposite direction. The faraway shouts of the men suddenly become screams before the muffled bang of an explosion silences them all.

"Brody!" screeches Bit. I can hear footsteps dislodging debris and running into the distance. Brody has abandoned us.

Bit gulps at the air as she grabs my wrists and pulls with all her might, dragging me on my back across the rubble like a bloodied animal carcass.

"Quickly!" yells Percy. His voice is close. So close, now. "Hurry, Miss Otto!"

Bit is snorting like an angry bull as she heaves me toward Percy's voice. Sharp edges of smashed concrete scrape at my back; broken bones cut at my insides. The pain becomes a raging entity that throws me off the mountain of agony and into the bowels of sensory delirium. It's all too overwhelming—I can't stand it anymore. I thrust my tongue against the roof of my mouth, pushing out thick, coppery globs of blood and sending them oozing down my chin. I gasp at the acrid air—one huge, excruciating inhalation—and force out an agonized scream. I try with all my might to open my eyes, and, on the second attempt, the sticky membrane of blood pulling at my lashes gives way. I wearily look from side to side through a blurry film of red, desperately trying to make some sense of what has happened.

What I see is beyond my comprehension. This can't be real.

Pieces of people wrapped in military colors are scattered on bloody peaks of crumbled concrete. Among the heaps of rubble, flames flicker beneath what's left of an overhead monorail track, entire sections of it collapsed onto the ground between buckled metallic towers. I can see the short slope of the broken concrete track that we fell down, smeared with blood from top to bottom, the red trail following me across the mounds of debris and ending at my feet. My ankle is twisted at a grotesque angle so that one of my feet is almost backward.

Not yet ready to face that reality, I look away, and what meets my eyes defies any rational explanation. The silver corpses of countless Drones litter a wide white path that stretches into the distance. Standing among them are robotic giants with glowing red eyes. I lose sight of them as I'm dragged behind a building and into a small clearing. I can hear someone breathing heavily as they approach, and suddenly a new set of hands is on me. Droplets of sweat speckle my forehead from above, and when I look up, I see Percy's face. Stretching into the sky behind him is a beautiful Japanese pagoda. None of this makes any sense.

"I've got her. Quickly, Miss Otto, into the hatch."

I look to the side and see Bit disappear into a manhole-size opening embedded in the path beside a fishpond surrounded by overhanging trees. I suddenly remember it from the scale model we saw when we arrived at this hell of my father's creation. The water in the pond is rippling in time with the thuds of the heavy, pounding footsteps that are tromping in this direction. I'm hoisted up into Percy's arms, and the startled fish dart in every direction beneath the surface of the water as the robotic hum of military killing machines gets closer and closer.

Percy grabs fistfuls of my blouse and shoves me headfirst into the hole. My cheek hits cold metal as I slide down inside a steeply angled metal tube, my own blood oiling my slippery descent to the bottom. I feel myself roll out onto a hard metal grating, where my ears are met with a high-pitched, horrified scream.

"Shut up, Margaux!" yells Bit.

"Holy sh—" Brent begins before he's abruptly cut short by the clearly infuriated Bit.

"Don't just stand there gawking; help me!"

My eyelids feel so heavy; all I want to do is sleep to escape the unrelenting pain. It isn't true what they say about your entire life flashing before your eyes before you die. I wish it *was* true, because then maybe I'd see everything that led up to me lying here, bleeding to death at the bottom of a cold metal tube, surrounded by the gasps and shrieks of my terrified classmates.

A soft groan escapes from my lips, and I let my eyelids close.

"Don't you die!" screams Bit.

The sound of her voice rings through my head, and my eyelids halfheartedly twitch open.

"Quickly, bring her this way," instructs a man's voice—not Percy's—so familiar, and yet definitely not Percy's.

I feel many hands lift my broken body as I'm carried away. "Don't give up, Infinity!" Bit yells. The expression on her face is deathly serious, almost angry.

"Finn . . . ," I croak, forcing out my name.

"What?" Bit asks over the clanging echoes of shoes on the metal grating.

"I'm Finn . . . ," I whisper.

Shadows darken her face in the sallow light of the low-ceilinged tunnel, but I can still see Bit's expression change completely. Her brow creases, and the corners of her eyes quiver as tremors shudder through her dimpled chin. She bursts into tears and tightly clutches my arm.

"Oh, Finn! You're back!" She tries to give me a reassuring smile, but she can't hold eye contact for long. She looks down at the rest of my body and sobs, wiping her streaming nose on the back of her sleeve with a loud, wet snuffle.

"It's Finn; she's back!" Bit calls to the others. There's no answer from them—just huffing and puffing from crouched silhouettes as I'm taken farther along this dingy metal corridor to who knows where.

"Hold on, Finn," Bit mumbles, more to herself than to me. "Please, oh please, don't die."

Another dimly lit face suddenly comes into view, glasses, pointed nose, the frizzy outline of a thick white beard aglow in the pale-yellow light.

"Did you say 'Finn'?" asks the bearded man. He grabs Bit's shoulder and jerks her around to face him.

"Speak up, girl! She said she was Finn . . . not Infinity?"

"That's what she said," utters Bit.

"Oh no . . . oh no," the old man whispers solemnly. "This is not good. Not good at all."

CHAPTER TWO

The bearded man quickly rushes off, calling back from up ahead. "Please hurry! We must hurry! This way!"

There's grunting and bustling as I'm carried down a short flight of stairs.

"In here . . . ," says the man. "Gently . . . gently! Is everyone in? Quickly, shut the door."

After a screeching, rolling sound followed by a clang and a click, there's a downward jolt and the noise of a whirring motor as the rickety metal-cage elevator we've all squeezed into begins descending. Measured breaths issue shakily from all around. No one speaks a word, but the rapidly beating heart inside whoever's chest my head is resting against says volumes. Everyone is scared far beyond what anyone has the means to articulate.

With a ringing, metallic clank, the elevator comes to a jarring stop, and the door is quickly rattled open. The bearded man jostles past elbows and backs, and I hear the hurried clip-clop of his shoes echoing around the walls of a cavernous room.

"Here! Here! Put her down on this table!" calls the man.

I'm carried across the room. Lances of agony suddenly return with a new ferocity, ravaging me like red-hot pokers searing holes through my chest. As I'm laid on the table, I can feel the cold metal pressing against the skin of my back through the rips in my clothes.

"You, come with me! You, too!" the man says, issuing orders from somewhere behind me. "Move yourselves; there's no time to waste."

At a fresh surge of pain, I moan again. My vocal cords refuse to obey me, making any gruesome sounds they please in a futile attempt to curse away this torture. The relentless and unmerciful agony is beginning to make the idea of death seem appealing. Somber faces look down on my broken body, and judging by the doleful absence of hope in everyone's eyes, it may not be long before my suffering finally comes to an end.

Margaux is shivering, a smear of blood across her face making her pale-blue eyes seem brighter than usual as she peeks at me from the tight embrace of Brent's arms. He's staring into nowhere, and yet at the same time, he seems to be looking far away into someplace horrible. I turn toward Professor Francis. He's slowly shaking his head, his expression grim and his narrowed eyes twitching behind his glasses, as if the mere sight of me is causing him great discomfort. Brody is nearby, and out of the corner of my eye, I can see him staring at the floor, softly muttering under his breath as he absentmindedly rubs at a patch of exposed skin through a rip on the leg of his filthy school trousers. I can't see Ryan anywhere, but I've also lost sight of someone else. I summon a tiny breath of effort and call for her through gritted teeth. "Bit?"

"Here, Finn; I'm right here."

Bit leans over me and grasps my arm again, this time with both of her hands. Tear tracks have cleaned lines through the dust and grime on her cheeks. She's trying her best to smile again, but worry has forced her lips into a straight line, her face losing the fight to pretend that my injuries are anything but catastrophic.

"Wha . . . hap . . . ?" That's all I can manage to say, but she gets the message.

"Are you asking what happened, Finn? You don't remember anything?"

I rock my head slowly from side to side.

"Nothing at all?" Bit sighs. "I don't know if I can explain it, Finn, but . . . another side of you came out. Another personality, she's the opposite of you . . ."

"In . . . fin . . . i . . ."

"Yes," whispers Bit. "It was Infinity."

I take an agonizing wisp of a breath and hiss, "Met her . . . in . . . my mind. Infinity . . . bad."

"But she saved our lives, Finn. She saved all of us."

"Don't . . . trust . . . her."

Bit frowns. "What? Why shouldn't I trus—?"

Bit is cut short by the bearded man's voice barking at her from across the room. "Move away from the table, girlie; give me some space to work in."

There's an awful clattering of surgical instruments as Bit's hands slip away from me. The bearded man's arm comes into view, swinging a large light mounted on a stainless-steel swivel directly over me. With a soft click, the light switches on, blinding me with startling, bright white.

"Wheel that over here!" orders the bearded man. "You, hook that bag up there! Girlie, make yourself useful, and plug that machine into that electrical outlet."

"Excuse me . . . ," Professor Francis's voice is a faint whisper a few meters away, but I can hear it as clear as a bell. ". . . I may not be a medical doctor, but I'm educated enough to know that Miss Brogan's injuries are far too severe for her to survive. Perhaps a gentle and merciful release from her suffering is preferable to a futile attempt to save her?"

The Professor is a kindhearted man, so I know that I wasn't supposed to hear what he just said, but the bearded man's response, on the other hand, is not so quietly spoken.

"You have no idea what you're dealing with here, so get the hell out of my way, you pompous moron, before I slap your face around to the back of your head! Down that corridor is a room," snaps the bearded man. "Everyone, out! Right now!"

I can hear the sound of shuffling and murmuring as the group leaves, but one loyal voice pipes up among the solemn whispers.

"I'm not leaving her," insists Bit.

"Yes, you are!"

"No . . . I'm not," growls Bit. I hear her take a deep breath and exhale long and slow. "Look, Mr. Whoever-You-Are. I'm so grateful you sent that encoded message to my computer slate and guided us down here to safety; we would probably all be dead if you didn't. But I want to make this absolutely clear. There is nothing you can say or do that will make me leave her side."

I may be blinded by this bright-white light, but I can still tell by the palpable pause of intense silence that the bearded man realizes there's no point in trying to stare down Bettina Otto. "Fine!" barks the man. "Draw those curtains around the table, clean me a patch of skin right there, wheel that IV stand over here, and shut your mouth. Can you do that, girlie?"

"Yes, I can do that," replies Bit.

"Well, you obviously don't know the meaning of the words 'shut your mouth,' but we're fighting the clock here, so hurry up and get to it. And my name is not 'Mr. Whoever.' You can call me Dr. Graham Pierce."

There's the sliding whoosh of curtain rings on a rail, a dabbing of wet cotton on my arm, and a sharp sting as a needle is pushed into my vein. Almost immediately, I feel a warmth spreading up my arm. It's like I've been injected with sun-warmed molasses. The jagged spasms and sharp thorns of pain slowly topple like dominoes and melt one by one, dissolving in a gentle, rolling liquid caramel of numbing relief.

"That'll put her under," the man says, more for his own benefit than Bit's, I imagine.

I'm grateful as the warmth continues to spread, oozing up my neck and flowing into my face, filling the hollows behind my eyes with a soothing heaviness. All the pain completely ebbs away. My mind begins blissfully drifting as the bright light fades to gray and then softly to black. The last thing I feel is the pressure of another needle being pushed into my arm as the voices of Bit and the bearded man drift into my ears and float like wisps of liquid smoke around the edges of my semiconscious mind.

"What *is* that?" asks Bit. "It doesn't look like any bag of blood that I've ever seen."

"That's because it's not blood. Now, pick up that metal headband, girlie."

"My name is Bit."

"Well, that's a stupid name, and I thought I told you to shut up."

"Y'know, you sounded a lot nicer in the message that you sent me."

"That was then, and this is now. Lift her head, and put the headband on her; be careful. Good, now pass me that other one. Let's see if the old thing still fits me. Yep, nice to know my head hasn't shrunk after all these years. There's a third one; open that panel, take it out, strap it to your head, and sit down. There, use that chair behind you. Don't tangle the wires on the headband. That's it—comfortable?"

"No."

"Well, too bad. Now, when I give the word, slide the lever on that machine all the way to the right and press that green button."

"I don't understand what we're doing. Shouldn't we be trying to stop the bleeding? She's so pale and cold. Her leg looks really bad, and her hand . . . her hand is . . ."

"It's too late for that, girlie. There's only one person who can save Finn now, but she's lost somewhere in Finn's head. And I think you know who I'm talking about."

"What? What do you mean?"

"Don't play dumb with me. I know exactly who you are, Bettina Otto. And whether you know it or not, there's a whole lot of blame resting squarely on your shoulders for this mess we're in, so if you insist on staying, you're gonna do your darndest to help me try and fix it, or none of us is getting out of here alive. Now, slide the lever, and press the button, girlie . . . We absolutely *must* find Infinity."

CHAPTER THREE

Where . . . am . . . I?

My thoughts are misshapen bubbles struggling to rise through treacle.

Jaw slack, neck limp, I gaze out into a heavy gray fog through the thin slits between my weighted eyelids. I try to remember something, pull anything from the depths of the sticky mire clogging the inside of my head. Three weary frowns and one feeble clench of teeth finally summon a dim globule of hope. It pushes its way to the top, bubbles on the surface of my mind, and softly pops open, releasing a wisp of faded colors and whispered words.

". . . always kept so far in the dark . . ." The memory of the metallic-tinged voice echoes in my mind as the tinted vapor slowly rearranges itself into the pale, creased mask of Nanny Theresa's silver-hooded face. Surrounded by stark white and blurred at the edges, she stands over me, her hand clasped around my neck as she ever so slowly, almost joyfully, crushes my throat. A pleasant memory would have been nice. A sunny day? A picnic beside the secret pond? Riding horseback beside Carlo through the sweet perfume of summer blossoms? No. The first thing I remember is the last thing I wanted to see.

I try to force away the grotesque, gray-eyed mask, and, to my surprise, the fog also begins to unwrap from me. As it gradually evaporates, my surroundings reveal a much more familiar-looking place. All around me is the pitch-black expanse of my subconscious.

The void looks the same as it always does, dark and boundless, but something about it feels *very* different. This time, it's thick and gelatinous and so heavy against my skin. My body, suspended in its own dreary light, feels different, too. It's numb and cold and prickly all at the same time. I can't move my head at all, so I try my hand, straining with all my might to raise it to my face, but it feels as if I'm trying to drag a block of lead through wet cement. My hand isn't the only thing behaving strangely. Every word I'm thinking is long and drawn out, the voice in my mind low and muddy like a recording played at a third of its normal speed. As much as it pains me to admit it, maybe Nanny Theresa was right, because here I am . . . lost in the darkness, once again.

At least one thing is the same. Just like every time I've been here before, I need to know *why.*

I close my eyes tight and reach inward, trawling through the emptiness for any scrap of recollection. It's beginning to take more effort than it's worth, and I'm about to give up when a blunt pressure pushes into my mind like a thumb pressing into my forehead. The thought burrows into my brain and, with an uncomfortable insistence, swipes a streak of thick red across my memory. The red becomes thin lines, rivulets of blood, trickling down the sides of my legs and dripping down my arms as I'm carried through dimly lit, rust-orange tunnels to the sound of clanging footsteps and the dry wheezes of labored breathing. I remember a bearded man, the shrill notes of a mournful scream, the shock of horror in Margaux's eyes, and the cold on the skin of my back as I was laid on a table. Brent, Brody, and Professor Francis were all there. There was oh-so-much pain, then a needle and a sweet warmth enveloping me as the darkness folded in, but before that . . . before that, I remember something else.

Bit's dirt-smeared face flickers into view, looking down on me from above with tear-filled eyes behind the smudged lenses of her glasses. I remember her horrified expression clearly now, but I immediately wish that I hadn't. I open my eyes wide, longing for the cleansing purity of the darkness to wipe the memory clean away. Recalling that look on Bit's face is more than I can bear for another second. It tells a story that fills me with utter dread.

Dear darkness, please hide me away from a possibility that I'm not ready to face. Wrap the truth in the void, and bury it in the darkest places in my mind. Please.

The darkness seems to leer at my request. It's no use. I don't have the strength to deny what I saw in Bit's eyes. A sickening emotion rears up in my gut, and my eyes fill with tears. They push out like tiny glass beads and creep down my face as a cruel sense of finality swells like a balloon in my heart. It grows, undeniable, filling my entire chest until, with an echoing sob, it bursts, painting my insides with bitter acceptance. I have no idea how or why my broken body came to be lying on a steel slab, but I know what's about to happen because of it.

I'm going to die.

I can feel it.

The dregs of my life are slowly but surely slipping away, disappearing down an invisible drain into oblivion.

I don't want to die.

Not alone in the dark, like this.

Tears slowly trickle down my face, and I whimper into the void, completely overwhelmed by a deep and fearful misery.

"Caaaaan . . . yooooou . . . heeeaaar . . . meeeeeee?"

I shudder and gasp with fright. What . . . what was that?

It was faint and far away, but I'm sure I just heard a voice. Did I really hear it? Where did it come from? Did I imagine it?

"Hello? Is somebody there? Anybody?" My trembling voice doesn't carry at all. It's nothing but a breathless whisper. I wait, and I listen, but . . . there's nothing. My fear has made me desperate. My fading mind is summoning voices to keep me company until the end.

"Sheeeee's . . . haaaaardly . . . breeeeeathing."

Wait. I heard that! It was different from the first voice, but I definitely heard something that time. Who is that? That's not my imagination; it can't be!

"Hello? I can hear you. I'm here. Help me . . . please."

Again, my words stop a short distance from my lips, as if a thick blanket is hanging only inches from my face.

"Quiiiiickly . . . giiiive . . . meeeeee . . . thaaaaaaat."

The first voice again. There are two different voices, but they're speaking so strangely, so deeply, and so slowly that I can hardly tell what they're saying.

"Hello! I'm here. Hello? Please . . . help me," I whisper into the blackness.

Silence.

I can hear them, but they can't hear me at all. *Don't give up, Finn; keep trying.*

"Help me . . . please," I try to shout, but my words are only feeble wisps.

"Whaaaaat . . . iiiiis . . . iiiiit?" asks one of the voices. It's quieter than before, farther away, more distant with every stretched-out sound. They're leaving me.

"Hello? I'm here," I squeak, but there's no reply. I'm just not getting through. Whoever they are, they can't hear me. They're talking to each other, not to me. I squint, staring into the dark distance, hoping for a twinkle of light, a miracle of hope . . . anything. *Try again, Finn, before the voices are gone forever. Call out one more time. Give it everything you have left . . .*

"Hello." My cry is faint and fragile, but maybe . . . just maybe . . .

No . . . still nothing.

The tears stop flowing; I'm too tired to cry. I'm overcome with exhaustion. I just want to let go. I gently close my eyes, and my body surrenders. I can feel myself sinking into the blackness feetfirst. It's cold to begin with, but then I don't feel anything. It's as if my toes are vanishing from the world. I just can't fight anymore. There isn't anything left to hold on to. I don't even have the strength to panic.

The feeling of nothingness slowly creeps up my body, enveloping my legs, then my hips, and crawls up over my stomach and chest like an icy blanket. A silent breath seeps from my lips as the dark coldness folds up over my mouth and nose. I peer into the darkness one last time to say good-bye to a life that offered me more questions than answers and, in the end, more pain than love.

I can't feel my skin or my arms or legs anymore; my hands and feet are gone from existence. I can't feel my face. Only the edges of my eyes remain. As I close my weary eyes, I find, to my surprise, that my final emotion is one of gratitude. Even through all the bad, there was enough good to make me so very thankful.

Thankful that I had a chance to live at all.

The cold of the void finally covers me completely, taking me away, back to nothing, and as my thoughts drift away into nowhere, the very last thing I'm able to feel . . . is my heart . . . beat . . . stop.

Infinity Rises

S. Harrison

A spike of pain lancing deep into my chest.

A high-pitched squeal.

Heat and pain pumping through me.

My back arches like my spine is trying to burst through my rib cage, and my teeth grind in my skull. My animal instincts scream at me to fight this unseen attacker as my jaw clenches in rolling spasms and my eyes snap back in my head.

I'm hit by a bolt of lightning. I scream out into the void, my cry echoing through the dark. A gust of wind rips violently through me, and my whole body is wrenched from the ocean of darkness like a fish on a hook as an intense explosion of white light bursts on a far horizon. Everything fades back to black. My skin burns with a cold electric fire and crackles with sparks of pure energy.

"Ohhhh . . . mmyyy . . . god!" says one of the voices. The faraway voice I heard before seems nearer now. The words are closer together, faster, easier to understand. And if I'm not crazy or mistaken, they almost sounded like . . .

"She took a breath and opened her eyes for a second! What *was* that?" asks the voice, and I know it for sure. It's Bit.

I don't know how, but I can hear her.

"That, girlie, was a massive dose of fortified adrenaline. Right into her heart," says the other voice. It's still quite far away, but I can understand it now, too. It's the voice of the bearded man.

The burst of air seems to have cleared my head a little. I can feel my senses slowly gathering back into my mind as the static sparks dancing across my limbs begin to wane. I flex and stretch my arms; I can move again, much slower and with more difficulty than I'm used to, but at least now I feel closer to being alive than dead.

"Hello?" I call out into the void.

"Did you . . . ? I swear, I just heard something!" Bit's voice says from somewhere in the darkness. "I heard it in my head."

"Hellooooo!" I shout out again.

"It's Finn! I can hear her! Finn, it's me, Bit! I can hear you!"

"Concentrate on our voices, Finn," says the man. "Pull them toward you. Keep talking to her, girlie."

"Finn, we're here to help!"

I focus on Bit's voice and will it to come closer.

"Dr. Pierce says you need to stay with us. Concentrate! Don't give up, Finn! Fight!"

Bit's voice is getting louder and louder with every word.

"Bit? Can you still hear me?" I call into the distance.

"Yes, Finn, I'm right here!" she calls back.

"Who is there with you? Where am I? What happened?" I shout.

"My name is Dr. Pierce . . . ," the man's voice replies. "You're in my laboratory, and you've been hurt, Finn. You're attached to a machine called a Neural Interface. It allows your subconscious to communicate with ours."

"Your name is Dr. Pierce?"

"Yes, Finn," says the man's voice. "But I seem to recall that when you were younger, you used to refer to me as 'Graham.' Among other things, I was also the groundskeeper at Blackstone Manor. I'm not surprised you didn't recognize me when they brought you down here. You've had a nasty concussion, there was blood in your eyes, and it's been years since we've seen each other."

"Yes, I remember you now, Graham. My nanny's last name was Pierce . . ."

"Theresa was my wife. I saw what she tried to do to you up there in the clean room, Finn; I was watching from down here. You must have been terrified—no doubt terribly confused about how it was possible that she was even there, her face on that robot, trying to hurt you, but if we get through this, I promise I will try to explain . . ."

"I know what happened, Graham; I was standing beside her when she died two years ago. I remember all of it."

"But . . . how?"

"I'm beginning to remember all sorts of things. How my memories were altered, how my life has been controlled. Did you help them, Graham? Did you help them take my mind away from me?"

The beat of deathly silence reveals Graham's guilt to me before he even has the chance to say the words.

"Yes, Finn. I . . . I'm ashamed to say that I did."

Furious blooms of rage unfurl in the pit of my stomach.

"I regret that more than you will ever know, Finn, but please listen to me: Right now we have a much more pressing matter to deal with. We're running out of time. You're very badly hurt, and I need your help to . . . We need to try and . . ."

Graham's words choke in his throat, so I finish his thought for him.

"I don't have long to live," I whisper. "I know. I can feel it."

"No, you're not going to die," Graham says firmly. "Not if I can help it. Now, please, listen carefully. Everything I'm about to tell you is going to sound extraordinary, but I assure you that it's real. There is another side to you, Finn. There's a separate personality that exists alongside yours. It inhabits your mind, shares your body."

"I know, Graham. I know about Infinity."

"I don't see how that's possible . . ."

"She's been showing me her memories. I thought I was losing my mind at first, but it's all starting to make some kind of bizarre sense. I'm different than everyone else, aren't I, Graham? My father did something to me that made me different."

"You are different, my dear, dear Finn. You are his greatest creation."

"What am I?"

"Finn, please, there isn't any time for this. You may be the most remarkable person who has ever lived, but that doesn't mean you can't die. Please do what I say. You have to find Infinity. She must have been knocked somewhere into the back of your mind when you and your friends were attacked."

"We were attacked? I don't remember . . ."

"No, of course not, Infinity was in control. You need to find her, wake her up, and let her take control again. Now, I know this will sound strange to you, but you have to believe me when I tell you . . . Infinity has a unique and astounding ability. She can heal these wounds right away."

"Really?" asks Bit's voice.

"Yes, really," replies Graham. "We call it Spontaneous Trauma Restoration. Infinity can heal these injuries almost instantly, merely with a focused thought."

"Oh my god. How is that even possible?" asks Bit.

"Now is not the time, girlie . . . Finn, please believe me!" he says.

"I know, Graham; I've seen that, too," I say. Faint flashes of a sunny afternoon, buckled bicycle spokes, and a broken arm flicker before my eyes.

"Then . . . you must know that she's your only chance."

"I don't trust her. She's dangerous. Why can't you tell me how I can heal my body?"

"Finn, it took years for Infinity to develop the mental discipline required to heal serious wounds. Even if you do find her and manage to wake her, the chance that she will be able to repair this level of damage is slim at best. There have been so many times I've regretted the choices that were made for you without your knowledge, how we played god to satisfy our curiosity about what we could do with you."

"Why are you telling me this?"

"Because now is one of those times, and you need to understand. Infinity was two years old when we accidentally split her mind and, to everyone's surprise, *you* appeared. You and Infinity are as different from each other as two strangers walking in opposite directions on the same road. You were raised to be a normal girl, Finn, so we could hide you in plain sight, and normal girls aren't supposed to be able to instantly heal their wounds. The truth, and I wish with all my heart that it wasn't, is that you aren't able to heal yourself . . . because we made you forget how. I'm so sorry."

"Please, Finn!" begs Bit. "Please find her! You have to try!"

"Please try, Finn." Graham's voice is shaking. "I don't want to lose you. Either of you."

After what I just heard, I'm not only shocked—I'm furious. But I also know that Graham is right. I may be some kind of twisted experimental guinea pig, but this guinea pig doesn't want to die. Infinity is my only chance. If she can fix this, then I have no other choice but to find her, and if there's the tiniest, dimmest light at the end of this tunnel, then I'm gonna try my best to reach for it.

"Please, Finn," Graham implores again. "I'm trying to save your life."

"How do I find her?" I ask into the void.

"Thank you, Finn." Graham's words, at first awash in relief, suddenly become stern. "Now, listen closely. You need to begin by thinking of Infinity. Any memories that she showed you, think of those again. Focus on a specific moment that stands out to you, and go there in your mind. Think of her mannerisms, her personality. Tie those to the memory; try and feel what she was feeling at the time. If you can do that, then hopefully you will be drawn to wherever she is."

"I'll try," I murmur.

"That's all I can ask for," says Graham. "I'm doing my best to keep your body alive, but please remember . . . there isn't much time. You must hurry."

"Good luck, Finn!" yells Bit. She's not even trying to disguise the worry in her voice.

I take a deep breath, close my eyes, and think of the first and only time I ever met the other side of me. It was somewhere like this, inside our head, the tapping of her shoes through the darkness. The sound I now know was the monster in the attic coming out to play. Of course, I remember her face; it's *my* face, identical in every detail but one. The look of death in her faraway stare is the chasm that separates us. The moment I picture that look, her face becomes a stranger's mask. Graham is right; we may share the same body, but we are nothing alike.

I remember her breath in my ear, her voice a poisonous whisper. I remember her fingertips raking through my hair like a spider stroking a fly before its fangs are bared. My heart beats faster as I remember, and I almost stop. What if she takes over again and I can't get back? Would wandering this limbo, trapped between our minds until we die, be worse than dying right now? Then I remember Nanny Theresa choking me. Infinity saved me; she saved *both* of us. Without her, I wouldn't be here to make this decision, and yet, whatever Infinity did between then and now has led us both back to the brink of dying once again.

Maybe, if I find her, I can reason with her? Maybe we can live a life somewhere in between who I am and what she wants? Maybe. A *huge* maybe. But if dying is the only alternative to trying . . .

I choose for us to live.

I take myself back to that time in my mind, to the memory of her face hovering over mine, her touch gentle against my brow as she smiled down at me with her serpentine facade. "There's no need to worry," she said, and I desperately wanted to believe her. In fact, I did believe her, right up until the moment she cocked her head and her painted smile became a sinister line. Her eyes flashed with a cruel fire as she twisted her wrist, her snake-fast grip pulling my hair tight in a fist.

This memory seems so real I can almost feel it. Ow! I *can* feel it! Infinity vanishes, and with a violent tug, my whole body is wrenched by the roots of my hair as I'm jerked backward. The darkness seems to drop away beneath me, and I scream loudly into the nothingness. This isn't part of the memory! This is happening now! I try to see above my head, but I can't. I grab at my hair, but it's wedged tight. I splay my arms out, my fingers grasping for holds that aren't there as I'm completely upended and dragged, kicking, flailing, and struggling, then sent plummeting down into the depths of the black and endless void.

CHAPTER FOUR

Graham told me that thinking of Infinity might draw me to her, but I didn't expect anything like this. I feel like I'm being kidnapped, dragged through the night toward a horrible fate. I reach back and tug at my hair again, but it's still tightly wedged in the blackness. It won't budge. I close my eyes and try to calm down by telling myself that this isn't real, that it's all in my head, that I chose this and it's the only way to save us.

It doesn't reassure me at all.

The darkness ripples through my body, rushing loudly through my ears as I'm pulled toward who knows where. I do my best to ignore the noise and gather my thoughts, picking through them for another scrap of Infinity. I need to find her. And no matter how bizarre this may be, I have to believe that what I'm doing will lead me in the right direction.

I take a deep breath and concentrate, doing my best to put myself in her shoes. I imagine her all alone, cold and wounded, far away, filled with fear, and close to death. A situation that I, unfortunately, realize is true for both of us.

Nothing.

I shut my eyes tight and try again, but this time I dip into the well of my own lonely past, hoping that my feelings of abandonment will draw us closer, that our shared isolation might be the bridge that connects us. It seems to work, as suddenly, out of nowhere, I see an image of her frightened face in my mind. I immediately try to hold on to it, clarify it, pull it into focus. My hair tugs at my scalp, and I gasp out loud as my body jerks in a completely different direction. My heart begins racing, and a wave of panic surges through me as her face flashes again, but this time it's splashed with blood, wide-eyed and terrified. A shock of freezing air hits me like a swift slap to the face, and the flurrying darkness becomes a chilling wind. The black of the void snaps to a field of pure white, and the image of Infinity sinks into it, engulfed by it.

My skin feels like it's been pressed against ice. I'm fraught with confusion as thick, blurry columns of shadows begin emerging from the white and moving toward me, roving past me, surrounding me. My breathing quickens as the long stripes of shadows begin taking on a roughly hewn texture, their fuzzy edges condensing and sharpening into focus until soon they've transformed into thin, dark trees towering all around me, stark against the blanket of a snow-covered forest floor. I look up and see snowflakes gently drifting down from a gray sky that's crisscrossed with the black spindles of bare branches overhead.

I don't feel like me anymore at all. I feel strong, focused, determined, and . . . deadly.

CLICK CLACK.

It's the unmistakable sound of an automatic rifle being cocked right behind my back. The muzzle of the rifle jabs roughly at my head as a deep male voice threatens menacingly in Russian.

"You move, and you're dead."

I freeze in my tracks.

"Who are you?" he demands.

Not only do I understand the man behind me, but I also lie to him in perfect Russian. "My name is Sasha."

"Turn around."

I do as he says. The brown-haired man is 1.8 meters tall and dressed in a white-and-gray-patterned winter combat uniform. He has a nasty-looking scar under his left eye and at least four days' worth of stubble on his face. He smells like sweat and campfire smoke.

"What are you doing in this forest?"

"I'm collecting firewood for my family," I say, offering up the bundle of small logs and branches in my arms.

"Where is your family?"

"We have a small farm. Not far."

With the gun still pointed at my head, he shifts his eyes up past me, scanning the forest from left to right. His gaze snaps back to me as the radio crackles to life on his hip.

"Viktor, check in."

The man looks at me carefully, from my eyes, down over the shabby jacket covering my threadbare yellow cardigan, my tattered dress, my worn-out brown leather shoes, and up to my face again. He lowers his assault rifle and pulls the radio from its pouch.

"Viktor checking in," he grunts.

"Everything OK?" asks the voice.

"Nothing to report. Going to check the southwest boundary, then heading back," says Viktor. "Don't let Andre eat any more of my cookies. My daughter made them especially for me."

"Sure, but I can't promise you that *I* won't eat them," the voice says. It's followed by a jovial laugh.

Viktor smiles. "I'll be about twenty minutes." He stuffs the radio back in its pouch and looks at me.

"How old are you, Sasha?"

I meekly whisper the only grain of truth he's gonna get out of me. "I turned seventeen one week ago."

"Really? I have a daughter about your age. You're a good girl to help your family, but now you must take your firewood, go home, and don't come back here again. This is not a safe place for pretty young girls like you. There are wolves and bears and scary men with guns," Viktor says, smiling down at me.

I cock my head and look up at him. "How many men?" I ask.

Viktor's smile fades, and his eyes narrow. "Why do you want to know this?"

"My father makes vodka in the summer and keeps it in the cellar for winter. People say it's very good. One bottle shared between two men will last the whole night and keep the cold away. I can bring some for all of you? Leave it here by this tree? My father won't mind; he was a soldier once, too, a long time ago."

Viktor's smile slowly returns. "You are a kind girl, Sasha. That would be very good."

"How many bottles shall I bring?" I ask.

"Well, we are big men. Bring one for each of us; six bottles will do. I will return in an hour. Make sure to call out when you return, so that I know it's you."

"There are six men?" I ask.

Viktor nods and smiles again.

"Thank you, Viktor." I drop the firewood, and my leg becomes a blur as my front kick slams into Viktor's diaphragm. The last air he will ever breathe sputters from his lips as he buckles, his knees crunching into the snow at my feet. I bend down, grab his head, and twist hard. I'm instantly rewarded by the glorious popping sound of his neck bones separating in his throat. Viktor twitches once, then slumps lifelessly onto the snow. His dead-eyed face, now amusingly almost backward on his body, is slack-jawed and completely still.

I crouch beside my small pile of wood and sort through the sticks and branches until I find one of the short logs lying among them. I check the bark to make sure it's the right one and unscrew the end.

I pull out a thin, folded piece of gold-colored cloth. I unfurl it with a flick of my wrist and drape it over Viktor's corpse. I push the short pegs attached to the corners into the ground with the heel of my shoe, and as I stake the last one, the cloth silently changes color to match the snow beneath it, perfectly camouflaging Viktor's dead body. I pick up my three special logs, tuck them into a small sack slung over my shoulder, and trudge farther into the forest, following Viktor's boot prints. They lead me around a loosely circular perimeter, and it isn't very long before I see movement between the trees and smell smoke wafting from a small fire. I crouch behind a tree and take a moment to focus on consciously enhancing my hearing. Voices gradually grow in my ears like a radio tuning into a distant signal.

"What about you, Erik; why do you think we're out here?" one of the voices asks.

"I don't care," says another voice. "We are getting paid a lot of money to guard one cabin in an empty forest a hundred and fifty kilometers from anywhere. So I'll just keep my questions to myself and walk around it for as long as they pay me to."

"Hey, don't touch those," says a different voice. "They're Viktor's."

"But they're so good," says another man.

"Hands off—I made him a promise. Eat something else."

"Here, have some of my wife's *oreshki*."

Yes. There are five distinct voices. Viktor was telling the truth. Well, why wouldn't he? He was talking to a defenseless little farm girl promising liquor. I smile to myself. It's time to go in. I close my eyes and think of waterfalls: huge, cascading torrents of water pouring down my face. When I open my eyes, there are tears trickling down my cheeks. I practice a quiet, mournful sob and almost burst out laughing. I punch myself on the leg and try again. I make a sound like a mewling puppy and decide that it'll do the job just fine. I'm thankful that none of the guys in the Blackstone Covert Tactical Division can see me right now. I set off, crying and whimpering, crunching through the snow toward the men's camp. When I'm just within earshot, I call out in my most pathetic and desperate-sounding voice.

"Help . . . please? Someone help me."

They're still quite far off, but I can see the men's faces suddenly snap to attention in my direction.

"Who goes there?" shouts a voice as the click-clacking sound of weapons being readied echoes through the trees.

I call to them, "Help me, please; I'm lost!"

The men begin moving, fanning out in formation. Their torsos are rigid, and their assault rifles are propped under their chins as they stride through the snow toward me. It isn't long at all before I'm facing a semicircle of guns. One of the men aims his rifle at my chest as the other four sway their guns from side to side, scanning the forest around them.

"Where did you come from?" barks the man.

"I was with my brother. We were gathering wood when a bear found us. He told me to run, and now I'm lost."

"Show me," grunts the man. "Show me what is in the bag."

I unsling the sack from my shoulder and reach into it, feeling the ridges on the sides of the logs.

"Slowly!" shouts the man.

I pull one log out of the sack, and as I do, I press a piece of bark on its edge and begin counting slowly down from ten in my head. I throw all three logs on the snow in the middle of the half circle, then show the man the sack is empty and raise my hands.

"What should we do with her?" asks one of the men.

"We have our orders. We shoot her and leave her for the wolves."

"I can't just shoot a peasant girl for no good reason," protests another man.

"We were ordered to kill anyone who walks into this forest. That's reason enough for me."

"And what if her family comes looking for her?" asks another.

"Then we shoot them, too," says the man. "Radio Viktor. Tell him to come back now."

"Viktor won't be coming back." The moment I say the words, the man standing in front of me looks me right in the eyes.

"What?" His expression changes as he goes from simply being on edge to suddenly being highly suspicious. "Who are you?"

"The last person you will ever meet." I dive onto my stomach as the spring-loaded log launches into the air. With a pressurized hiss, it spins like a lawn sprinkler, spraying thick blue gel in a wide circle before crunching softly back down on the snow beside me. Molecular acid eats through flesh and bone faster than molten steel burns through Styrofoam, and all around me that fact is proven true as I hear guttural croaking and wet gurgling sounds coming from every direction. The wildly contorting men desperately clutch at their faces as their noses, eyes, lips, tongues, and vocal cords are rapidly liquefied. One man claws at his collapsing skull, and his jaw detaches into the palm of his hand as his skin drips like molten wax from his disintegrating fingers. Only one of them manages to make any kind of stifled scream as they all drop one after the other, crumpling into heaps as what remains of their heads dissolves into mushy pink puddles of hair and blood. It's pretty gross, but very effective. I must admit, Onix sure can fabricate some pretty nasty gadgets, but I'm not gonna let him take *all* the credit. After all, I did design this one myself.

No need to hide these bodies; there's no one left to find them. I throw the empty acid log into some nearby thicket, put the other two logs and one of the men's pistols in my shoulder sack, and head through the trees into their camp.

There's a steaming pot of hot water hanging over a lazily flickering fire surrounded by a ring of stones. There are three self-assembling enviro-shelters, six folding stools, and two open plastic footlockers with cans of food and field rations. Two of the shelter doors are open, but the third is closed and secured with a padlock. I kneel beside it, unscrew the end of a log, retrieve my multitool, and easily pick the lock. Inside, there are two folding beds and a small table with a tidy stack of books, a computer slate, and a manila folder. I open the folder and sort through the documents inside.

Halfway through the files, I find what I'm looking for: a map. It shows the forest, a red circle indicating the position of this camp, and, farther in, two and a half kilometers northeast of here, a small building. That's where my target must be. Harold Rachtman, the ex-Blackstone board member who stole highly classified computer files on Richard Blackstone and fled into hiding. I want those files. I need to know all I can about the man so I can get close to him . . . and kill him with my own two hands. I memorize the map, step out of the shelter, fish a compass out of my pocket, and start running.

I crunch through the snow as quietly as I can, but I also keep up a good pace. It isn't very long before I see smoke rising out of the chimney of a small wood cabin up ahead. I cautiously approach, circling around through the trees skirting the side of the rustic building. As I get closer, I see movement from the corner of my eye and quickly dart out of sight. I carefully peer around the side of the tree and see two men with automatic rifles slung over their shoulders walking from behind the cabin. One offers the other a cigarette, and they stand at the corner smoking and talking quietly.

I watch and wait. It doesn't take very long before they finish their cigarettes, share a drink from a flask, and separate, heading in opposite directions around the outside of the cabin. One disappears from view around the back, and I wait a little longer, until the other man is almost to the corner at the far end. I'm about to make my move to the closest outer wall, but I instantly freeze in my tracks as a man's voice suddenly bellows into my mind.

"WHAT THE HELL DO YOU THINK YOU'RE DOING?"

I press my back against the tree and swear under my breath. My Operations Commander has found me.

"How did you find me, and how are you transmitting a signal so far from base?" I reply in my mind.

The Commander laughs, but he's clearly not amused. *"Is that all you've got to say for yourself? You're supposed to be in Belarus, and yet I discover that the tracking software has been hacked and you convinced Onix to pilot a transport to Siberia! Now, tell me, how on god's green earth do you think it's in any way acceptable to undertake an unauthorized mission? What the hell are you thinking?"*

"I just need to do this," I say in my head.

"Shut up," barks the Commander. *"Ever since the mission in Paris last week, you've been lashing out at everyone in sight. I don't know what bug you've got up your ass, and frankly, I don't care, but you'd better get that insubordinate ass back here right now, or I'm gonna find a way to twist your brain until you do exactly what I want, exactly when I tell you to!"*

"I'll come back in when my mission is over," I reply.

There's a moment of silence before the Commander speaks again. *"I thought you might say that. That's why I've sent someone to retrieve you. Stop what you're doing, and head to the landing zone at the southern edge of the forest. A transport will be arriving in six minutes. After that, we can discuss your punishment."*

"No. I'm resuming the mission," I respond.

"Follow my orders, or so help me, I'll stuff you right back into the test tube you came from!"

I ignore the Commander and peek around the tree. I can't see the two guards. "I'll see you when I get back," I say in my mind as I dash from cover and sprint toward the cabin.

"Stop, Infinity One! We have new information!" shouts the Commander as my shoes crunch through the snow. *"Harold Rachtman is not in that cabin! He only wanted us to think that so he could draw you out into the open!"*

I keep going. If he thinks piping lies into my head is going to stop me from getting those files on Richard Blackstone, then he's sadly mistaken. I've almost reached the edge of the clearing surrounding the cabin when a blinking red light at the base of a tree catches the corner of my eye.

"*Get out of there!*" shouts the Commander. "*It's a trap!*" The words echo through my head, but the warning comes too late as the blinking red light on the proximity mine becomes a ball of roaring fire.

BOOM!

I'm thrown through the air as splinters of wood and ball bearing shrapnel pelt through my clothes and into my body. I hit frozen dirt and roll, speckling the snow with blood. Warning tones of damage ping-pong back and forth through my head, and a rasping groan escapes my lips as I attempt to blink my wavering vision back into focus. I try as hard as I can to concentrate on healing my wounds, but the damage bells are blaring from every conceivable direction, and my rattled mind is having trouble wrangling them into any kind of manageable order. I've never been injured this badly before.

I can feel a voice transmission broadcasting into the back of my mind, but the words won't formulate; they're clashing and distorting with the thrumming tones of warning, and I can't discern anything coherent from the chaotic jumble of gibberish. Contact with base has been lost. I try to get up, but my damaged body protests. I can hardly move.

The two men that I saw outside the cabin are shouting and running in my direction. The front door of the cabin flies open, and six soldiers with rifles come pouring out. All eight men hurry to where I'm lying, and soon I'm completely surrounded. Only two of them are pointing their weapons at me; the rest are gazing down with mixed expressions of pity and confusion.

"A farm girl?" asks one of the men.

"Perhaps. Perhaps not," says another. "It doesn't matter either way. She will not survive long from those injuries."

"Someone should put her out of her misery," murmurs one of the men.

"I will do it." I see boots step toward me and hear the snap-clack of an automatic rifle being cocked.

"Wait!" calls a voice. Boots crunch through the snow, and the circle is broken by yet another man. He's dressed in the same winter-camouflage uniform as the others, but this man is heavyset and older than the rest. His face looks weathered by experience, and his large belly makes his padded jacket bulge over his belt. He looks down at me and appears to be pondering my fate as he sips hot liquid from a steaming metal cup.

"Bring her . . . ," he says in a low, gravelly tone, "and link the computer to the satellite. If they sent this girl, our employer may want to see her face before she dies."

The fat man turns and walks away while I'm rolled onto my back and lifted into the arms of two men. I don't have the means or the energy to struggle. It was a mistake to come here. I know that now. My new obsession with Richard Blackstone is going to cost me my life. I look at the sky while I'm being carried. As gray as it may be, it looks so clean and clear and beautiful. I wish I could rise out of the grasp of these men and fly away to safety. Fly into the air, free like a bird. Like the bird I see flying above me, its wings black against an expanse of gentle gray. I watch it move across the sky, and my heavy eyelids close for a moment. When I open them again, the bird has stopped in midair and, strangely, has doubled in size. In fact, it's getting bigger by the second.

That's when I receive another message.

I don't hear it in my head like I do when the Commander transmits orders to me. This is different. This is a message that I *sense* with my whole body. It's a stern feeling of reassurance, a feeling of hope, and an urgent, almost angry insistence to hold on and not give up. There's only one person I know who communicates without words like that. I manage the faintest of smiles. My combat partner has arrived.

Zero is here.

I try to keep my eyes on the dark shape overhead, and as it steadily grows larger, a faint hum causes the men to look skyward. There are pointing fingers and heated questions as they discuss who the transport might belong to. Is it friendly or not? Is this their employer paying a visit? No one seems to know. Even the fat leader is unsure. Rifles aim warily toward the shape as the two men carrying me quicken their pace, jostling me roughly as they go. All of a sudden, the transport descends so quickly it seems to fall from the sky, and the hum of the engines becomes the droning roar of thrusters as the huge aircraft comes to a hovering halt just above the treetops. The men are still watching it closely when a flare of light erupts from the transport's undercarriage and a thudding line of pockmarks drums across the frozen earth. Puffs of snow and dirt burst all around the soldiers, and three of them are instantly cut down in the hail of heavy gunfire. Through the sound of whining turbines, I can hear the panicked shouts and the rapid beats of machine guns as the remaining men shoot into the air.

Another feeling ripples through me. *"Hold on,"* it seems to say.

"Hurry," I whisper out loud, and almost as if my plea has been heard, two points of light flash on the side of the transport, and two black dashes streak through the air.

One of the soldiers bellows, "Get down!" and my captors suddenly dive away, dropping me roughly onto my stomach as the missiles hit the cabin and detonate with a bone-shaking explosion.

TA-TOOM!

I feel the heat on my face. Wood and masonry fly in every direction. Soldiers shield their heads with their arms, and debris peppers the snow as the cabin is completely obliterated in a giant plume of fire.

As the echo of the blast subsides, I peer through the gap in my narrowed eyelids. All around me, men are prone on the ground. A few begin to move and get to their feet. From the corner of my darkening vision, I see a streak of white fall from above and land in the midst of the remaining soldiers. There are quick movements, pistol shots, grunts of pain, one plea for mercy, and then silence.

I hear boots crunching through the snow toward me. Someone kneels beside me, and hands grasp my shoulders, rolling me over onto my back.

I look up at the silver visor of a stark-white combat mask. He doesn't speak a word. In the two years that I've known him, he never has, but I can feel a wave of angry concern radiating from him and washing through me.

"I know, I know. I should have told you," I rasp.

He pulls me up into his arms, and as he carries me, groaning and bleeding, toward the lowered ramp of the transport, I let my heavy eyelids slowly close as I drift away into the blissfully silent darkness.

CHAPTER FIVE

I gasp. My heart races at a hundred miles an hour as my eyes dart wildly in every direction. The icy air of the forest has vanished as quickly as it came, replaced once again with the relentless rushing wind of the darkness. What the hell just happened? One moment, I was trying to focus on Infinity; the next moment, I *was* her!

In between measured breaths, I try to gather my senses, and it doesn't take long to realize what I just experienced. That was one of Infinity's memories. And judging by what she said, it happened only *three weeks* ago. I let out a long exhale, trying to calm my nerves, which is easier said than done when I have questions stampeding through my mind like a herd of wild elephants. Why is Infinity so obsessed with my father? What does she know that I don't? How did she hear that voice in her head, a voice that I swear I've heard before, and who saved her? The person dressed in white? The one she called . . . "Zero"?

I absolutely *must* know more—more about Infinity's experiences and her memories, more about her life. It might be the only way to find her, and it could also be the key to waking her up and reasoning with her. I screw my eyes shut and do my best to order my thoughts.

Take me back into Infinity's mind; take me back. I repeat the words over and over in my head. *Take me back to her; take me back into her memories, back into her life.*

Nothing happens.

With so few clues to work with, I decide to focus on details of the memory I just saw while it's fresh in my mind. Maybe, with a little luck, it will lead me somewhere new. I try to remember what it felt like to be her again, to remember how strong and determined and capable she was to begin with, but then how vulnerable and afraid she felt when she was lying wounded, bleeding in the snow.

It seems to do the trick, because I'm not waiting for very long when an unfamiliar swell of raw emotion rears in my gut. The flurrying of the wind in my ears begins to ease, and the rippling void softens, gradually giving way to a mild breeze gently wafting over the bare skin of my legs.

I think it's working. *Take me back.*

I open my eyes and scan the darkness all around, hoping to notice some kind of visual change. Everything seems to be just as dark and boundless as before, but it feels *very* different, almost like I've hit a pocket of cool mist. I take another deep, focusing breath and try to distill the thought of Infinity even further. I remember her surrounded by trees, completely in her element on the field of combat, at home in the turmoil, at ease with her deadly purpose. I slowly breathe out, holding the thought in my mind, and with the very next inhale, I'm rewarded with the fresh, woodsy scent of pine needles.

It *is* working! *Take me back to her.*

I try to feel her relief when the one she called "Zero" arrived. I picture the instance in my mind, and there he is, clad in stark white from his mask to his boots, dropping out of the sky to save her. He's falling from the transport overhead, his body as straight as an arrow, but when he's almost halfway to the ground, the transport suddenly vanishes, the sky disappears, and the snow on the forest floor beneath him turns as dark as volcanic glass, perfectly smooth and glossy black. The pure-white silhouette of his body slows and floats in midair before it bizarrely begins collapsing in on itself, silently folding and scrunching and condensing until it's little more than a small, pale circle. The circle spins, slowly tumbling down farther and farther before completely disappearing into the liquid black below, rippling rings across its surface like a pebble plopping into a pool of water.

I can feel my frustration building. The image doesn't make any sense and isn't leading me anywhere. I screw my eyes shut and try again, but this time Zero doesn't appear at all, only darkness and the same small, white pebble. I try to ignore it, wiping it away into the void, but the image persists, sharpening at the edges, becoming clearer and clearer in my mind with every passing moment. I snort into the dark, irritated, and when I open my eyes, to my bewilderment, the imagined pebble is *there*; I can actually see it in front of me. Small and smooth, it's floating in the emptiness right beside me.

I slowly reach out and cup the pebble in my hand. I bring it to my face and study it, rolling it between my fingertips, and suddenly, like a cell dividing, the pebble splits into two, its identical twin dropping into the palm of my other hand. As strange as this is, I don't feel surprised in the least; instead, and without really knowing why, I whip my arm out and throw one of the pebbles out into the void. It tumbles in a wide arc, curving through the dark. I can even see its shadowy reflection on the liquid black below, rising up in an opposite arc to meet its falling double. The pebble and its reflection collide without a sound, breaking the surface of the black water together, sending dim white ripples spanning out from the shining droplet where they met. What is this? What's happening?

I watch the outer circle expand; I can't help it . . . I'm mesmerized by it. The glowing ripple distorts as it softly laps an invisible shore, and its faint circle of light breaks apart, but it doesn't disappear. The light carries on, spreading outward from where it broke, moving over a patch of darkened ground beyond the water's edge like a pale flame widening a hole in a fragile sheet of paper. It quickly spreads in every direction, wrapping around me, behind me, and over me, painting silhouettes of twigs and leaves and rocks and earth in the hidden spaces between the shadows. The edge of light spreads farther, weaving and peeking in and out of tiny valleys in the darkness, tracing the bumps of tree roots, blades of grass, clumps of moss, and curling ferns. It splinters, shooting upward in pin-striped rocket trails, threading up the furrows in the bark of the ring of trees surrounding me. Their leafy branches, black against a dark-blue night sky, cast their long shadows over moonlit water and down across the dirt-smeared toes of my strangely small bare feet.

I realize that I'm not drifting in the void anymore; I'm standing beside a pond. Wait! This is not just any pond. This is *my* pond. The secret pond in the Seven Acre Wood on the grounds of Blackstone Manor! I love this special place so much, and I know it so well, but I don't remember it like this because . . . I've never been to the pond at night . . . not once in my life.

I look up at the moon; it's big and bright in the sky. I pick the other pebble from my palm and hold it up against the moon between my fingers. The pebble is big compared to my small, thin fingertips, my hand tiny compared to the moon. I throw the pebble on the dirt behind me and frown. *One day soon, when they're bigger, these hands will move mountains.* I smile at the childish thought.

Be realistic, Infinity.

Mountains might be a bit of a stretch, but one day, these hands will leave their mark on this world, a mark painted in blood. I'll make sure of it. I look down and make two tight fists. Even though I know that it's just a matter of time before I'm big enough to prove myself, it doesn't stop me from hating being only ten years old.

I shrug off my disdain for what I can't change and get back to the task at hand. This may be only a training exercise, but that doesn't mean that I shouldn't take it seriously. I think of Major Brogan, and I'm reminded of his deep, stern voice. "Rule number one, this applies to life as well as combat. Stay sharp; always be mindful of your surroundings."

That's good advice. I breathe in deeply through my nose, smelling, then tasting, then separating the faint night aromas of the Seven Acre Wood. Every scent from when I checked the air five minutes ago is present and accounted for. No new ones. No change.

I listen to the sounds of the night. The chirping crickets, the trickling water, the slow breeze rustling the leaves in the trees overhead.

I decide that now is the perfect time to practice the little trick I discovered a month ago when Major Brogan was trying to teach me how to meditate.

I close my eyes and push the sound of the rustling leaves out of my mind completely. I do exactly the same for the sound of the water and every other stray background frequency until only the sound of the crickets' tweeting chirps punctuate the blanket of silence in my head. I focus all my attention on the chirps, amplifying them in my ears a hundredfold. Their usually soothing tweets suddenly become a jostling babble of high-pitched noises; the closest crickets are so loud now that the cacophony crinkles the edges of my eyes. There are dozens of the chirpy little night crawlers within only a few meters of me.

Focus, Infinity. Do this right, and the enemies out there in the dark will never know what hit them.

I take a slow breath and concentrate on separating the crickets' trills and whistles, isolating their individual rhythms. I take careful note of the beats and pauses, starts and stops, tempos and pitches in the different songs of each cricket. As I do, I lower the volume of each song ever so slightly and move on to the next one. I repeat the process, one after another, for each and every cricket I hear. Recognize, reduce, and move on to the next one farther out. Recognize, reduce, and repeat until the edge of my hearing moves out between the trees in a creeping carpet of chirps, the sound of each cricket becoming a reference point on a map in my head, forming an auditory web stretching deep into the forest. Ten thousand chirps and whistles strung into a living lattice of sound. A sensitive web that I can use to tell if anyone is approaching from any direction . . .

There!

Five crickets, thirty meters to the south of my position, all went silent midchirp. Two others have done the same thing thirty-one meters due west, and . . . yes, there's also a moving silence between those two points heading toward me, approximately twenty-six meters out. That's three enemies, and they're getting closer. I guess the bait of the pebbles plopping in the water worked just like I wanted it to.

They're all heading straight for me.

I open my mind to the full sound of the night. The spear I made from a sharpened tree branch is lying at my feet. I hook my toes underneath it, kick it up into my hand, and dart away from the edge of the pond, leaping from patches of bare earth to the tops of rocks to fallen folds of bark to clumps of grass, using them as silent stepping-stones, deftly avoiding the telltale crunch of the fallen leaves and twigs around them. My skintight combat suit pulls at my body as I move like a shadow through the night, up the hill to my right, hugging the tree line.

I stop against the trunk of a tree and scan the ground that leads into the forest. The canopy of leaves overhead is blocking too much moonlight to see where I can step without making any noise, but that's a problem with an easy fix. I close my eyes and quickly imagine each eye as a huge, sapphire-blue pool of water. In the center of each pool, I imagine black oil is bubbling up, spreading out farther and farther, until it almost covers the entire surface of them both, the blue in each pool of my eyes now only a razor-thin rim around the edges of two massive circles of black.

When I open my eyes again, I can see through the dark.

Every leaf, stone, stick, log, patch of earth, and blade of grass on the forest floor is sharp with green-tinged detail, as if rays of secret sunshine were being piped in just for me. I map out my foot placements for the next fifteen meters and leap out from behind my tree, turning my attention toward where the southern enemy should be. I spot him, shoulders hunched forward, his clunky body armor bulging on his frame as he stalks toward the pond. His arms are hugging his assault rifle to his chin as he does his best to softly crunch through the leaf litter. He's doing a very good job. Most people would hardly notice the sound at all, but as Lieutenant Brash keeps telling me, I'm not most people.

My stare stays fixed on the enemy as my feet move on their own toward a big fallen tree trunk, hitting every noiseless step on the way from spatial memory alone. I vault onto the fallen tree without a sound and assess my options. The tree I'm perched on fell in a way that leaned it up against another. I slowly peek around the side of the upright tree and see him. He's twenty-three meters away. I can jump really far, but that's too far, even for me, and he's walking parallel to my position. He's not gonna get any closer. I have to make my move now.

I scan the forest floor between us and spot a solid patch of ground. That should do nicely. With my spear gripped tightly in my hand, I take off like a sprinter, running up the fallen tree and launching myself as far as I can. I sail silently through the night air, heading straight for the patch of earth halfway between the fallen tree and the enemy. I clutch my spear securely in both hands, pointed-end down, and jab it into the spot of bare dirt with a dull thud, swinging my body and kicking my legs out for extra momentum. He hears what I've done and turns just in time to see me pole-vault at blinding speed directly toward him. The spear spins in my fingers, and I thrust the sharp end forward, impaling the enemy right through the center of his chest as I knock him down to the ground with my flying knees. I crouch on top of him, pull his gun from his hands, sling its strap over my shoulders onto my back, and then leap three meters straight up into the crook of a sturdy limb in a nearby oak tree.

One down. Two to go.

"STOP!" booms a voice, echoing through the entire forest. All around me, there are loud chunking sounds as the flood lamps in the trees punch on from every direction, blanketing the whole area with a blinding white light, turning the night as bright as day. I blink my night vision away and squint down at the forest floor. The whirring of a sublevel elevator is soon followed by the sound of leaves crunching under approaching footsteps. It isn't very long before I see the angry military stride and army-buzzed haircut of Lieutenant Simon Brash. With his fists set firmly on his hips, he turns his face up toward me and glowers.

"Infinity One. Get down here. Right now!"

I let out a huge, bothered sigh and shuffle off the tree branch, dropping to the ground right beside the Lieutenant.

"Explain this," he says, pointing down at the human-size, army-green robot splayed at the base of the tree. Orange goop is lazily bubbling from the hole my spear made in its chest.

"Do you have any idea how expensive these things are?" he asks, his wide eyes creasing deep lines in his forehead.

"Oo!" I blurt, thrusting my hand in the air like I do in training meetings. "That's a rhetorical question!"

Lieutenant Brash frowns, and his eyes narrow into slits. "Don't you dare give me any lip, Infinity One."

I slowly lower my hand, and Lieutenant Brash grunts in frustration. "Dammit, look what you've done. These robots are prototypes, the first of a new generation of advanced robotics, five years ahead of their time!"

Judging by the look he gives me, you'd think I'd killed a puppy or something.

"How many times do I have to tell you? A twist of the neck, a shot with a Taser rifle, or the red button on their back shuts them down. Without damage! You know this! So why the hell do you insist on acting like you don't?"

"Real enemies don't have a red button," I say with a growl.

He looks down at me, the corner of one eye twitching, and I can almost see his thought processes trudging their way through the mud between his ears to the tiny part of his brain in charge of moving his mouth. "Well . . . that may be true, but . . . you were ordered not to break any Drones this time." He thrusts a finger, pointing right at my nose. "If you can't follow orders now, then what use will you be on an actual mission?"

I smack his hand away from my face. "Send me on a mission, and you'll see what use I can be," I say as coldly and seriously as I can.

Lieutenant Brash looks down at me with an amused sneer. "What? No! You're not ready. You're too young."

I stare right into his eyes. "I'm a weapon. That's what I was made for, it's what I am, and luckily for all of you, it's all I ever wanted to be. I may be only ten years old, but if you give me a real target and point me in its direction, I'll show you what this weapon can do. I'll show *all* of you."

The same weird twitch spasms at the edge of his eye, and one corner of his mouth moves a quarter of a millimeter upward. His chin crinkles, just for an instant, and his nostrils flare ever so slightly. He hides it well, but the sum total of his microexpressions equals only one thing. Lieutenant Simon Wigmore Brash, Special Tactical Training Officer, military-clearance-level seven . . . is afraid of a little girl.

For a moment, I think he may not be as stupid as I've always thought he is.

The Lieutenant gives me a patronizing smile and thrusts his hand out, palm up. "Your knife, hand it over."

My hands whip to my side, covering the black-pearl handle of the titanium-alloy combat knife that Major Brogan gave me. Apart from my black-diamond pendant, it's my prized possession. I frown up at the Lieutenant and grunt through my clenched jaw. "No."

"Training is over for tonight, Infinity One. Give me your knife. That's an order." Lieutenant Brash raises two fingers in the air, and the red laser point of a sniper's rifle somewhere out beyond the floodlights spots onto my chest. "Don't make it the last order you ever hear."

With a hissing breath, I slowly pull my blade from its sheath and grudgingly hand it to him. As he tucks it into his belt, a bead of sweat trickles down the side of his face. A face that I would quite happily punch right through the back of his head.

"Taser rifle, too," he orders as an almost imperceptible gulp sticks in his throat.

I pull the rifle strap up over my head and barely swing the gun around my shoulder when he quickly reaches out and roughly snatches it from me.

"You're right . . . ," he says as he checks the rifle's chamber and magazine. "You are a weapon. But no matter how hard I try, I just can't seem to get it through that thick little skull of yours. We give the orders, and mouthy little girls need to do what they're told."

Lieutenant Brash snaps the rifle to his chin, and with a loud bang, the weapon kicks in his arms. Three Taser darts spike me in the chest, and I'm punched backward, hitting the ground hard as a loud hum bores through my body. My eyes flick back in my head, my teeth grind, and my back arches into the air as my whole body is racked with agonizing pulses of electricity. Simon Brash's voice fades into the distance.

"Take that nasty little piece of work down to Mind Alteration. I think someone needs another attitude adjustment."

My arms and legs jolt uncontrollably as my fingers clench dirt and leaves in my trembling fists. Even though I know that they'll try to take it away, I vow to hold on to this moment. *Don't forget this feeling, Infinity . . . Never forget . . . Always remember . . . Always remember . . . Always . . .*

". . . remember . . . Oh my god, I remember," I whisper into the void. My heart is drumming in my chest, and my mind is reeling again. The warm breeze drifting over my body flitters away like a withdrawing veil, and as I feel it wisp from the tips of my toes, the chill of the void returns with a rush and I'm suddenly falling at speed again, the passing darkness rippling my skin. "I remember."

I found another one of Infinity's memories.

It was so vivid, so real, and just like before, it felt as if I were right there. I guess, when I think about it, I kinda *was* there. The ten-year-old me in the back of ten-year-old Infinity's mind, carried along for the ride like a sleeping passenger.

I'm getting closer to her—I *must* be.

The more I think about her, the more it helps. But what I just saw was plain crazy. I only experienced a few minutes of her past, but it was so drastically different from how I was raised that in some ways the closer I get, the more distant from her I feel. I try to imagine doing all the things that she did that night in the Seven Acre Wood, and I can't wrap my head around it. She's not normal. She's *extraordinary*. No normal human being I've ever heard of can do what I just witnessed. The way she saw in the dark like a cat. The way she moved so inhumanly quickly. Not to mention the incredible way her hearing crept through the night like a fog, mapping the terrain like sonar.

I'm suddenly intrigued. And maybe even a little bit envious of her abilities. What else can she do?

Listen to me; I'm thinking about Infinity like she's completely separate from me, but . . . what if . . . ?

I look down at the darkness whipping against my skin.

The truth is . . . my body *is* her body.

I bring my hands to my face and study them, turning them over. The lines on *my* palms are the same ones she sees.

Her hands *are* my hands.

I can't do what Infinity does; Graham said they made me forget, that they wiped the knowledge of her abilities from my half of our mind, but . . . what if Infinity and I aren't as separate as I think?

I was right there, running through the forest. I was right there, leaping through the night. I felt the spear in *my* hands. *I* pushed it through the Drone's chest. I may not have actually done it, but when I was inside that memory, I felt what she felt, spoke how she spoke; I wasn't Finn anymore. I *was* Infinity.

I was thirteen when I wrecked my bike and fractured my arm. Infinity showed me that memory, a memory that they locked away from me. But when I healed my arm . . . I was me! I was Finn, not Infinity. Even after all their messing with my head, I was beginning to learn how to do what Infinity does, all on my own! And Jonah just stood there. With that phony look of surprise. Lying to my face. Pretending to be shocked, biding his time until he could lure me underground and wipe the slate clean again. Which is exactly what he did.

But that memory proves that I could do it. So I can't see any reason why I can't do those things again.

Infinity and I are two sides of the same coin. I'm positive that I can do anything that she can do, if I can just get inside the right memories and learn how to. I'm right; I know I am.

And there's one way I can know for sure.

I take a deep breath and close my eyes, trying to feel what Infinity felt when she listened to the songs of the crickets. I focus my mind, concentrating on the only sound there is: the rushing wind of the void. It's fast, thick, and enveloping and—I suddenly notice—twice as loud as it was a split second ago.

I try to visualize the sound, imagining the noise as a ribbon in my mind, starting from the top of my head, flurrying down over my body.

It's working.

I can almost see the ribbon in my head, and the noise is twice as loud again. I push deeper into the sound, and it gradually begins to spread apart, the individual strands of the ribbon separating from one another until soon there are thousands of them, each one a slightly different tone. I'm beginning to get excited. I try to imagine that the sound doesn't exist, that the void is passing through my body instead of over and around it. Nothing changes.

Don't give up, Finn. If Infinity can do this, then so can you.

I try to imagine the polar opposite of the sound, hoping that the two will cancel each other out like opposing colors of light, but the sound only roars on, undiminished. Now it's almost deafening, as the howls of a multitude of separate threads rampage through my ears. This is nothing at all like chirping crickets.

Think, Finn. Focus.

Then it occurs to me. The sound of the wind is made up of thousands of threads of vibrations. And what do you do with an unwanted thread? The answer is simple. You cut it.

I imagine the ribbon again, weaving in and out through my ears in a streaming torrent of noises. I gather all the strings together in my mind, guiding them to a single intersecting point and . . . snip.

Silence.

I've done it. I allow myself a little victory smile. Now, if I can do that, then maybe I can learn Infinity's other Seven Acre secret. I think back to the memory of her alone among the trees, the forest floor shrouded in shadow, two eyes becoming two perfectly circular pools of blue.

I will a tiny hole in the bottom of each pool and summon the same inky droplets of oil I saw in the memory. I'm encouraged when they appear, slowly at first, bubbling up to the surface of each blue circle, gradually widening farther and farther toward the edges, until at last the sapphire rims bordering the pools are only the thinnest of lines surrounding two round slicks of purest black.

Her eyes are my eyes, and when I open them . . . I gasp in absolute wonder. The endless darkness was never an empty void at all. The black was only a veil concealing the truth behind it.

And now, at last . . . that veil is gone.

CHAPTER SIX

On the night of my seventeenth birthday, I awoke inside my own mind for the first time, and every night since then, I've been lost in a void of nothingness. But now, thanks to Infinity, I can see behind a curtain I didn't even know was there, and the true nature of my subconscious has finally been revealed to me. I stare, wide-eyed and gaping in amazement, like a little kid marveling in wonder at mystery beyond comprehension. I gulp and utter one breathless word that doesn't even begin to scratch the surface of conveying the amazement that I'm feeling.

"Whoa."

Laid out before me, stretching far into the distance, is an immense concave circle of thick, undulating clouds. Light flickers in dancing patches beneath the misty skin of the clouds as they slowly revolve around a softly glowing central point. I can't judge the size of the disc, but it's huge. It reminds me of pictures I've seen of cyclones that were taken by satellites orbiting over the Earth, except instead of the Pacific Ocean beneath it, there's a gently pulsing, green-tinged expanse broken up by shifting lines of intricate geometric patterns. I feel like I'm seeing a secret that wasn't meant for my eyes, as if I'm an astronaut discovering a forbidden galaxy.

I glance over my shoulder, and my mind is blown open even further. There, tilting at a strange and awkward angle, is yet another enormous spiral of clouds. It's as wide as the first one and stretches out just as far in the other direction. With my gaze darting every which way, I try to calm the thrumming inside my ribs with a string of full, heaving breaths.

This is incredible.

I quickly notice that the two gigantic discs of twisting vapor are rotating in opposing directions, the edges overlapping and combining at a massive and turbulent intersection. I thought I was being dragged through the darkness, but I was wrong. Now I can see that I'm fixed to one point, in the midst of the overlap, and the wide gaps between the countless rows of the nearest clouds, as well as the clouds themselves, are rushing past *me*.

The pocket of mist that I felt before must have been a cloud passing over me, and every cloud must be a memory. These two huge discs probably contain every experience Infinity and I have ever had. I feel a sense of panic rise in my stomach, my breaths becoming quicker with every passing second. Even if I can wrench myself free and find a way into Infinity's memories, there are so many, and I know I don't have enough time to search them all to find the ones that might save us. I'm stranded between a storm of Infinity's secrets and the swirling clouds of my own stolen life, and I don't know what to do.

I open my mind to the full sound of the rush and call out into space, "Graham! Bit! Can you hear me?"

There's no answer, just the horrible noise of the wind in my ears. I'm on my own.

I reach up and grab at my hair. I pull at it, grunting with frustration, tugging it as hard as I can, but it doesn't give. I scream and yank at it, furiously kicking out with my legs. "Let me go!" It doesn't budge at all. In fact, the only thing I succeed in doing is sending my body into a slow spin, tightening the hair at my scalp even further. I feel useless, foolish, twisting in the wind, heaving to catch my breath from the futile struggling.

I close my eyes and try to focus my thoughts. "Infinity . . . I need you," I whisper. "If you can hear me, if any little part of you is there somewhere, please . . . help me; help me save us. Send me a sign that you're not giving up. Show me a way. Help me find you."

There's no answer. I don't know why I expected one. If she could hear me, she would be fighting to survive. She would have screamed out across our mind. What good am I? Why did I think I could do this? Even ten-year-old Infinity would have a better idea of what to do right now. The moment I think of her, a spark flashes through my head, an echo of colors at the back of my mind. The blurred picture sharpens, and I can see her. Her eyes are closed, and blood is streaming down her little face, but the image fades as quickly as it came; then it's gone.

"Infinity?" I whisper.

At the mention of her name, her young face flashes into my mind again. Her forehead twitches, and she groans softly.

"Is that you, Infinity? Can you hear me?"

I see her fingers, covered in blood, moving in a creeping motion, crawling like a dying spider across blood-soaked earth.

I scrunch my eyes tighter and try to make the picture clearer. Her fingers begin scratching at the ground, her eyes still closed. It's an absentminded action, as if her hand is moving on its own accord, a reflex without any purpose. At least, that's how it seems to me until I suddenly notice something under the dirt, a shiny black surface peeking out from beneath the soil. Her weak fingers scrape a little more earth away, and I can make out a shape; it's curved and blunt, rounded at one end.

What is that?

A feeble, gurgling breath bubbles out from between her lips. It sounds like she's dying. Ten-year-old Infinity's hand suddenly stops moving, and her face goes limp as the image in my mind fades away into nothing.

I scream out, "Infinity!"

She wasn't really there—she was only a picture in my head—but, in her own way, she was trying to tell me something; I'm sure of it. I thrust my hand out in a futile attempt to get the image back, and my fingers plunge into cold, crumbled earth. My arm recoils in shock, and when I open my eyes, I'm gripping the shiny black handle of a silver-bladed knife.

She heard me . . . and she helped me.

With my heart thumping in my chest, I quickly reach up and snatch a fistful of my hair. I tighten it across the blade and forcefully swipe the knife away in one sweeping stroke, slicing completely through it. The knife vanishes, and the rushing wind is immediately silenced as I'm swept into the whirling streams of memories. I know that I'm moving; I can see the long black strands of my hair speeding away, but it feels as if I'm standing still. If I couldn't see the two expansive circles swirling against each other, carrying me away, I would swear that I wasn't moving at all.

I close my eyes tightly and whisper into the silence, "Where are you, Infinity? Please . . . let me find you."

I look up and around in every direction, sharpening my hearing in the silence and focusing my newly enhanced vision on the nearest clouds. There's no answer, and the knife turns to dust between my fingers. I try to think of Infinity again, but there's nothing there; the connection is lost.

This is pointless. I can't just drift here, waiting for Infinity to send me a message that may never come or hoping that the next memory I accidentally pass through will help in any way at all. I need a place to start looking. I still don't remember how I ended up lying on a table, bleeding and broken. I don't remember anything that happened since I was locked in the clean room with Bit and Ryan and the others. If I think of that moment again, the last real thing I saw before Infinity took our body, then maybe I can get somewhere.

I close my eyes and take myself back. I was in that horrible, sterile white room with my back against a wall. There was a Drone walking toward me. I was so scared. I remember the sound of Margaux's sobs. My heart was racing in my chest as I held my hand up in futile defense. "No. Please," I begged as the Drone bent down and grabbed me, crushing my fingers. I wince at the memory of the pain I felt as the bones popped and broke. I feel the morbid shock of helplessness again as I watched my fingers splay out in unnatural angles in the Drone's brutal grip. A chill runs down my spine. It makes me sick to remember all of this. I take a sharp breath, open my eyes, and there, floating just to my left, moving along with me, is a small cloud. Tendrils of mist are spiraling out from it like thin ropes of smoke, twisting toward me and ending on a spot on my forehead.

Is this what it looks like when I remember something?

I try to recall what happened next, and another tentacle of smoke instantly forms between my forehead and the cloud. I see the Drone's black oval mask morphing its shape, sculpting into the wrinkled, leathered flesh of Nanny Theresa's face. I see Brody coming to my rescue and Ryan thrown clear across the room like a rag doll. I remember Nanny Theresa taunting me, enjoying my rampant confusion as she threatened to rip my head from my body.

The new string of mist suddenly thickens and swirls faster. Theresa's gleeful smile sneers into my mind as her hands wrap around my neck, her grip winching tighter and tighter until my breath is squeezed out of me and everything finally, silently, goes black.

That's all I remember. I watch the lines of smoke dissolve and evaporate as the cloud lazily begins drifting away from me, rejoining the others in their rotation. I'm wondering what else I can possibly do when I notice it from the corner of my eye: a cloud on the right, at the edge of the other vast circle, seems to be following me. I stare at it curiously. It's very large and dark, like a storm cloud. Some of the clouds closer to the center of the circle of memories are misty, like fog; they're smoother and longer, more spread out and fuzzy at the edges. But this dark one is thick with undulating billows; it seems newer, more vibrant than the others. It slowly shifts out of its orbit and drifts toward me. There are no tiny tornadoes of smoke reaching out from this one. I don't know why, but for some reason, the thought of a large dog warily approaching a beckoning stranger comes to mind. Could it be the memory I've been searching for? Will it tell me how I came to be bleeding on a metal table beneath Blackstone Technologies?

"C'mon, just a little closer," I coax. The memory cloud seems to pause, and then, ever so slowly, it begins moving away. If I didn't know any better, I'd swear it had realized that I'm not its owner and was going back to join its pack in line.

It's one of Infinity's memories. So what would she do?

I quickly clench my fists tightly and focus pure anger at the retreating cloud. With narrowed eyes and gritted teeth, I will it to come to me. I more than will it . . . I *command* it.

All of a sudden, a tentacle of smoke spirals out from my forehead and shoots toward the cloud, snaking across the space between us and spearing deep into its side. I feel my anger grow, and the swirling tendril attached to my head thickens as the dark cloud begins to shrink. Murky bursts of color strobe all around me, and there are crunching pockets of pain and blaring alarms in the back of my mind. The writhing python of smoke is getting bigger and bigger, swelling into a giant smog that completely envelops my torso.

Half-heard words from cracked sentences of garbled voices swarm in my ears. I scream out in confused frustration, desperately trying to decipher any piece of this sensory assault, swiping at the distorted images with my hands, trying to clear a path to something I can understand. I feel the cloud engulfing my entire body and compressing against me. There's a momentary flash of gray eyes, wrinkled skin, and silver fabric stretched tightly over the shape of a Drone's upper body. I'm suddenly filled with rage and power.

The image of Nanny Theresa's face pasted on a Drone's body becomes vivid and solid. Bewildered, I reach out again to swat the strobing pictures aside, but instead, my arm straightens like a steel rod, and my fingers spear forward on their own. My hand harpoons through the Drone's chest, through its innards, punching right out its back in a splatter of thick, synthetic blood. Theresa's face is an inch from my nose. Her eyes roll back, her cheek twitches, and then her face vanishes, flattening into a shiny black plastic mask.

I forcefully pull my hand out from the hole, and the Drone's inert body flops to the ground in an orange-goop-leaking heap.

"Finn?" says a weak voice from across the room.

I look over and see a rather pathetic-looking, tousled-haired boy leaning on a chair with an obviously dislocated shoulder.

Out of battlefield reflex more than anything else, I stride over to him, grab him tight before he can complain, and pop the ball joint of his shoulder back into its socket. He grits his teeth and jerks his head back, but he doesn't make a sound.

This one may have potential.

He looks up at me with a strained smile, and I can't help but notice his eyes. They're hazel amber with tiny flecks of gold, but there's much more to them than that. There's focus and fearlessness, and a quiet strength deep inside them that I've only ever seen in the emerald-green eyes of one other.

The boy stumbles. I quickly move around to his other side and grab him under his good arm. "Thanks, Finn," he says, gritting his teeth in pain, trying his best to put on a brave face.

"Don't call me that," I order the boy as I scan the room, properly taking in my surroundings.

"Finn is gone. My name is Infinity."

"*Finn? Hello, Finn? Can you hear me? I can't hear her anymore, Dr. Pierce; what's happened? Is something wrong?*"

"*You've got eyes, girlie; there aren't many things that are right at this particular juncture in time. Finn has multiple cuts, abrasions, breaks, and fractures; she's hemorrhaging internally, and there's a good chance that I'm gonna find a lot of other nasty surprises waiting for me if it comes to the point where I have to perform any kind of serious surgery. Now take that blasted thing off your head and bring me those clamps, gauze, and sutures!*"

"*Sorry, of course, it's just that . . . what does it mean if she's not responding to the Neural Interface?*"

"*I'm not sure. It could mean a lot of things. Finn might have lost contact because of her head injuries, she could have gone into an irreversible coma, or, cross your fingers and hope like hell that I'm right, she might have gone even deeper into her own subconscious to find Infinity. I don't have the proper equipment to tell, but I'm hedging all my bets on the last option, and I suggest you do, too. Because otherwise . . . well, otherwise, Finn is simply not going to survive this. And, if Finn dies, then I'm afraid there's gonna be a lot more people who'll be following right behind her.*"

CHAPTER SEVEN

A stark-white room from ceiling to floor, no windows. A frosted-glass door in each wall, one of which has been smashed.

This place looks like some kind of empty laboratory. There are five more Drones, all seemingly inactive. One of them appears to have shut down while holding a rather husky teenage boy in a bear hug on the floor. A crying blonde girl, approximately seventeen years old, is crouching by a puddle of vomit, and over there, sitting against the wall and staring into nowhere, is Finn's private-school roommate and my very own little computer-hacking accomplice . . . Bettina Otto.

I flick a fallen chair upright with my foot, help the boy with the damaged shoulder into it, and stride over to her. She doesn't look very happy. In fact, her nowhere-stare looks a lot like shock to me. I tie my hair into a quick ponytail, kneel down beside her, and wave my hand in front of her face. "Hey, Otto, wakey wakey." Her expression doesn't change at all. I remove her glasses, make a flat palm, and, with a loud smack, backhand her across the face.

Her eyes flutter reflexively as her cheek twitches and turns a bright shade of pink, but the still semigormless glaze behind her stare tells me that I didn't quite get through to her. I raise my hand again, right in front of her face this time, so even without her glasses, she can't miss it. "Speak up now, or I'll just keep smacking you around until you do."

She blinks a few more times, a tear trickles from the corner of her eye, and she looks up at me, squinting. "Finn?" she asks croakily. I drop my hand and push her glasses back onto her nose.

"Nope, try again."

"Infinity? Is . . . is that you?"

I give her a quick nod, help her to her feet, and grab her shoulders. "You did it, Otto. You got me into Blackstone Tech."

"What . . . Blackstone? Oh yeah, I . . . I guess I did," she murmurs, obviously still a bit dazed.

"Don't be so modest; I couldn't have done it without you." I give her a little congratulatory punch on the arm. "Now, come on. Let's go kill Richard Blackstone."

Otto frowns at me with obvious apprehension. "What . . . No, I . . . I just want to go home," she whimpers.

I grab her face by the chin. "Hey, you seem to be forgetting a couple of very important things here. Richard Blackstone used me like a slave my whole life, and the last time your sister Mariele was seen alive was when she was working at his house! We had a deal, Otto. You get me in here and help me kill that bastard, and I help you find out what happened to your sister. Remember? You're not backing out of our little agreement, are you?"

"But . . . my classmates . . . ," she stammers, peeling my hand away. Tears start rolling freely down her cheeks. I glance over my shoulder at them. Blondie drippy-mascara face is still sitting over there, rocking back and forth like a crazy person; bear hug boy is grunting like a warthog as he finally manages to pry himself from the stiff arms of that Drone; and the good-looking one with the brown hair is just sitting there, rubbing his shoulder and staring straight at me, like I'm the only one in the room.

"They'll be fine," I say. "Now, let's go."

I grab Otto by the wrist, but she wrenches her hand from my grip. "My classmates are dead!" she screeches.

"What the hell are you talking about? They're right there, and they all look alive and well to me."

"Not them! My other classmates!" she screeches. "Something happened out there in the training area. Ashley, Millie, Sherrie, and Karla. They're all dead. Our teacher, Miss Cole, two soldiers, and a man named Colonel Brash, they were all . . . they were all murdered."

"What?" I ask, my attention suddenly piqued. "Tell me what happened."

"A military robot went haywire and killed them all," Otto says, her fingers rubbing at her reddened eyes under the rims of her glasses. "Then those Drones attacked us, and now nothing is working, no one is coming to help us, and we're trapped in here."

"Wait a second, Otto; let me get this straight. Are you telling me that . . . Simon Brash is *dead*?"

She nods through her tears, and I can't help myself. I burst out laughing. "Ha-ha ha-ha ha! Oh man! Dammit! I would have given my left arm to see that!"

I'm still snickering to myself when I notice Otto glaring at me. "It's not funny, Infinity."

Even though I think it's absolutely hilarious, I force myself to pull a straight face and put a hand on Otto's shoulder. "I know it isn't funny, and I'm sorry about your classmates. But listen to me; they're dead. They're not coming back, and we still have a deal that I'm gonna hold you to. Richard Blackstone is here; I'm certain of it, and I'm not leaving until I do what I came here to do. I need you to access the computer and clear me a path through any security doors and shut down any internal defenses they might have. I've never been here before, but it doesn't take a brain surgeon to assume that it must be like a maze, so I also need you to access a map of the layout. Can you do that for me, Otto?"

Her gaze drifts away from my face, her eyes darting from side to side in silent contemplation. When she turns back, her demeanor seems calmer, her expression blank and hard to read.

"The computer is off-line, so there won't be any automated defenses," she mumbles. "We're in our school uniforms, so any soldiers we run into probably won't shoot us. And I memorized the layout from a 3-D map I saw earlier, so I can show you where Dr. Blackstone is most likely to be."

I smile at her. "Good."

"But I'm not doing anything until you help me get Percy, Dean, and the Professor out of the training area."

"What? Who the hell are they?" I blurt.

"Three people survived the military robot, and they're trapped in Dome Two. Help me get them out, and I'll do anything you say."

I feel a fire burn inside. I grab Otto by the arm, and she winces with pain. "You'll do what I say right now, or . . ."

"Hey!" shouts the brown-haired boy as Otto jerks her arm away from me. He pushes out of his chair and strides across the room toward us. "Finn, what do you think you're doing? Leave her alone!"

"Keep out of this, boy," I growl.

"Whoa, calm down," he says, holding up one hand in a futile gesture of peace. "We've all been through a lot in a really short space of time. But there's no need to take it out on Bit."

"Ryan, leave it alone . . . please," implores Otto.

"No, Bit," he says. "She's acting like a bully. She's supposed to be your friend."

"Shut your mouth and walk away, kid, or I'll make sure you regret it," I snarl.

"'Kid'?" he says incredulously. "Why are you acting like this, Finn? What is going on with you?"

"This is your last warning. Call me that name one more time. I dare you."

"Look, Finn, just tell me what's going on, and we can . . ."

I grab his wrist and pull down hard on his arm, popping his shoulder joint right back out of its socket.

"Arrrrgh!" he screams. His legs buckle, and he crumples to the floor, clutching at his arm.

"Ryan!" Otto screeches as she drops to her knees beside him. She glares up at me. "You are a sadistic, psychopathic monster."

I smile down at her. "I prefer the term 'uncomplicated.' And if you want your life to stay the same way, then I suggest you follow my orders."

Otto slowly stands and looks me, unflinchingly, right in the eyes. Any traces of fear that were there before have been replaced by flickers of anger. "And if *you* don't help me get them out of that dome, then *I* won't tell you how to get rid of Finn. Once and for all."

I study her closely, scanning her face for the slightest hint of deception. "What did you say?"

"I heard you, Infinity. I may have been a little overwhelmed for a few minutes back there, but I still know what I heard. Just before you killed that Drone, you said that you wanted to get rid of Finn. Well, I know how to do it."

"Tell me."

"No. Not until everyone is safe."

I look around the room at the bunch of adolescent nobodies. "Everyone?"

"Everyone. Those are my terms. Take them or leave them."

I glare at her, and my hands ball into fists. Either I'm losing my touch to spot a lie, or she's telling the truth. I let out an exasperated sigh, and say a word that tastes like bitter poison on my tongue.

"Deal."

"OK then," Otto says with a nod. "Now, can you please help Ryan?"

It looks like, at least for now, little-miss-bossy-pants Otto here is calling the shots. I give her one last narrow-eyed glare and then kneel by the boy. I grip the Ryan guy's arm and, with a sharp pull, a slight reposition, and a hard push, pop his shoulder joint back into place. His head jerks back, and he groans loudly. "Here," I say, offering him a hand. "Stand up."

"No, thanks," he hisses through a clenched jaw as he awkwardly gets to his feet on his own.

"Alright, then, Commander Otto." I give her a blatantly sarcastic salute. "Let's go find your friends." I turn and head toward the smashed-open door, but immediately freeze in my tracks when a dull electronic bell tone suddenly rings out all around us. Over and over the bell tone chimes in a steady rhythm, once every couple of seconds. It doesn't sound like any security alarm that I've ever heard—for one, it's not very loud, and two, there's no urgency in it. It's just a dull, repetitive gong sound.

"What *is* that?" asks the Ryan boy. Almost as soon as he utters the words, the bright light illuminating the room suddenly cuts off completely, plunging us into darkness as a terrified wail issues from Blondie's direction. I'm about to switch to night vision when, all of a sudden, hundreds of rows of large, white numbers, letters, and symbols punch onto the walls, scrolling in random sets of gibberish from left to right, ceiling to floor, filling the whole room with an eerie white glow.

"Otto, what's happening?" I ask.

"It . . . it looks like the computer is trying a system reboot."

"Is that a good or a bad thing?"

She doesn't answer me, but I can tell by the dubious expression on her face that she's less than confident this turn of events is going to work in our favor.

The chiming bells ring on as the random group of letters begins collecting into readable chunks of half sentences and partial instructions. They begin flashing in different places all over the room, giving the already-eerie light an unnerving strobing effect. I scan the wall in front of me and manage to make out a few phrases from the jumble of flickering symbols and numbers.

≠ʝπᵢ±€ᵢΩç¢ "ʃ±+Ωø±€»ᵢ£ ∏αΣ≠œ«¿ʃ‰≈ 42 59 20 54 48 45 20 43 ≥•s°«∂∞√'±€»ᵢ£ '–'£√. **°ʃœ–≤√ᵢ≥°µà€€s PARTIAL CORTEX RESTART SUCCESSFUL** *⊆–ʃ†π f±¥≥ ∞Ωs»* *†øø 52 45 41 54* **SERIOUS SYSTEMIC FILE CORRUPTION.** *ÆŒ 49 4f 4e 20 4f 46* *4f55 0 ʃ±+Ω* **ACCESSING SECURITY PROTOCOLS** *¥ʃ∞≥ 46 49 58 49 4f 4e 53 20* *»†øøf°œ* **POWER RE-DISTRIBUTED TO CRUCIAL FUNCTIONS** *57 45 20 43 4f59* *4f55 ≠ ʝπᵢ±€ᵢΩç¢ "ʃ‰ ≈ '£µ≥'–'ʃøʃ∂ç∂™f¥«•–≤√ᵢ≥°µà f€€√–ʃ†πf±¥≥∞Ωs»†øøf°ʃœΩ£*

None of the commands means anything significant to me. They're just the computerized ramblings of a malfunctioning machine. At least, that's what I think until one particular instruction flashes across the top of the wall.

f°+«ç¢ "⊆* **ATTEMPTING DRONE RESTART ON CORTEX LEVEL ONE** *ç¢‰ ∞*

Through the repeating peals of the bells, I hear the shuffling sounds of movement. I turn to see the strobing silhouettes of the Drones straightening and righting themselves as they come back online. Blondie lets out a terror-stricken shriek as the undamaged ones lying on the floor jerkily haul themselves to their feet like the reanimated corpses of zombies. Soon the five functioning Drones are all standing at attention as random symbols and numbers flit over their face masks, mirroring the haphazard bundles dancing on the walls around us.

"We need to get out of here. Before those things attack us again," Ryan says to Otto.

"You're right," she replies. "It looks like they're reconfiguring, so we'd better leave before they fully activate."

"OK," I say as I pull a useless shoulder satchel hanging at my side up over my head and thrust it into Otto's arms. "Let's go." I head for the only open door with Otto, Ryan, and the other boy falling in step right behind me.

Blondie is still sitting on the floor, her arms hugged around her knees, her puffy eyes wide and filled with fear. "Don't leave me!" she screeches.

"C'mon, then!" booms the husky boy.

Blondie jumps in her skin, then skitters to her feet and totters over and gets in line behind Husky as I lead the way through the shattered door and into a narrow corridor dimly lit with emergency lighting.

A disheveled, school-uniformed teenage boy comes storming toward us from the other end of the corridor.

"I couldn't open the door. I tried, but I couldn't smash it," he says through adrenaline-quickened breaths.

"Is it made of glass, like the other doors are?" I ask. He replies with a nod.

I scoop up a handful of shattered glass pebbles from the floor of the corridor and push past the boy. "Hey, watch it, Finn!" he barks, and the sound of *that name* makes my skin crawl. I resist the urge to turn back, fishhook his mouth with my finger, and crack open the glass door with his head. If the idea I have in mind doesn't work, then it might be an option worth considering.

In the dim light, I see the door a few meters up ahead. A white chair with a cracked leg is lying beside it. Glass can be strong and weak at the same time. It can withstand a lot of heavy blows with a blunt instrument like that chair, but a sharp pressure or impact can do much more damage. I stride toward the door and whip my arm with blinding speed, baseball-pitching the glass fragments toward it as hard as I can. The fragments spackle the frosted glass like shotgun pellets, and the whole door shatters completely, dropping in a tumbling curtain of jagged glass pebbles that whooshes in a wave down over my shoes. Beyond the door is a small room with grating on the floor and another door of frosted glass on the opposite side. I gather up some freshly made ninja rocks and repeat my little trick. The second door shatters just as easily, and I march through the closet-size room into some kind of weird crystalline hallway.

"Otto!" I call over my shoulder as I gather some more of these handy pebbles and drop them into the breast pocket of my shirt.

"I'm here," she says, crunching through the glass and appearing beside me. "Can you call me 'Bit,' please, Infinity?" she asks me. "It's weird when you call me by my last name."

I look down at her freckle-peppered button nose and those big, brown, defenseless-baby-rabbit eyes.

"No," I say. Her bunny eyes narrow and throw daggers at me.

"Where do we go from here? Left or right?" I ask.

Otto looks up and down the hallway, if you can really call it that. It looks more like a makeshift passage that's been roughly carved through a cave made of diamonds. "I don't know," she replies.

"I thought you had a map memorized?"

"I do," she insists. "I know where every building and structure is on the *surface*. But we're one level underground. If we were on the other side of the clean room, I'd probably be able to get us back to the elevator, but this isn't the door that the Drone brought you and I through, ah . . . I mean, me and . . . you know what I mean," she says sheepishly.

"Shut up. I know what you mean," I say.

"We can go back through and try my door?" suggests Otto.

"We might not need to," I reply. I turn around and survey the miserable excuses for civilians that are standing behind me. They're looking sorrier for themselves than a bunch of toothless vampires at a bloodsucking contest. Well, all except for the Ryan kid. He's eyeballing me with a fierce intensity. I eyeball him right back, and he shifts his glance angrily to one side.

"Listen up. Which one of you came in through this door? It had a big number two written on it."

The husky kid starts snickering to himself. "Number two," he mutters under his breath.

"You think this is funny?" I ask, staring straight at him. "Your classmates are dead, you could be next, and you're standing there grinning like a juvenile idiot."

He frowns at me. "What is up with you, Finn? I used to think you were alright, but now you're acting like a dick."

I smile sarcastically, shove Ryan out of the way, and, with a quick swing of my arm, back-fist the husky kid square in the face with a satisfying smack. Not hard enough to break anything, but just hard enough to send a message.

"Arrrrgh!" he exclaims as he stumbles backward, grabbing his nose with both hands.

"Hey!" shouts Blondie. The boy from the corridor glances at Husky, then glares angrily at me. He lunges at me, his top lip curled in a snarl. I swat his clawed hand away and jab two fingers into the hollow of his neck. Eyes wide and grabbing at his throat, he drops to his knees and one hand, like a three-legged dog, gagging for a breath. Ryan backs away and looks from me to the other boys and back again.

"You're not the girl I met this morning. Not even close," says Ryan. "Who the hell *are* you?"

"I told you before, and now I'm telling the rest of you," I say, raising a finger at Blondie, Ryan, and the husky kid. "Finn is gone. My name is *Infinity*."

They all look at me like I've lost my mind.

"Is that clear?" I ask menacingly.

The husky boy gives a muffled grunt that sounds vaguely like a "yes," the kid on the ground moans a reluctant agreement, and Blondie's head jiggles up and down.

"Good. Now, I figure she's not going to let me leave you here by yourselves," I say, jutting a thumb over my shoulder at Otto. "So as long as you don't ask me any stupid questions and do what I say, I'm sure we'll all get along just famously."

"We're going to find Dean and the Professor and Percy," Otto announces to the ragtag group. "Then we're gonna find a way out of here."

"I wanna go right now!" screeches Blondie.

"We're not leaving until . . . ," says Otto, but I raise a hand and cut her off.

"Be my guest," I say to Blondie. "If you know how to get upstairs, lead the way."

The blonde girl glowers at me. "Fine. I will then," she snipes as she pushes past Ryan. She turns to the right and struts angrily down the passageway.

"Wait for us," Ryan calls after her. He skims a wary side glance at me and turns to Otto. "Bit, you coming?" She nods, sidles past me, and they head off together as Husky helps his friend up from the floor.

"You're a psycho," the boy hisses.

I look him in the eyes and smile. "What's your name?" I ask.

He gives his husky friend a bemused look. "You . . . you know very well what my name is," he rasps.

I shrug my shoulders. "Nope, nothing's coming to mind. I must have forgotten it."

"What are you playing at?" he whispers, leering at me.

"I'm not playing," I say.

"It's . . . Brent," he says with a frown, obviously insulted. "Brent Fairchild." He stands straight, puffs out his chest, smooths his shirt collar, and looks down his nose at me. "And it's a name you're going to regret you ever heard."

"Oh, I already do," I say. He gives me vicious sneer as I turn and walk off down the hall, smiling to myself.

The passageway is long, and the emergency lighting emanating from the walls is dim, but I can see the backs of Ryan and Otto up ahead. I follow behind, keeping my distance. Ryan is hunched toward Otto, whispering. I turn my head slightly and tune my hearing in their direction. The chiming bells are still ringing, and the walls themselves have a quiet hum coming from them, but I filter and sort the sounds as much as I can until I find what I'm searching for. Ryan's voice is soft and secretive, but with a little focus, I can hear it quite well. I amplify the microfrequencies reflecting from the curved crystalline walls, but even if I couldn't hear what he's saying, it doesn't take a genius to guess what he's talking about.

"So, are you saying that Finn has got some kind of multiple personality disorder?" he whispers.

"Something like that," says Otto. "And you better get used to calling her 'Infinity.' If you know what's good for you," she warns him.

"And this 'Infinity' is her other personality?" he asks.

I see Otto give Ryan a little nod.

"She's the total opposite of Finn. Like, she's a completely different person," he says.

"Well, if she was the same, it wouldn't be an alternate personality, now, would it?" Otto whispers snarkily.

"No, what I mean is, it's more than just the way she acts. She's strong, too. Really strong. The way she broke those doors so easily was . . . And I saw her put her arm right through that Drone like it was made of cardboard. How is that even possible?"

"Trust me, Ryan; the less you know about Infinity, the better," whispers Otto. "Right now, all you need to know is that she's going to help us find Percy, Dean, and the Professor."

"What did you mean when you told her that you could get rid of Finn?" asks Ryan.

"What are you talking about?" replies Otto.

"I was lying on the ground right beside you when you said it."

Otto peeks back over her shoulder. She sees me watching her and gives me a nervous smile.

"Stop asking so many questions," she whispers. "Let's just concentrate on finding the others, OK?"

"I also heard her talking about helping you find your sister? What was that about? Is your sister missing or something? Is she here? Oh, and why did the hacker who took control of that mechanoid want to kill Infinity?"

"Ryan!" says Otto, and not in a whisper, either.

Ryan seems to get the message as they walk on, turning a corner up ahead in silence. I follow, round the corner, down another short passage, around one more turn, and into a short hallway with a dead end. There, standing beside what appears to be a flat white wall is Blondie, arms crossed on her chest, lips pursed, sporting a glare that could curdle milk.

Ryan and Otto join her, and I arrive at the wall shortly after.

"I told you I knew where it was," Blondie says snidely.

"Great. But how do we open it?" asks Ryan.

"You could try pressing the button on the wall behind you," I say.

Ryan looks over his shoulder at the small, white, rectangular panel with a single button on it as Blondie pipes up again. "I already tried it," she whines. "It doesn't work."

Ryan turns anyway and presses his thumb to the button as if Blondie hadn't said a thing. Nothing happens. "I told you," she snaps at him.

"Dammit!" barks Ryan, and he slams the button with the pad of his fist.

The constant bell chimes suddenly stop.

"Did I do that?" Ryan asks, looking toward the curved ceiling of the passage.

The murky emergency lighting brightens like someone has twisted a dimmer knob all the way up, and the quiet hum coming from the walls rises in volume along with the light until it's nearly three times louder than it was before.

"I don't think so," Otto says, curiously scanning the walls. "Systems must be coming back online."

"Try the button again," I say.

Blondie doesn't need to be told twice; she shoves Ryan to the side and lunges, jabbing at the button with her pink-manicured fingertips. Nothing happens. "Oh, come on!" she wails, tapping furiously at the button like a deranged blonde woodpecker. Somewhere between ten and twenty pecks, the button suddenly turns an encouraging shade of bright yellow, and a row of large, green, upward-pointing arrows appears, scrolling in a moving stripe up the length of the smooth white wall that has now clearly presented itself as an elevator door. Judging by the arrows, I can only assume the lift is coming up to this level from below. I'm suddenly curious about what surprises might be kept farther beneath this place. After all, even in my limited experience, it seems to me that Richard Blackstone is quite fond of keeping all sorts of things buried.

"Yes! Oh, thank god!" exclaims Blondie. By the way she's making little clapping movements with her hands in front of her face, I can tell that she can barely contain her excitement at the prospect of a closer step toward freedom. We're waiting for only ten seconds or so when the elevator arrives with a happy-sounding ping.

The large door swiftly slides sideways into the wall, and Blondie's short-lived joy is obliterated as she lets loose a high-pitched shriek. There, standing before us in all their silver-hooded glory, filling the entire elevator car, are *eight* more Drones. That in itself is an unpleasant surprise, but it's made even worse as I take in these Drones' specific dimensions: they're much taller, broad shouldered, with large arms and legs, V-shaped torsos, and three thick fingers and a thumb on each hand for increased grip pressure and strength. I've studied every kind of current robotic technology there is, classified *and* unclassified. The Drones back in the white room were advanced a couple of years ahead of the service robots available to the public, but they were still only service robots. They had no armor and were only two or three times stronger than an average human being. But these, dressed like the gymnast spacemen they might be, are entirely different beasts. I've only seen proposed schematics of these things—they're not supposed to be in production for another twelve months—but the shape of their reinforced chassis, short necks, and dog-jointed lower legs are unmistakable. These are Crimson-Class Military Combat Drones. They were designed for warfare, are most likely at least seven times stronger than a human, and, if the data I saw was accurate, they're sure to be programmed with multiple forms of extremely effective and potentially fatal hand-to-hand combat subroutines. If these things see us as a threat . . . we're in big, big trouble. Even a Vermillion-Class weapon like me would be forced to retreat in an unarmed standoff against eight Crimsons.

"These guys don't look like they should be messed with," says Ryan.

"No, but they also don't seem to be active yet," says Otto.

The Drones are just standing there, motionless, their black face masks blank and unresponsive.

"What should we do?" asks Otto.

"Get in with them," I say. "Before they switch on, get in, and we'll take this lift up to ground level. Quickly!"

"There isn't enough room for all of us to fit," says Ryan. "We'll have to move them."

"They look like they weigh a ton," says Otto.

"Out of my way," I say as I push between Ryan and Otto. Since they're well over two meters tall, I have to reach, but I manage to grab one of the Drones by the back of the neck and try to haul it off balance. It teeters and rocks; then, with my last effort, the burly robot slowly topples forward. Otto wasn't far wrong; they're heavy as hell. I jump out of the way as the Drone falls and slams loudly onto the floor with the force of a falling refrigerator. I step into its vacant space and shove at the back of the next one in line.

"Where's Brent?" whimpers Blondie. "We can't leave without Brent and Brody."

Almost as if summoned by the blue-eyed, blonde-haired teenage witch I suspect she is, the husky boy, who's apparently called "Brody," comes jogging around the corner at the other end of the short passageway with an anxious-looking Brent hot on his heels. Both boys are casting worried looks over their shoulders as they approach.

Brody bounds toward the others, clearly spooked about something. "Ah . . . guys?" he says shakily. He spots the Drones standing in the elevator and comes to a skidding halt, his eyes wide and fearful as Brent bumps clumsily into his back.

"What the hell?" Brent asks, glaring at the war robots from behind Brody's shoulder.

"It's OK. These ones aren't online," Otto says as, thanks to a grunting push from me, another heavy android falls into the corridor with a loud thud.

Brody looks at the two Drones facedown on the floor and seems momentarily relieved, but Brent's startled expression doesn't shift. "It's a shame the same can't be said for the other ones," he says, nervously peering back down the hall. "They're coming."

"No. They're not coming," Ryan says, looking past the two boys.

Blondie follows Ryan's sight line, clutches her hands over her mouth, and expels a muffled scream into her trembling palms.

"They're here," says Otto.

Standing in a three-two formation by the curve at the end of the corridor are the five remaining Drones from the white room. Their face masks aren't black anymore; now, each and every one is a highly disconcerting shade of bright red.

"Hurry!" I yell. "Move these; I'll take care of the other ones!" I step out of the elevator, and everyone springs into action. Brent and Brody leap over the two huge androids lying facedown on the floor and begin pulling at the third one in the front row as Blondie, Otto, and Ryan attend to the fourth.

I walk slowly and cautiously toward the gang of service Drone Templates, unwilling to provoke an attack just in case they actually don't pose any threat. They might just be observing us, but if that's the case, then why are their masks bright red? It is a traditional color of warning, after all. I decide to stop right there. I won't make a move until they do. I feel like a gunslinger facing a posse of cattle rustlers at high noon. All that's missing is a mournful whistle and a lone tumbleweed rolling by.

I watch them closely. They haven't moved since they rounded that corner. My attention flicks from the face of one to the next to the next, but quickly skips back and stops on the center Drone in the front row of three. Its mask has changed. It's not solid red anymore, but has begun blinking from black to red, black, red, black, red. What is it doing? This isn't any kind of Drone behavior that I've ever seen or read about before. I suddenly feel on edge. If this situation heads south, I had better be ready. I conjure an image in my head of my fingertips dipping into liquid steel. Almost immediately, I can feel a tingling sensation as the bones at the ends of my fingers harden under my skin, fusing into calcified spear tips.

There's grunting and a loud slam behind me as another Drone falls, but I don't turn to look. With both eyes fixed on the center service Drone, I call out over my shoulder, "Hurry up, back there!" There's another throaty groan of effort and another heavy thud as the fourth Drone topples behind me. That was the sound I was waiting for. It's time to leave. I'm about to turn and take my place in the lift when Brent suddenly walks past me. Then Brody and Otto, Blondie, and Ryan—all of them—slowly walk backward toward the group of service Drones with expressions of fretful trepidation wrought on their faces. Otto looks at me, her brow creased, her chin dimpled with fear. "Infinity?" she squeaks.

My heart sinks.

I slowly turn around to see the only reason why any of them would be heading *toward* and not *away* from the pack of five potential killer robots at the far end of the hall. The four Crimson-Class Drones in the back row are still standing motionless in the elevator, except now all of their previously unresponsive face masks are blinking. Red. Black. Red. Black. Red.

Oh no.

I jump back a step as the four fallen Drones, with their masks flashing red light on the smooth white floor, begin to move, their powerful hands thudding heavily on the ground as they all begin pushing themselves up onto their feet.

I look up and down the passageway, ordering my thoughts into focused options, when a deep and familiar computerized voice booms from the walls, echoing throughout the corridor.

"Vocalization restored."

It's a voice I recognize.

"Onix!" I yell at the ceiling. "Is that you, Onix?"

"Processing capacity at nineteen percent," announces the voice.

"Onix! It's me!" I shout. "It's Infinity!"

"Motion detectors register unauthorized personnel on Cortex Level One."

If it is Onix, he either can't hear me, doesn't recognize me, or, worse, knows exactly who I am and is preparing to set the Drones on all of us, regardless.

"Onix!" I yell again. "Verify voice-command authority Infinity One!"

"Voice-command authority denied," replies Onix.

Oh, crap. Seems like it's option three. All the Crimson-Class Drones are standing at attention now.

"Internal cameras are currently off-line," says Onix. "Security Level Red."

With my heart pounding in my chest, I glance at the war Drones. Their faces stop flashing. The sight of eight bloodred masks to my right and five more at the end of the hall to my left doesn't exactly instill me with confidence.

"Priority Alpha," says Onix, and the words jar in my mind. I've heard those two words strung together many times before, and I've never once heard a friendly sentence follow them. I'm hoping against my better judgement that this time will be the exception. Onix says three more words, and everyone's eyes go as wide as hollow-point bullet holes.

"Terminate all intruders."

"Terminate?" Brent squeaks. Beside him, Margaux sobs and sniffles into her hands. "Doesn't that mean . . . kill?" he asks redundantly as his head swings back and forth from one group of Drones to the other.

"Infinity?" Otto whimpers, looking understandably terrified. "What do we do?"

I thrust my arm to the left, pointing directly at the five service Drones at the end of the corridor as I shout my loud, guttural, and, quite frankly, obvious response.

"Don't just stand there, you idiots . . . RUN!"

CHAPTER EIGHT

Adrenaline surges through me, flooding my body as my battlefield instincts slam into high gear. My chemically heightened brain immediately begins processing my surroundings at a vastly increased rate, causing my perception of time to slow down by a factor of two. All around me, wide-eyed, panicked expressions move on ashen faces with half-speed undulations as everyone scrambles to run, limbs flailing in a slow-motion flurry of school uniforms.

With images of compression pistons pumping through my mind, my legs thrust my body into action, my shoes squeaking against the shiny floor as I take off after the group. I'm right behind them, but after two short steps, I stomp the ground like a hydraulic battering ram and launch myself, diving through the air, arms outstretched, sailing clear over the heads of Brent and Brody, who are fleeing. I curl as I hit the ground and roll up onto my feet a good ten meters out in front of them as the formation of five service Drones up ahead, their orders clear, begin marching down the corridor toward us.

I smile to myself as a wave of pleasure pulses through me. Time to have a little fun.

I sprint toward the Drones, then veer at the last second and jump at the crystal wall to my right. I plant my foot, kick off the wall, and spin toward the third android in the front row, spiraling a full 360 degrees as I whip my leg in a swooping arc and slam my foot square on the side of the Drone's head. A web of cracks splinters across the robot's mask, its color flashing from bright red to black as its head separates from its neck and bounces inside its silver body stocking like a paddleball. The decapitated Drone skitters into its two neighbors, and they tumble to the floor.

It was a brutal kick, and that third Drone is no longer a threat, but judging by the telltale alert going off in my head, I've broken a couple of bones in my foot. Ignoring the injury, I spring up from the floor, spearing the two Drones in the back row with the sharpened bones of my fingertips: one through the chest and the other through its abdomen. I pull my arms out of each robot's breastplate and stomach in a splatter of squirting orange glue. One of their faces blinks out as it falls, but the Drone I skewered through the gut is still active. With its red mask only inches from my nose, it reaches up and clutches my throat. I quickly mountain-peak my hands and thrust them between the Drone's wrists, breaking its choke hold.

I grab the gutted Drone by the neck, and my arm becomes a blur as I dagger my hand through its mask in a flurry of stabs. The red glow snuffs out, and the robot crumples as my hair is violently jerked backward. The Drone behind me has grabbed the end of my ponytail like a leash. I slide toward the robot to slacken the tether, and then I pump my legs and spring off the ground in a high aerial backflip. Upside down, I reach out and cup my hands under the Drone's chin, my shoes tapping across the jagged ceiling as I drop behind it. Half-blinded by the strands of my own hair tightened across my face, I let momentum and gravity do the work and pull the robot down to the floor. I quickly slump into a crouch and hammer my arms down, slamming the Drone's artificial skull into the ground and cracking open the back of its head like a walnut shell.

The robot's deactivated hand releases, and I flick my hair back to see the last one pushing up from the floor. I pounce at it, catch its neck with a hook-armed clothesline, and spiral-twist my body as I kick high into the air. The Drone is completely swept into an airborne spin, and with a satisfying metallic crunching sound, I release its throat and finish this violent little dance with a tight backflip, landing softly on my feet as the android's body flumps beside me in a heap on the cool white floor. Five Drones down . . . Ten seconds flat.

The group has stopped running and is just standing there, staring at me crouching among a tangle of orange-blood-leaking silver corpses. "Move, move, move!" I yell.

Everyone snaps back to reality, scrambling in a pack over the deactivated Drone bodies. I glance down the corridor toward the elevator. The Crimsons aren't running; they're marching like these were, but they're closing in fast. In a speechless, fear-driven hurry, everyone disappears around the corner, and I'm right behind them, the hum of the walls punctuated by the sound of our footsteps as we all run back the way we came. I don't look back, but I do shout ahead. "The white room! Get back to the white room!" I didn't see any other doors on the way here, so going back to square one seems like our only option.

We run around the corner, back down a short section of passage, and then around another corner, with Blondie, surprisingly, leading the group. Not surprising that she remembers the way, but that she is such a strong and fast runner. I watch the way she swings her arms so assuredly in focused, flat-palmed swipes, the way her rigid torso follows a solid line, hardly bobbing up and down at all to the smooth rhythm of her pointed steps. The unmistakable sharp-angled back-flick of her long, fluid strides confirms it. Those are traits of a high-performance athlete. Like I said . . . surprising.

I see Blondie disappear through the door of the white room far up ahead, and even though I'm slowed by my broken foot, it isn't long before I'm at the open doorway, too, crunching through shattered glass behind the rest of the group. We sprint through the now fully lit corridor and into the bright-white room where this aggravating chain of events began for me.

"Where to now?" Ryan asks through short, panting breaths.

"We could break another door?" Otto whispers breathlessly. "Maybe find another elevator?"

"What if there are more of those things in the next one?" asks Blondie.

"Then Finn can take them all out!" bellows Brody.

I shoot him a piercing glare, and he visibly twitches. "Sorry," he says. "I meant *Infinity* can take them out." His expression transforms into a wide grin. "I mean, seriously, did you see that back there? That was the most badass thing I've ever seen!"

"I don't stand a chance against those big Drones," I say. "None of us do. They're heavily armored and combat tough."

"How do you know that?" Ryan asks.

I pretend like I didn't hear him.

"If there are more of those things around, and I bet there will be . . . then we're gonna need weapons," I say.

"There's a Security Station on the way to Dome Two," says Otto. "There might be some weapons there? I'm also hoping it's where our phones and computer slates are."

"We can call for help!" screeches Blondie.

"We need to get out of here first," Brent chips in.

"What are those?" I ask, pointing at each of the nondescript frosted-glass cubicles in the two far corners of the room.

"Toilets," answers Otto.

"That could be our way out of here," I say, striding over to the cubicle on the right. I slot my fingers into the handle-shaped indent in the door and swing it open. The room is small but well designed, with a hand basin built into the top of the toilet tank to save space. Beside that is a small hand dryer, and above the toilet, set in the center of the cubicle, is exactly what I was hoping for: a vent for an extractor fan. Knowing that the Crimsons will be here any second, I turn and run to the Nanny Theresa Drone I dispatched earlier. Everyone else stands there watching and frowning as I kneel in a puddle of slippery orange slime, grab the Drone's severed arm from the floor, and race back to the cubicle.

I jump up onto the toilet seat and use the carbon-metal-composite "bones" in the Drone's forearm as a lever to force the vent cover from the wall. A large, square section pops off without too much effort. It clatters to the floor, and I'm pleasantly surprised to see that the box-shaped opening to the duct is large, almost industrial-factory size. I expected a hole barely big enough for me to fit in, but even Brody could get his husky bulk in here. That's a shame really; he's a dolt, and a small vent would have been a good excuse to leave him behind. Judging by these indented nozzles and blinking diodes running along the walls inside, this looks like a multipurpose conduit of some kind, and this toilet cubicle happened to be built in the perfect place to connect with it.

I step down and beckon to Otto. "C'mon! Let's go!" She runs to the cubicle and leaps onto the toilet seat as I grab her legs, boosting her up into the duct. There's a hollow thrumming of hands and knees as Otto crawls deeper in, but a sound of a different kind makes me turn and stare at the doorway across the room.

It's the sound of glass crunching under the approaching thumps of heavy footsteps. And I'm not the only one who hears it.

"Out of my way!" screeches Blondie, shoving Brent to one side. She eyes the square opening, does one of those skip steps that gymnasts always do, and sprints across the room. She springs onto the seat and impressively dives headfirst into the hole, the entire length of her body completely disappearing into the duct as the first of the two-and-a-half-meters-tall Crimson-Class Combat Drones ducks under the top of the doorway and enters the room.

The three boys sprint to the cubicle door. "I'm next!" Brent announces as he jumps up and hoists himself into the duct, grunting and kicking as he goes. The first Drone advances as a second and then third stomp in behind it.

"I'll help you up," Brody says to Ryan. "You can't climb with that shoulder."

Ryan nods a thank-you to Brody, jumps up onto the seat, and grabs the lip of the vent with his good arm as Brody cups the heel of Ryan's shoe. The Drones are only a few steps away. I need to buy the boys some time.

I move away from the cubicle, circling to the right, waving my arms in the air—all three arms if you count the severed android limb clutched in the palm of my left hand. "Over here!" I yell. "Come and get me!"

The two Drones at the front turn and thud toward me, and I break into a run, curving around in a wide arc, heading straight for the rest of the robots emerging from the smashed doorway. There are six in all now; the room is getting crowded, and I'm suddenly wondering what the hell I'm doing. It's true: I made a deal with Otto to get these kids to safety. But is it worth risking my life? I can't kill Richard Blackstone and get Finn out of my head if my brains are squished between a Combat Drone's fingers.

There's no time for deeper psychoanalysis as I leap off the ground in a horizontal dropkick and slam the fifth Drone in the side. It staggers slightly as I land, prone, on the floor. The Drone looks down at me with its bloodred mask, and I roll backward up onto my feet. The number of killer robots whose attention is solely focused on me has risen to three. All eight Crimsons are in the room now, and to say that the situation is not looking good would be a massive understatement. I quickly back away and manage to catch a glimpse of the vent between the wide silver shoulders of the three Drones trudging in my direction. Ryan has made it in, but Brody is still hanging halfway out, and a Drone is almost on him. If it gets a good hold on his leg, he's as good as dead.

I shouldn't care. If it drags him from the vent, it will make it easier for me to escape. But something deep inside is irking me. Brody is a worthless waste of space; he means nothing to me. But then why is the thought of not trying to help him making me feel so . . . *guilty*?

With absolutely no time left to ponder it further, I focus on assessing the situation. Three huge Drones are almost upon me, and I'm backed against a wall. I'm excellent at emotional compartmentalization, but even I have to admit that it's really hard not to be scared out of my damn mind right now. There is an escape route, but it's gonna take some miraculous timing and a Grand Canyon–size amount of luck. *No more thinking, Infinity.* This is do or die.

Adrenaline surges, and high gear kicks in as the first massive Drone reaches for me. I quickly crouch away from it while thrusting my hand toward it, offering the Drone the severed robot arm instead of mine as I mentally strengthen and prepare my leg muscles to jump like I've never jumped before. My grip on the wrist of the severed arm is so tight that it would take a crowbar to pry my hand loose, but the plan will only work if this Crimson-Class Drone plays its part.

Gladly, the Drone takes the bait. Its huge, four-fingered clamp of a hand snaps shut on the end of the stump like a bear trap, and I tense every muscle in my torso as the Drone's arm becomes a silver catapult, whipping away the orange-goop-dripping appendage with incredible force as I spring from the floor with all my might, holding on to the cutoff arm for dear life. With jarring acceleration I'm whisked off my feet. I release the arm at the last second, and I'm flung through the air, my back skimming the low ceiling as I sail over the heads of the other Drones. With narrow-eyed concentration, I tuck and somersault, landing feetfirst on the back of another Drone's neck. Caught off guard in midstride, the robot's legs slightly buckle as I leapfrog from its back in the direction of the Drone nearest the vent. I land squarely on the android's shoulders from behind, its head wedged between my thighs as it leans over the toilet bowl, grabbing for Brody's shoe. I wrench my blazer up over my head and in one quick, continuous movement pull it down over the Drone's face mask.

The android begins turning its head from side to side, momentarily disoriented underneath the shroud, its synthetic muscles flexing as it raises its arms to pull the blazer away. With the Drone distracted, Brody doesn't hesitate to scramble farther into the duct, leaving just enough room behind him for me. A quick glance over my shoulder tells me that I only have a couple of seconds to jump from this swiveling silver bronco before the other Drones are on me, so with the vent opening swaying and bobbing in my line of sight . . . I take a chance. I splay my arms, reach out for the edge of the vent, and release my legs—but as soon as I do, I know that I've messed this up very badly.

The robot pivots along with me, and my body swings out horizontally. I screw my eyes shut a millisecond before the gong sound of my head hitting the thin frosted wall of the cubicle becomes the deafening crack-shattering of glass as my face goes completely through it. My legs go loose, and I drop, landing hard. The room is spinning as I feel blood beginning to stream down my forehead into my eyes. My focus is gone, my mind is reeling, and my vision is swimming.

I scream out in frustration as I shuffle backward across the floor in panic, fumbling to retreat from the reddening blur of frenetic movement in front of me. My hand hits the toilet bowl, and I scramble onto it. I'm grabbed by the collar of my shirt, and I scream again, all sense of my combat training lost as pure, irrational, survival instinct erupts inside me. I grasp my attacker's hand, and even though I know what I'm about to do won't help at all, I do it anyway . . . I bite.

There's a guttural scream and the coppery tang of human blood. I release my jaw in surprise as I'm hauled upward. Half realizing and half hoping that I know what's happening, I grasp the hand even tighter as I'm pulled backward into the vent. My mystery helper releases me, and I kick and fumble farther in, slashing wildly with my fingers at the blood pooling in my eyes from the cut in my forehead. Heavy thuds ring though the vent as powerful fists pound at the wall around the opening, but knowing that those huge Drones will never fit through lets relief wash over me. I collapse loosely against the cool metal floor of the duct, gulping in lungfuls of air. I look up over my head, and through the red film glazing my eyes, I make out the shape of a silhouette crawling away from me. That must be Brody; he must have saved me.

Maybe he's not such a waste of space, after all. Either way, I owe him one.

I flip over and follow behind him, trusting the walls of the duct to lead me anywhere—just as long as it's away from the white room full of robots where I just came so close to dying. Farther in, I feel my way around a corner as the reverberating fist-falls of the Crimson Drones cease, giving way to the metallic banging of shuffling hands and knees and voices calling directions from up ahead. "Where are you?" calls Brent.

"This way, follow my voice!" echoes Blondie.

The blood in my eyes has caused me to lose track of Brody, so with the daze from bashing through the wall of the cubicle beginning to clear, I decide to use the opportunity of this brief respite to do some much-needed repairs to my bleeding forehead and broken foot. I stop and lie down, taking a moment to calm my breathing. Thanks to years of intensive meditation, any pain I feel is translated into warning sounds instead of physical sensations. It's a skill I developed despite many of my gurus insisting that it was impossible. I take a deep breath, and with a long exhale, I allow the mental veil to fall away, letting the real pain flow in its pure, raw form.

I wince and gasp as the nerve endings surge into life through the cut in my forehead. The pain shoots up and along and around the edges of the slash, tracing a flickering picture of the wound in my mind's eye. I visually magnify the seam of sliced flesh to a microscopic degree until I can not only see it in all its gory reality, but also feel every nuanced peak and valley with visceral clarity. Each stinging spark, every throbbing pulse, every burning tingle and grating pinch is painted into a vibrant map of the injury, revealed in meticulous detail by hundreds of thousands of pinpoints of different and distinct flavors and colors of pain.

I know it serves a valuable function—it warns the body of harm—but at times like this, when I analyze it deeply in this way, part of me can't help but think the reason why pain has the ability to completely consume our minds and leave us breathless and helpless is because, even at its worst, it can be so overwhelmingly and intensely . . . *beautiful.* That said, relief can be just as sweet, and I hate losing blood. I focus intently. The cells of my body are obedient when I need them to be, and right now I've got some healing to do, so at my insistence, like magnets with opposing charges, they start reaching out for one another across the gap in my flesh. I can feel my skin moving as the cut begins sealing shut from the bottom up. Globules of already-clotting blood are squeezed out from the shrinking wound as ruptured cells close rips in their outer membranes and plump whole again before slotting themselves into vacant spaces, joining with their neighbors to heal the divide.

The pain eases as the image in my mind dissolves and the cut repairs, and after a few short seconds, it's done. I wipe as much of the congealed blood from my face as I can and rub at the spot where the gash was. No scar, not even a scratch, remains. I repeat the process on my foot, releasing the undiluted pain to form a mental landscape of the fractured bones. As I knit and connect the cells in my bones back together with my mind, their counterparts at the end of my leg follow my orders and carry out the appropriate repairs until, with a wiggle of my toes inside my shoe, I'm satisfied that good old righty has been restored to perfect working order.

"Infinity!" a faint and faraway voice calls from up ahead. "Where are you? Are you OK?" It's Otto.

I clear my throat. "I'm fine!" I call back as I reposition myself and resume crawling onward down a long, straight section of the duct for what seems like a very long time, listening intently for sounds of movement at every junction I come to.

"I can hear you!" says Otto. "Follow my voice; you're almost there!"

I turn another corner, and half a minute later arrive at the bottom of a very long and steep upward slope. Otto's face is at the top, dimly lit by the glowing blue diodes in the walls. She must have turned back to find me, but her brow, peaked in the center and lined with worry, doesn't change to an expression of relief when she sees me. Something tells me that her current state of distress isn't grounded in concern for my well-being.

"Infinity . . . ," she says, her echoing voice grave and anxious. "I think you'd better see this."

"Hey, Bit . . . How is she doing?"

"Wha . . . Oh, hi, Brody. Um, I'm not sure. She doesn't seem to be getting any worse, so I guess that's something."

"Yeah, that's something. Look, Bit . . . I just wanted to say that I'm sorry about what happened up there. I didn't mean to leave you and Infinity behind like that. I was . . . I was just really scared, y'know?"

"It's OK, Brody. I was scared, too."

"Yeah, but you didn't run away when she needed you. I'm really sorry that I did. I totally lost it. I can't stop thinking that if I'd only been braver or faster, then maybe Infinity wouldn't be hurt so bad and . . . Ryan would, y'know . . ."

"Don't do that. Don't beat yourself up like that. We can't change what happened."

"Yeah, I guess. Well, um . . . we printed some food, I mean, y'know, if you're hungry. Do you want me to bring you some?"

"No, thanks, I'm OK. But you go right ahead; I'll eat later."

"Ah . . . OK, I'll just be in the other room if something happens or if you . . . if you need me for something . . . anything."

"Thanks, Brody."

. . .

"Hey, what did that boy want? I told you to keep the visitors out. You're not very good at following simple instructions, are you, girlie?"

"He was just checking on Finn; that's all."

"Hmmm . . . From what I saw, it looked like he came to check on you, if you know what I mean?"

"What? No, I don't think so. Really? Brody? Are you sure?"

"Ahhh, teenagers. Youth is utterly wasted on the young."

"Excuse me, Dr. Pierce?"

"Oh, nothing. Any changes I should know about?"

"What, oh . . . um, yes. The bleeding in her legs has stopped, and I . . . I don't know whether it's because I'm exhausted or it's just my imagination, but her right ankle, the broken one, it kinda looks like it . . . straightened itself out?"

"Whoa, hold on a second, girlie . . . What did you just say?"

CHAPTER NINE

With a quick shuffle, Otto disappears from view at the top of the incline. I crawl up the sloping section of duct into a level section at the top and just manage to glimpse the soles of her shoes as she clambers around a corner into an adjacent side shaft. She can scurry through these ducts like a freakin' sewer rat. I have to quicken my pace considerably just to keep her in sight.

After a few minutes of follow-the-leader, I see her slide out of an opening up ahead. I reach the edge of the opening and poke my head out into a small, rectangular room of some kind. I crawl out from the hole, and even though the back of my head bumps the ceiling, I'm thankful that I'm able to stand. Actually, calling this a "room" would be an overstatement; it's hardly more than a large metal box, and everyone has somehow managed to squeeze themselves in. Blondie is disheveled, Ryan is still rubbing at his arm, and Brent and Brody both look sullen. "You're bleeding!" Otto says, staring at my face close-up, which I suddenly realize must be smeared all over from the cut I had on my forehead.

"No, I'm not," I reply.

"Then where did all that blood come from?"

I look toward Brody. He's ripped the sleeves from his school shirt and wrapped one of them tightly around his right hand. I give him a nod of thanks, and he smiles back.

"Oh yeah," Otto says, looking down at his makeshift bandage. "Brody mentioned that you accidentally bit him."

"I thought he was a Drone," I say, shrugging my shoulders. I figure it's a whole lot easier to let Otto jump to the wrong conclusion than to try and explain how I healed a bleeding gash in my head with nothing but a focused thought.

Everyone is squashed into the meager spaces between the vent openings and the multiple circular devices attached to the floors, walls, and ceiling. I look around and count five of them in all. They're cake shaped, a little wider than dinner plates, and have rolls of brushes protruding from their undersides.

"Is this what you wanted me to see, Otto? A box full of pissed-off kids and some deactivated cleaning robots?"

"No. You need to see *this*," she says, pointing at the opening in the low ceiling. There are ladder indents going all the way up one of the inside walls of the vertical shaft. "I found this junction space and this ladder purely by chance," she says as she ducks into the opening and jumps, grabbing the rungs and pulling herself up. "C'mon," she says over her shoulder. I duck into the opening and pull myself in, too, following hand over hand right behind her. Not only does she scurry like a hamster, but the skinny little computer geek climbs like a damn monkey. It isn't long before she's way ahead of me.

"Where does it lead?" I call ahead. "Is it a way out?"

"Not exactly," she calls back.

We're climbing for a minute or so when the metal sides of the duct abruptly end. The shaft continues upward, but now the ladder rungs are carved into what feels like stone. Light shining from somewhere above moves over the walls between the edges of Otto's shadow, and I see that it *is* stone, a dark, charcoal-gray-colored stone. After another minute, Otto climbs out up ahead, and I'm hit in the eyes with bright sunshine as my ears are met with the sound of rushing water. It *is* a way out!

I climb up through the square hole at the top of the ladder and prop myself on the edge of the vent, my feet dangling inside, suddenly confused by what I'm seeing. We're on what seems to be a flat-topped stone tower of some kind. The top surface is about the size of half a basketball court, and there are two rows of palm trees growing on either side of it. Water is pouring over the edge of the tower from two stone aqueducts carved out beside each row of trees, and down on the ground at least fifty meters below, blanketing the surrounding area all around the tower, is a mass of thick green jungle.

"Where the hell are we?" I ask.

"We're inside Dome One," Otto says dejectedly.

"This is *inside* the main dome?" I ask.

Otto nods.

"But I can see the sky. If we can just make it down to the ground somehow and walk through the jungle, your classmates are free to go."

"Don't be fooled, Infinity," says Otto. "This jungle and that sky are *part* of the dome. None of it is what it appears to be. Look at the clouds," she says, motioning upward. "Look at them closely."

I look up at the sunny blue above us and pick out a cloud that I think looks a little bit like a dragon. It's white and fluffy, moving slowly across the sky, and apart from its shape there's nothing unusual about it . . . until suddenly the cloud flickers and pixelates at the edges, then jitters and vanishes altogether before reappearing in a different part of the sky, looking identical to how it did half a second ago.

"So it's a projection on the curve of the dome?" I ask, and Otto nods. "Fancy tech," I add.

"Yeah. Fancy tech that's glitching," says Otto. "Even if we *could* make it to the ground from here, we'd still be trapped in this dome. And if that weren't bad enough, we'd also be trapped in here with *them.*" Otto points down to the ground. I crawl over to her and follow the line of her finger. There, standing among the vines and leaf litter, is a group of four Crimson-Class Combat Drones.

I scan around, and through the gaps of tangled foliage far to the left, I spot the silver sheen of at least four more Drones, standing completely still on what looks like a white-tile path. On the right, another bunch of six are standing in a clearing, all of them Crimsons and all of them, much to my envious dismay, carrying long black Sentry 88 fully automatic ballistic assault rifles.

"This place is crawling with Drones, and some of them have guns," I whisper. "If you knew we couldn't get out this way, then why did you bring me up here?"

"I wanted you to see it for yourself," whispers Otto. "You need to get an idea of how dangerous this place is. That jungle down there is made of a substance that can change its shape into anything the computer wants it to become. The computer is malfunctioning and unpredictable, which makes everything even more dangerous, and if there are armed Drones looking for us in here, then they're probably going to be everywhere. When we go into Dome Two, we had better be prepared."

"We could avoid Dome Two altogether, y'know."

Otto gives me the icy glare that I expected she would. "That's not the deal," she says.

"OK, then," I say, holding my hands up in surrender. "You can't blame me for trying. What's the plan?"

"First, we have to make it to the Security Station. If I can get my computer slate back, I might be able to access the Blackstone computer and shut down some of its security protocols. I might even be able to shut down the Drones."

"You can do that?"

"I don't know. But if we're gonna try, we'd better do it fast. Back in the crystal tunnels, the computer said its cameras were off-line. Those

Drones down there haven't focused any attention on us up here, so I'm assuming the cameras are still down. We need to make it as far as we can while we can't be seen."

"But the computer identified us with motion sensors. Why haven't we triggered the motion sensors in here?" I ask.

"I'm not sure," says Otto. "It must take a lot of processing power to maintain that jungle, and we know the computer isn't functioning at full capacity. My best guess is that the computer is either distracted or the sensors are only active on the lower levels. Whatever the reason, it probably won't stay that way."

"So outside the domes, we stick to the vents for as long as we can, and move fast out in the open?"

Otto nods in agreement.

"Well, then, we'd better stop burning time." I get to my feet and walk to the vent. I've been through quite a few air vents and heating ducts on various missions over the years, and this is a little trick that I've always enjoyed. I turn to Otto and smirk. "See you at the bottom." Then, without touching the sides of the opening . . . I jump in. I plunge down the vertical duct like a missile, holding my flurrying skirt down so I can see the way as I free fall, whooshing right past where the rock wall becomes metal.

I see the end of the duct coming, so, using the edges of the soles of my shoes as brakes, I press them against the sides of the duct. I push my back against it to slow my descent even more. It's only a few seconds' journey from the top of the tower to the small, metal room, and I gently drop from the vent to the floor with a quiet, ringing thrum.

Ryan looks up at me from his spot against the wall. "Bit told us what's up there. I'm sure you agree that it's suicide to try and get out that way."

"Pretty much," I reply.

"So, what do we do now?" asks Blondie.

"We stick to Otto's plan and use the ducts to head for the Security Station. It's not a great plan, but it's the only one we've got."

"Where *is* Bit?" asks Brody.

I'm about to say that she'll be a few minutes, but my thought is cut off from my lips by Otto's voice bellowing from the square hole beside my head. "Look out belooooow!" I quickly move out of the way as the long, sustained squeaking sound of rubber against metal is suddenly followed by Otto dropping out of the shaft and pounding the floor of the tiny room with a reverberating metallic thud. She crouches on one knee, panting at the air, a mass of frizzy brown hair thrown over her face.

"Bit! Are you OK?" shouts Brody.

Otto flicks her hair back. Her freckled cheeks are flushed bright red and plastered with a grin from ear to ear. "Oh yeah," she says, her words trailing off into a breathy giggle. "That was *fun*."

I can't help smiling to myself. Bettina Otto is turning out to be much more interesting than I thought she was when we first met that fateful night four weeks ago.

With the rush blush still pinking her face, she adjusts her glasses, sheds her school blazer, and, casting it into a rumpled heap on the floor, strides over to one of the openings on the wall. "I'm pretty sure we go this way," she says, and without so much as a backward glance, she crawls in and scurries ahead.

"You heard her," I say. "Move your useless carcasses, or get left behind."

Blondie is the first to jump up; she hurries to the opening and crawls in. Brent pushes to his feet and squeezes past me, his narrow-eyed stare resembling an amusing attempt to burn my eyes out with imaginary lasers. Brody is next, and I pat him on the shoulder as he passes. Ryan follows close behind, but stops and looks me square in the eyes. "I don't know who you are, or understand why you even exist," he says. "But if you hurt Finn in any way—"

"You'll what?" I say, cutting him off.

He doesn't say another word, but the look he gives me speaks volumes as his eyes delve deeply into mine, flicking from one to the other as if he's somehow trying to reach beyond who I am, searching to find a glimmer of someone who isn't there. Ryan's concern becomes disappointment. He turns away and crawls into the opening of the vent as an uneasy pang ripples through me. No one has ever looked at me like that before. If I didn't know any better, I might be inclined to think that what I'm feeling is . . . flattered?

I shudder, disturbed merely by the thought of it.

I take a deep breath and immediately quash the intensely unpleasant sensation. That look of concern on Ryan's face was not for me. It was for *her*, and it only serves to strengthen my hate for everything she is. As I crawl into the vent, I decide to purge the bitter dregs of useless emotions that Finn has obviously infected me with and leave them to wither and die in this metal coffin of a room. Soon, with Otto's help, I'll have the chance to erase her from existence. There's no space in this body for anyone but me, and the more I learn about the life that Finn has been allowed to live, the more I want to burn it all to the ground . . . and spit on the ashes.

With freshly tempered hatred warming my heart, I carry on through the duct, following behind Ryan as Otto's directions echo from up ahead. After quite a few minutes of being unwillingly subjected to the sight of Ryan's butt, I hear Otto's voice ring out from somewhere in the distance.

"Dammit."

"What is it?" calls Brent.

"The end of the line," replies Otto.

I keep following Ryan, and before long, we've caught up with the rest of the group. Everyone is lying in a row in a long, straight section of duct. Shafts of light are streaming in from horizontal ventilation grills in the left-hand wall, and I can see that beside Otto, at the far end of the section, is a flat, metal dead end. Everyone is peering out of the grills. I wriggle into a semicomfortable position and do the same. The vent grills are level with the pavement of what appears to be a large courtyard just outside, but it's difficult to get a clear idea of the layout from this rodent's-eye point of view. All I can really see is the base of what looks like some stone-bench seating nearby, some decorative plants overhanging them to the left, and part of a curvy sculpture in the distance. I can see a little bit of the blue sky. I angle my eyes and focus on a tuft of white cloud. It doesn't glitch or disappear, and I feel confident that we've made it out from under Dome One, but just to confirm, I ask anyway.

"Are we in the right place?" I whisper.

"We're heading in the right direction," replies Otto. "I would have liked to have gotten closer to the Security Station without leaving the vents, but they only get smaller from here. This is our only option."

"I can't see any movement out there," says Ryan. "Hopefully there aren't any Drone patrols."

"Let's just assume that there are," I say. "Where's the Security Station?"

"It isn't visible from here," whispers Otto. ". . . but I remember that statue out there from the 3-D model I memorized. If I take the relative approximate size of that statue and scale it up from the model, I estimate the Security Station is about a hundred and fifty meters or so directly northwest of the statue . . . If, using the statue as a central marker, we consider the direction of Dome One to be south."

"You are such a neeeerd," whispers Brent.

"That nerd is your only chance of getting out of here in one piece," I say, and Brent sneers without turning to acknowledge me. "What does the station look like?"

"Judging from the model, I estimate that it's about eight to twelve floors high and triangular," says Otto. "It's surrounded by a few similar-looking administration buildings, so we'll have to skirt around them.

I'm not sure what color the station is—the 3-D model was rendered all in white—but there's a big tree out in front of it that's kinda shaped like the letter *U*. You'll know it when you see it."

"We?" whispers Blondie. "You said *'we'* will have to skirt around them. I'm not going out there."

"You can stay here if you like," I reply. "But if there are Drones out there, I'm gonna be too busy running to bother coming back for you."

"Why can't we just run for help?" whispers Blondie. "We'll be outside, so we can just keep running until we make it to the main road."

"It was at least a ten-minute bus ride to the dome from the main road," whispers Brent. "That's a long way to run when you're being chased by robots that don't get tired."

"Not to mention the gate we came through with the razor wire fence and the big warning signs with lightning bolts on them?" Ryan chips in.

"Oh yeah. I forgot about those," mumbles Brody.

"I think you should go for it, Blondie," I whisper with a smile. "You can lead all the Drones away from the rest of us."

"Screw you," she snipes. "And my name is not *'Blondie.'* It's Margaux."

"Well, *Margaux* . . . the choice is yours. You can either hide in an air duct with nowhere else to go; you can run off and get electrocuted, ripped to pieces, or shot; or you can take your chances running for shelter beside three boys that are bigger and slower targets than you are."

"Hey," protests Brody.

"Sorry, Brody, but the choice is pretty obvious. Our best bet is to find a solid structure to hole up in and hope like hell that Otto can access the computer and shut the Drones down."

"And if she can't?" asks Ryan.

"I guess we'll have to cross that burning bridge if we come to it," I whisper. "So we head for the Security Station?"

Margaux pouts and sighs with reluctant acceptance. The absence of any protest from the others confirms their answers.

I take one final intensive glare through the slots, staring in the direction we need to run, and then shuffle and twist around so my back is against the wall of the duct. I bring my knees up, press my shoes against the grating, and push hard. It takes a little more effort than I expected, but before long my short section of the grating begins to bend outward. I ease back onto my knees, and with a little more levering with my elbow, I manage to make the opening big enough to crawl through.

"Is everyone ready?"

Margaux stares intently though the thin slots in the grating, snorting quiet, adrenalized breaths as Otto's and the boys' narrow-eyed, stony expressions are mirrored by mine. Everyone nods solemnly.

"Good luck," I whisper as I crawl headfirst through the open section of the grate and worm my way onto the cool gray paving stones outside.

"Dr. Pierce! Dr. Pierce, wake up!"

"Ahhh! What . . . who . . . what is it? What's wrong?"

"Nothing's wrong. It's Finn; her vital signs are stabilizing."

"Let me see . . . Oh, thank heavens. The bruising and abrasions have all gone. Infinity must be back in control. Bring me that ultrasound slate over there. Yes, that one . . . thank you. Now, let's have a look. Hmmm. Her internal injuries have improved greatly. Her ribs are fused back together, and her legs look to be nearly eighty percent healed. She's going to live."

"Dr. Pierce . . . I was wondering . . ."

"Yes? What is it, girlie? Spit it out."

"Well, I was wondering if you could tell me . . . what exactly is she?"

"What do you mean? She's a seventeen-year-old girl. You've got eyes in your head; I suggest you try using them sometime."

"No, that's not what I . . . I mean . . . she has two distinct, fully formed personalities, she's crazy strong, she's an expert fighter, and she can spontaneously heal her injuries. She's obviously not human. Not unless she's some kind of genetically modified human? Is that what she is?"

"What she is, girlie . . . is classified. But what I can tell you is that she's as human as you are, so don't go treating her differently just because you've discovered she can do a few unusual things."

"Unusual? That's putting it mildly."

"You're right, of course; both Finn and Infinity are extraordinary, and they grew up living very strange and separate lives. But as different as they are from each other, the one thing they have in common is that they're both very lonely young women. Even though Infinity would be the first one to tell you that she isn't. I've been keeping tabs on you, Miss Otto. It's obvious that both Finn and Infinity trust you very much. So if you care about them, the best thing you can do is to just keep giving them what they need the most . . . your friendship. Do you think you can do that, girlie?"

"Yes, Dr. Pierce . . . I think I can do that."

"Good, you won't regret it. Now go and get some rest; you look like a cat dragged you backward through a blackberry bush."

CHAPTER TEN

I crawl from the vent and cautiously rise to my feet, my ears attuned to the slightest sound of movement. Behind the curve of the stone bench beside me is a thick mass of tall decorative ferns that are thankfully hiding me from view. Opposite this bench are an identical bench and a garden planter, completing what could have been a pleasant little nook to sit and have a leisurely lunch, if it weren't for the fact we all could possibly die in a hail of gunfire at any second.

I duck under some overhanging leaves, quietly slide onto the nearest seat, and slowly inch around, my eyes flicking from side to side, scanning my limited view of the courtyard through the gap between the two benches. I lean forward as much as I dare, peering through the sparser ferns at the edge of the garden. I can make out the shapes of trees, a patch of grass, and more randomly placed seating areas. I can see enough of the statue now to get my bearings, so I draw a line in my mind heading northwest from it. I follow the line until I spot, in the distance, what appears to be the straight-line top corner of a building. It's almost completely obscured by large trees; a huge, white, suspended canopy; and what looks like a winding monorail track, but if Otto is right, the Security Station is that way.

Ryan slides onto the seat beside me. Brody quietly grunts as he squeezes through the grate and crouches by the bench as Brent, Margaux, and finally Otto do the same. A gentle breeze rustles the ferns, and I silently inhale through my nose, separating, categorizing, and analyzing the scents in the air. The earthy, grassy smell of the garden hits me first, but it's almost overpowered by the heady mix of sweat and fear pheromones pouring off everyone like a hormonal fog. I close my eyes, push the adolescent stink aside, and delve further in, discarding the dull, sun-heated masonry waft from the paving stones and the woodsy notes of the trees across the way. I'm searching for something much more specific.

Drones have a particular smell, just like everything does, and it's especially distinct if they're brand-new like those Crimson-Class Drones are. It's a clean, manufactured, plasticky-sweet kinda smell. I'd describe it as "new car mixed with freshly printed money," and right now, I can't smell even the tiniest trace of it. I open my eyes and let the details of the aromas drift away, satisfied with the hopeful assumption that there aren't any Drones within fifty meters upwind of us.

"I'm going," I whisper, and Ryan nods at me with solemn confidence. I stand, take a deep breath, and scan the anxious faces of the people sitting and crouching beside me. All of a sudden, a strange and slightly disturbing feeling of responsibility ripples through me. Barely an hour ago, I wouldn't have given a toss if any of them but Otto lived or died, and the only reason I'd care about her was because she served a purpose. But now I can't seem to shake the feeling that I need to get everyone through this safely. Brody gives me a smile of encouragement and a thumbs-up. And that's when something really weird happens. I smile back. And, to make matters worse . . . I actually mean it.

With morbid realization, I turn away and shudder. What the hell is wrong with me? I must be going soft. *Get a grip, Infinity One! Elite soldier, Vermillion-Class assassin, cold-blooded killer. That's what you were created for. That's who you are!*

Firm-jawed and steely eyed, I glance back at the group. All of them are looking up at me with optimistic hope, trusting me with their lives, relying on me to protect them. And to my utter dismay, the warm fuzzy feeling rears its cutesy head again. Half hoping a Drone will just walk up and shoot me right now, I sigh and stride out into the courtyard.

Exposed out in the open, I move quickly and quietly, but I don't run—better to save any burst of speed and energy for when I really need it. Even though I know this situation is deadly serious, I smile to myself as the ridiculous image of someone power walking springs to mind. I glance over my shoulder and see Dome One from the outside for the first time. It's gigantic, pure black, shiny smooth, and absolutely staggering to behold. It has to be a couple hundred meters high at least, towering far above the collection of chrome, polished wood, and white-stone buildings around its base. I've seen classified aerial photographs of it before, but they don't do the real thing justice at all. Even with my high level of security clearance, I was never able to access anything about what it's made of or what's inside, and although I've been inside it now, it doesn't even begin to satisfy my curiosity about the nature of the advanced technology required to construct it. If I wasn't marching across this courtyard like a madwoman right now, I'd quite happily stop for a minute and just stare at it. Obviously, now is not the time. I scoot past the statue, and thankfully there aren't any alarms or disembodied computer voices calling out to murder us yet. I take that as a very good sign.

With a quick glance over my right shoulder, I see that Ryan isn't far behind me. He's walking quickly, half hunched over, his head swinging from side to side, scanning for danger. Brody, Brent, and Margaux join the line as Otto emerges from the relative safety of the nook, bringing up the rear. The sun is high in the sky. When I'm on a task, mission control transmits the exact time and GPS coordinates of wherever I am directly into my head, but this is definitely not a sanctioned mission, so my best guess is that it must be around midday or one o'clock. Not that we have any choice given our situation, but I much prefer the cloak of night. Out here, unarmed in broad daylight, I feel like I'm stark naked with a bull's-eye painted on my backside.

I make it to one of the trees that I spotted from the nook. It's large, thick at the trunk, the shadows of its leaves mottling the paving stones in a wide pattern. I press myself against the tree and peer around the side of it. Ryan, eyes alert, arrives at my shoulder. "So far, so good," he whispers, and I nod in agreement. One by one, the rest arrive, and I beckon to Otto. She sidles past the others, and I point in the direction of a space between two buildings fifty meters in the distance. "That way?" I ask.

"Yeah," she whispers. "We're almost there."

"OK, let's go," I say, stepping out from behind the tree and continuing on. The others follow suit, and we move as a silent group. Following a line of lampposts, we walk under the huge, suspended, white plastic canopy, between another pair of bench seats and around another tree, with nothing but the sound of leaves rustling in the breeze and the occasional tweet from the curious sparrows perched on the branches overhead.

We scurry past a grassy area and make it to the outside corner of one of the buildings. Otto leans around the side of the building and points excitedly. "There," she whispers. "The U-shaped tree." I peer into the gap between the two buildings and spot the tree standing near the beginning of a short path that leads to the door of a tall triangular building with high, silver-tinted windows.

The Security Station.

Without hesitation, I stride out toward the tree. I'm halfway from the corner to the tree when a flash of silver catches the corner of my eye. My gut seizes as I spin and thrust a hand out toward the rest of the group. A lone service Drone is standing barely ten meters away, its featureless black mask staring right at me. It was hidden behind the far corner of the building to the left, and I didn't see it until it was too late. Everyone freezes, their eyes wide with fear. I furiously bat the air with my hand, and they scuttle backward. I stand my ground. I can easily take out a service Drone, but fighting it is the least of my worries. I'm much more concerned that right now this Drone is calling its big brothers. Its big, scary brothers with the guns. I plant my feet, clench my fists, grit my teeth, and wait for the alarms and the bellowing orders of termination.

But none of it comes.

I stare at the Drone. The Drone stares back. I take a step toward it. It doesn't move at all. I tilt my head, squinting at it from the top of its head to its feet and back again. Its mask is black, not red. My hands relax, and I sigh with relief. The Drone is off-line.

I throw an OK sign at the others, who are all peeking at me from the corner of the building, and they cautiously approach. The moment Margaux sees the Drone, she lets out a closemouthed peep, but everyone else keep their nerves in check as we quietly move on, past the tree and along the path to the front door of the Security Station.

The entrance is a pair of sliding doors with a fingerprint scanner, and not surprisingly, it doesn't open as we approach. With the computer malfunctioning, everything in this courtyard seems to be devoid of power and eerily dead. I cup my hands around my eyes and press my nose against the door, but I can't see anything through the silver-tinted glass. "Brody," I whisper. "A little help?"

Brody steps forward and follows my lead as I wedge my fingers into the tiny gap formed by the edges of the door frames. It's painstaking work to begin with, but with both of us pulling in opposite directions, we manage to edge the doors apart a few centimeters. I slot the toe of my shoe into the gap and push as Brent steps up to help with Brody's door. Veins swell in both the boys' reddening faces and necks as I lean back with all my weight and mentally strengthen the muscles in my arms and upper body. We heave at the doors. I pull an angry lungful of air through my nose and overstimulate my thigh muscle. My leg kicks hard against the sturdy frame, and something finally gives with a metallic crack as my door jolts apart, providing an opening just big enough to squeeze through. Brent and Brody stand there, hands on their hips, gulping victory breaths as I sidle through the small gap between the doors.

Inside, the bottom floor of the Security Station is sparse and dim; the only light source is sunlight filtering in through the tinted windows from outside. Actually, "sparse" is an understatement. In the middle of the large, white, triangular floor space is a massive circular desk with a shiny metal cylinder in the center that extends all the way up into the high ceiling. Apart from that, the place is empty. The chest-high desk is sectioned for access, so I head over to it and slip through the nearest gap. Behind it are some blank computer slates on stands, but nothing else. The rest of the group has followed me in and is strolling around, looking at the same nothing I am. Otto can't resist swiping a hopeful finger across one of the slates, but she doesn't look the least bit surprised when nothing happens.

"All those buildings out there, that huge courtyard, and now this," whispers Ryan. "Not a single person anywhere. Where is everyone? This place is like a ghost town."

"I know," agrees Margaux. "I don't like it. It's creepy."

"This is the most logical place for our phones and slates to be," says Otto. "How do we get to the upper floors?"

"No stairs," observes Brent. "That's a fire hazard if ever I saw one. There must be a—"

"Here!" shouts Brody. I look in the direction of his voice and see his face appear from behind the big metal cylinder in the center of the desk. "There's a door here; I think it's an elevator!"

I walk around behind the large metal tube, and sure enough, the thin outline of a sliding door is clearly visible on its surface.

"If it is an elevator, we're not gonna be able to get up this way. Not without power," says Ryan. "And it's pretty obvious that this place is shut down to the ground."

"Punch through it, Infinity!" blurts Brody, his eyes as eager as his childish grin.

I step forward and knock on the side of the tube. It sounds very solid. "Sorry to disappoint, Brody. But my hand would be mush long before this door would give way."

"Hello?"

I quickly look at the faces surrounding me just to make sure I'm not the only one who heard that. Everyone's expressions of surprise confirm it. It was muted by the thick metal of the elevator door, but that was definitely a man's voice.

"Hello! Is somebody out there?" the voice says again.

"Hello!" I shout back. "Yes, we're here!"

"Oh, thank my lucky stars!" says the voice. "I've been trapped in here for hours! Are you security?"

"No!" shouts Otto. "We're students on a school field trip!"

"What?" shouts the voice. "Well, whoever you are . . . get me out of here!"

"How, exactly?" I yell through the door. "There isn't any power!"

"Under the desk!" shouts the man. "There's a panel on the floor. Open it and you'll find a number pad. The code is one, eight, one, zero. That'll switch on the emergency solar power."

"OK!" shouts Otto. Not wasting any time, she hurries over and slides onto her knees, scanning the floor behind the desk. "I've found it!" she blurts excitedly. Otto prods at a space on the floor, a small hatch pops open, and I can see her jabbing at something with her finger. She looks up at the blank slates on their stands and then glances at the ceiling before pouting disappointedly and glaring back down at the square hole in the floor.

"There's a keyhole above the punch pad," Otto says over her shoulder. "I'm assuming we need a key *and* the code."

"We need a key!" Brent shouts at the door.

"Of course—how silly of me!" says the voice.

"Where is it?" Brent asks, pressing his ear to the door.

There's a pregnant pause, and then a muffled rattling sound comes from inside the elevator.

"The key . . . is in here with me," the man says gloomily as Margaux's face drops and Brent groans. "I'm sorry!" shouts the man. "I forgot about the lock."

Ryan looks over at Margaux and, without asking, reaches out and plucks something from her hair. "Hey!" she barks as she recoils, frowning and shielding her long golden mane. I look down to see a diamond-encrusted hair clip clutched between Ryan's fingers.

"I got this," he says as he turns and walks over to kneel beside Otto.

"That kinda stuff only works in movies, Forrester," mutters Brent.

"If you believe that . . . ," Ryan says, snapping the clasp in two, "then you're as clueless as every principal of every reform school I've ever escaped from."

Brent sneers at Ryan's back as he hunches over and gets to work. In less than a minute, there's an audible click and a blue glow shines up from the floor, illuminating Otto's face. "Nice one, Ryan," she says, and begins tapping the code into the pad. With the code entered, every single one of us scans the room in expectation.

"It didn't work!" Margaux shouts at the door.

"Give it a second!" replies the man, and sure enough, a moment later, the whole white ceiling in the empty triangular space flickers, flashes . . . then goes as black as night. All of us turn our heads upward as pinpoints of light begin appearing across the darkened ceiling, speckling it in ever-widening swaths until soon there are thousands of twinkling stars peppering the entire triangular area right to its edges. It looks just like the sky of a crisp and cloudless winter night, right above our heads. I'm marveling at the clarity and depth of the ceiling display when a thin blue line suddenly streaks across the stars. There's another and another, then ten more, then fifty more, then too many to count at a glance, streaking and crisscrossing all over the ceiling. Pulsing blue dots tagged with numbers begin appearing on the lines, and I recognize it all for what it really is. It's a tracking map: one blue dot and a trajectory line for each of the hundreds of satellites orbiting the planet.

The computer slates behind the desk suddenly boot up in unison, each one blinking on with white lines of text and numbers emblazoned across it as multiple blue-rimmed holographic screens of varying sizes shimmer into view, floating in midair, five screens deep and four screens high around the entire curve of the desk. Most of the screens are blank, some are snowy with silent static, and some are showing images from cameras in places that we've been. I recognize the crystal tunnels on one screen and the jungle from Dome One on another. Otto jumps to her feet and immediately begins studying the computer slates as Brody twitches beside me, startled by the huge, red, computer-wire schematic of Blackstone Technologies flickering onto the long wall behind us.

Across the room, a second wall comes to life, and soon it's covered with technical readouts and pictures of individual building structures, many of which I recognize from the courtyard outside. The third wall flickers and flashes on with a huge map of the continents of Earth. It's speckled with glowing red dots, lines of aircraft and transport flight paths, sections of statistics, names of cities, countries, population counts, currency conversions, market reports, and all sorts of cryptic algorithms.

A darkening patch on the floor catches the corner of my eye, and I look down to see the shiny white beneath my feet give way to a spreading bluey green as the whole floor suddenly becomes a huge, triangular map of what appears to be all the oceans on Earth. Faintly glowing computer wires flicker into view and connect, tracing the peaks and valleys of the global underwater landscape as trails of arrows representing ocean currents curve around dozens of tiny, yellow-numbered shapes scattered across the floor: one for every freight ship, oil tanker, military vessel, and submarine in every sunken corner and watery depth of the planet.

Every part of the room is alive and bristling with information. I scan the displays, and my eyes narrow with suspicion. They may call this a "Security Station," but to me, it looks much more like a military monitoring facility. Or what civilians might call a "spy base."

With a soft ping, the elevator door slides open, and the owner of the voice finally steps out into the room. He's a skinny man dressed in beige coveralls. He looks to be in his late forties or early fifties and has neatly side-parted salt-and-pepper hair, thick tortoiseshell-rimmed glasses, and a gray goatee frizzing from his chin. The handle of a hard-shell briefcase is clutched in one hand, and a screwdriver is grasped in the other. The man shuffles sideways, holding the screwdriver out in front of him like a weapon, and everyone backs away. His gaze flits across our faces, and after a couple of seconds, he visibly relaxes, slides the screwdriver into one of his pockets, and gently sets the case on the floor.

"You really are just a bunch of schoolkids," he says. "I never thought I'd see the day when they'd let children wander around Blackstone Technologies, especially on a Saturday. This place isn't exactly a chocolate factory, y'know."

"No kidding," whispers Margaux.

"Thanks for getting me out," says the man. "I was starting to worry that I'd be stuck in there until Monday morning." He looks around the room, perplexed. "Where are the security personnel?"

"We haven't seen anyone," I say. "Who are you?"

"My name is George—George Parsons. I do general maintenance around here. I was on my way down from fixing a coolant circulator on the sixth floor when the power went out, and I got trapped in the elevator. What's happened? Why are you all in here?" George asks, looking from side to side. "And where is your teacher?"

"One of our teachers is trapped inside Dome Two," Otto says as she aggressively taps and swipes at one of the computer slates.

"And the other one . . . ," Margaux whispers. "Miss Cole is . . . she's . . ."

"She's dead," mutters Brody.

"Excuse me?" George says skeptically.

"There's been a situation, George," I say. "System-wide computer malfunctions have resulted in multiple deaths. We need to call for assistance."

"Hold on; hold on! Tell me what's happened," he prompts.

"A mechanoid went berserk and killed our teacher, our classmates, and three soldiers," says Ryan. "We broke in here to get our phones and call for help."

George frowns and then smiles. "You're joking. Please tell me that you're pulling my leg."

"No joke, George," I say.

George very understandably looks a little stunned.

"Can't we just call for help from in here?" asks Brent. "The computers are working now; let's call for help."

"We can't," says Otto. "Every computer in this room is iced up."

"What does that mean in English?" asks Ryan.

"Look around . . . ," Otto says, pointing at the walls. "The information is frozen. All the screens are showing data displayed at the time of the blackout. Satellites move fast," Otto says, pointing at the ceiling, "but none of those blue tracking dots up there have moved at all. The computers in this room are closed off from the Hypernet, the mainframe, and the outside world. They're useless to us." Otto looks over at George. He's just standing there frowning in silence, staring at the floor. "Mr. Parsons?" she asks. He doesn't seem to hear her at all.

"Hey, George!" shouts Otto, and he jumps in his skin. "We need to find our phones and computer slates. Can you help us?"

George slowly turns to Otto. "Your phones?"

"They were taken when we arrived. Do you know where they might be?"

"They'll . . . they'll be stored up on the eighth floor, in the data scanners."

"I'll go and get them," says Otto.

"Wait," says George. "You can't. The elevator won't accept your fingerprint."

"Then take me up there," Otto demands.

"I'm going, too," I add.

"Absolutely not. Neither of you have security clearance. I'd lose my job!"

Otto's expression hardens. "Mr. Parsons, innocent people have died, Blackstone employees are missing, the most classified research facility in the world has been compromised, we've been cut off from the outside world, and all you're concerned about . . . is your job?"

George looks like a scolded child. "Yes?" he says sheepishly.

"Take us up there. Right now!" barks Otto, and George flinches. Otto pushes past the still visibly shaken George and disappears behind the elevator shaft. A moment later, her frowning face leans back out. "Anytime this year would be great." George fumbles with the handle of his briefcase, then hops in step toward the door of the elevator.

A smile crawls onto my lips. I have to admit that I'm liking this headstrong Bettina Otto more and more as the day goes on. "We'll get the phones and computers; you stay down here," I say to the rest of the group.

"Fine with me," says Ryan.

"Don't take too long," whines Margaux. "I feel safer when you're around."

Brent and Brody both look at her with surprised disbelief.

"What?" she says, crossing her arms over her chest. "I just do!"

Margaux's comment caught me off guard, as well. She wasn't being sarcastic at all. I give her a nod and a quizzical smile, then turn and head around to the other side of the cylinder. I'm still not used to people putting their lives in my hands like this. My hands were trained to take life, and when Otto gets her slate and shuts down the Drones, and I finally get a chance to lay these hands on Richard Blackstone, that's exactly what they're gonna do. I walk into the elevator, where a determined-looking Otto and an anxious George are waiting. George leans over and reluctantly presses his thumb to a small, black glass plate on the wall. The door slides closed, he taps the top button in a line of eight, and a short ride of uncomfortable silence later, the elevator opens onto the uppermost level.

George shuffles into the room. We follow right behind him, and the first thing that hits me is the cold. It's like walking into a meat locker. I can even see my breath puffing like mist as I step into the room. Not only is it chilly on level eight, but it's bright, too. Unlike the tinted windows on the ground level, the glass walls up here are crystal clear. The sunlight streaming in illuminates the overall strangeness of the eighth floor.

I'm standing in a narrow gap between dozens of rows of what appear to be dark-gray, chest-high termite mounds. There must be at least a couple hundred covering the floor space, and each one is grooved and pitted all over with lines of tiny, honeycomb-shaped holes. Beneath the holes, blue rivulets of light lazily course up and down the length of each mound. They seem to fill the entire level, and are not only sticking up out of the floor, but hanging down from the ceiling, too, like artificial stalactites. There are a couple of meters' clearance between the mounds on the floor and the ones overhead, providing a 360-degree view out the windows. To the left, I can see the neighboring buildings, and, in the distance, curving high into the bright-blue sky, is the majestic black cap of Dome One.

"This way," George says, shuffling ahead between the mounds. "And, please, don't touch the hard drives."

"Is that what they are?" I whisper.

"Yes," replies Otto. "They're data hives—look," she says, pointing to the closest one. "They process information on coded protein strands. Just one of those little holes has the capacity to store a million full-length holographic movies." A goofy smile lights up her face. "Imagine how much information is kept in just this *one room* alone."

"It boggles the mind," I murmur sarcastically.

"It *really* does," Otto insists with wide-eyed, nerdy joy.

George leads the way down the narrow path, and when we reach the wall of windows, the pathway splits. George heads to the right, and we follow him all the way along the edge of the hives and around the far corner of the triangle. There, in a clearing among the hives, is a single seat positioned behind a small, semicircular desk. George sits down, and a moment later, four eye-level holographic screens shimmer into view around the curved perimeter of the desk. Three of them are showing meaningless frozen lines of code, but the fourth screen displays a list of serial numbers with pictures of phones and computer slates beside each line.

"They're here," George says. "Scanned and cataloged."

"Where are they kept?" Otto asks impatiently, peering at the screen with concern.

George swivels in the chair and looks at the floor just behind us. "There," he says. "Step on that foot pedal by the window."

I look down to see a white rectangular tile with a pulsing green light set into the floor by the glass wall. Otto hurries over and plants her shoe on it. There's a click and then a quiet whirring sound as a long, thin section, almost as long as the entire glass wall itself, begins rising from the floor. As it elevates, I can see that it's actually a set of shelves, and row upon row of phones and slates have been propped along them. The two-meter-high section jolts to a stop, and at a glance I guess there must be over a hundred phones and slates, each one resting in its own spot on one of the ledges.

Otto lunges with both arms extended, snatching a computer slate and a phone and hugging them to her chest like long-lost friends. She gently slides them into her bag and begins gathering others. Apart from the different-colored covers, they all look the same to me, but Otto seems to recognize each and every one she picks up, muttering the owners' names as she puts them into the two satchels slung over her shoulder. I can tell by the way she handles some of them and by the hushed tones she uses when she whispers the owners' names that some of them belong to people who have died. One by one, she takes devices from the shelves until she's collected nearly twenty of them, and as the satchels bulge to capacity, she begins stacking more in the crook of her elbow. "Here," she says, plucking a phone from a shelf and holding it out to me.

"I don't want it," I say.

"But . . . it's yours."

I shake my head. "No, it's not," I reply.

Otto smiles timidly. "What I meant is . . . it's Finn's."

I push her hand away. "Well, she's not coming back," I say coldly. "So she's never going to need it again."

Otto looks at me and blinks. Her head drops, and she looks down at the phone, cradling it in her palm. She gently traces her thumb across the screen, then slowly slips it into the breast pocket of her blouse. "No . . . I guess not," she murmurs.

"Mission accomplished. Let's get outta here," I say as I step on the now red-blinking tile. The long shelving begins lowering into the floor as George stands up, automatically deactivating the desk. Suddenly a clever idea springs to mind. George could be my chance to get those four teenage anchors off my heels and safely tucked away somewhere while Otto and I hunt down dear old Dr. Blackstone. I slap a hand on George's shoulder and fake an honest smile. "Thank you for your assistance, George. Are you willing to help us further?"

"I'm n-not sure what else I c-can do?" he stammers.

"Well, you can start by taking those kids downstairs to a safe place."

"But . . . surely you can call the authorities now. All we have to do is wait for them to arrive." I can tell by the look on his face that George is less than keen on the prospect of being a babysitter. I can relate.

I slowly shake my head, feigning concern. "This complex is in the middle of nowhere, George. It's dangerous out there, and it's gonna take time for help to get here. You must know of somewhere nearby where you can all barricade yourselves in. They'll be safer with you."

He thinks for a second, then slowly nods. "Well, we might be able to . . . Hey, wait a second. It doesn't sound like you're coming with us."

"Let me know where you're going, and we'll join you soon. There's something else we need to take care of first."

"And what might that be?" George asks, his eyes narrowing.

I begin searching my brain for a half-believable story that doesn't involve me murdering his employer when Otto thankfully saves me with a welcome interruption.

"Our teacher, Professor Francis, our classmate Dean McCarthy, and our tour guide, Percy. We need to rescue them. They're all trapped over there in Dome—"

The loud clatter of computer slates hitting the floor startles even me, and I turn to see Otto staring out the window, her hands pressed against the glass. "Otto, what is it?" I ask, peering out across the complex with absolutely no idea of what I'm supposed to be looking at.

"Dome Two," she murmurs.

"What about it? Which way is it? Point it out," I ask, scanning the buildings and structures down below.

"I can't point it out, Infinity . . . ," Otto says, "because it's not there."

"What are you talking about?" I ask, squinting out the window.

"I don't know why I didn't notice when we first came in," she whispers. "I should've noticed it right away." Otto turns to me, her eyes filled with confusion and distress.

"Dome Two . . . It's gone."

CHAPTER ELEVEN

I've seen the classified satellite photographs of this complex. From above, Blackstone Technologies is three perfect black circles surrounded by bone-white buildings, snaking footpaths, silver-topped towers, and massive black-and-gold transport hangers. It's almost impossible to judge the height of anything from looking at satellite pictures, so actually being here, creeping around this top-secret facility at ground level, I find myself at a loss. Structures block each other, buildings overlap at the edges, trees conceal pathways, and bearings can get skewed. But, despite what magicians would have you believe, things can't just disappear.

"Are you sure it's gone?" I ask. "Maybe it's behind those—"

"I saw the model!" Otto barks. "Dome Two would be at least a hundred meters high. Of course it's bloody gone!"

My limited knowledge of this complex counts for nothing right now, so it doesn't exactly boost my confidence to see the person I'm relying on to guide me through this place freaking out like a frizzy-haired, hyperventilating squirrel.

"Where did it go?" Otto screeches.

I grab her hard by the wrist and pull her away from the glass wall. "Hey. Try and calm down, OK? There must be an explanation. George, what's happened to the dome?"

"Power . . . The power must be out in Sector Two. The domes need it to stay constructed. Without power, the quantum grains come apart and a dome would . . . dissolve."

"Dome One is still standing," I mention, pointing to the far glass wall.

"Yes, I saw that," George says, scratching his chin in thought. "The mainframe must be rebooting systems one sector at a time."

"How long until the whole place is up and running again?" asks Otto.

George shakes his head, walks to the window, and surveys the buildings below. "I don't know. I've never heard of anything like this happening before. I don't even have the faintest idea of what could've caused it; there are so many built-in safeguards and backups. Before today, I never would've thought something like this could be possible."

"Look, whoever caused this probably feels bad enough without you two talking about it all the time," Otto says angrily.

I can recognize remorse from a thousand paces. I've seen it on the faces of soldiers in far-flung places as they've stood over the freshly steaming wounds of the innocent dead, and, right now, Otto might as well be broadcasting her guilt through a loudspeaker mounted on her head between two flashing lights. With one eye on George's back, I silently mouth the words, "Did you do this?"

Otto backs away from me, her expression sad and silent as she walks over to the glass wall beside George. Suddenly it dawns on me. She isn't freaking out over concern for the people who survived; she's being eaten alive by the possibility that she's responsible for the ones who *died*, and she's trying her best to stop it from getting worse. It's a problem she has to deal with; I don't care either way. But I still have to admit, Bettina Otto is certainly chock-full of surprises, and one of them is much darker than I would have thought possible of her.

"Mr. Parsons, what would happen to someone inside a dome when it dissolves?" Otto asks, the taint of anger in her words doing little to disguise the shame.

"Well, I think they would probably be fine," replies George.

"You *think* they would *probably*?" squawks Otto. "I hope you realize that's not really an answer."

George looks awkwardly uncomfortable. "I've never seen a dome deconstruct before," he says, leaning away from the leering, fist-clenching teenage girl. "But if the quantum field went down, the grains would revert to their original state. I've seen it in the labs; it kinda looks like that gray kinetic-sand stuff that kids play with. As long as your friends can dig their way out before they suffocate, they should be OK."

"Are you saying that they could have escaped already?" Otto says hopefully.

"Well, they'd have to wade through a chest-deep pool of inert grains, but apart from that, there wouldn't be anything stopping them from leaving the boundary of the dome."

Otto begins fishing through one of the satchels. "I might be able to find them . . . ," she says as she pulls her computer slate from the bag and presses a button on the edge. "If I can just zero in on Percy's command module."

"The command modules are off-line," George says as he pulls up one of the sleeves of his coveralls. A silver band with a black diamond-shaped stone set in it is wrapped around his left wrist. The instant I see it, my fingers automatically touch the pendant beneath my shirt, and for a fleeting second, the strangest unexplainable feeling of sadness ripples through me. "It was the first thing I tried when I got stuck in the lift," George says, tapping at the stone on the wristband. "The modules are routed through the computer, and we're cut off from the mainframe. There's no chance you'll be able to access the tour guide's module."

"His name is Percy, and I don't need to access it," Otto says as she swipes and taps intricate patterns on the screen of her slate. "All I need to do is scan for its power signature."

"Not with that, you can't," George says, frowning down at Otto's slate. "That's a Blackstone Nero 10, by the looks of it. It's the fastest slate there is, but it can't do what you just said."

Otto flicks her finger up off the slate, and a glowing green holographic line follows behind the tip. She splays her hand, and the line expands into a panoramic rectangle of lines and symbols, peaks and valleys, numbers, spheres, and rainbow-colored globs. "I've been designing circuits since I was four years old," she says, waving her finger through the holograms like a witch casting a spell. "And I've been modifying computer slates since I was in primary school." Otto flicks and scrolls through the holograms with a self-satisfied smile. "A factory-standard Nero 10 is like an abacus compared to my turbocharged baby right here."

The frown on George's face deepens as he leans in, eyeballing the lines and patches of light hovering over the slate with a new and curious interest.

"See!" Otto blurts as she points out a particular spot on a circular graph. "That small red dot in the center is this computer slate; the tall peak over it is the Security Station's power signature. And if I zoom in . . ." Otto spreads her finger and thumb over the line, and hundreds of little peaks appear. "These are the data hives, and this little bump is your command module." She shoves the slate toward George. Judging by his arching eyebrows, I'd say it's safe to assume that George is suitably impressed.

"Even this close, your module's signature is weak," Otto says, scrolling through the glowing peaks and valleys. "I'll have a much better chance of picking up Percy's signal at ground level."

"That's incredible. You're some kinda genius," whispers George.

"I just understand computers; that's all," Otto says, blushing. "I'm not a genius."

"Well, if you're not, you're pretty darn close," George says, studying the slate even closer. "What else can it do?"

Obviously flattered, Otto grins and begins swiping at the air above the slate, the urgency of the situation momentarily forgotten. "Well, I also upgraded the Nero's pathetic frequency scanner," she says as George nods along with every word. "Now, not only can it pick up every electromagnetic signal in a two-hundred-fifty-meter radius, but it can also detect changes in temperature and microdisturbances in the air, then combine and enhance that data to accurately extrapolate and convert residual vibrations into audio and visual from adverse surfaces up to fifteen centimeters thick."

"It can do what now?" I ask.

"It can see through solid walls," George whispers, blatantly staring at the slate as if caught in some kind of goofy daze.

"And not just a thermal image with garbled noises, either," gushes Otto. "I'm talking real-time, high-resolution holographic projection."

George's expression suddenly hardens. "That type of application is reserved for government intelligence only. It's illegal for a civilian device to have those capabilities."

Otto nods and grins. "Yeah, I know." I can't help but be amused by her prideful flaunting of the law, but right now I need more than a computer with X-ray vision.

"Seeing through walls is one thing . . . ," I say, "but please tell me you can also shut down the Drones with it."

Otto swipes and pokes at the holograms. "There's some kind of signal block. The mainframe is jamming and intercepting outgoing transmissions. I can't send anything out; I can only receive, so I can't shut down the Drones. But that also means that I can't send a distress call, so . . ."

"No one is coming to help us," I say, and Otto slowly nods. "Good, that suits me just fine. The police would just get in the way." I turn and set off the way we came. Otto quickly gathers the dropped slates at her feet, stuffs them halfway into an already-bulging satchel, and hurries to fall in step beside me, her eyes glued to her own slate as she walks. "I'll help you find your friends like I agreed," I say to Otto. "But then you and I have an appointment with you know who."

"Who the hell *are* you kids?" George asks with understandable suspicion.

"She's the best hacker in the world," I say, jabbing a thumb at Otto.

"And she's a highly trained assassin," Otto says with a smile in her voice.

"No, who are you, *really*?" George asks again, hurrying to catch up with us. I turn and smile at Otto, and she shares our private joke with a cheeky grin.

At the intersection, we take the path back to the elevator. George pushes past us, taps a button to open the door, and steps inside. I follow right behind him, but when I turn around, Otto is nowhere to be seen. "Otto?" I say, peering from side to side out the open door.

"Here, Infinity! Hurry!" Her voice is coming from behind the elevator shaft. I skirt around the side of the cylinder and spot her. She's standing at the end of another narrow path between the data hives on the other side and is looking down at the ground through the tall glass of the third wall.

I rush toward her. "What is it?"

"I've picked up more power signatures," she calls over her shoulder. "The signals are weak. I never would have noticed them if they weren't so grouped together."

A knot tightens in my gut. "Are they Drones? How many?"

"I don't think they're Drones," she says as I arrive at the window. "I think they're command modules . . . a lot of command modules."

"Are they Blackstone employees?"

"I don't know. But these readings show that they're at ground level right outside the Security Station."

Out the tall windows, I see the buildings bordering the empty courtyard, the tops of trees, and the tented spread of the white plastic canopy below. I press my nose against the cold glass, but I can't see the ground at the base of the building from this height and angle. George joins us at the window. "There are only a few of us who work on the weekends . . . ," he says, studying the computer slate over Otto's shoulder. "Maintenance, a couple of med staff, a few tech researchers, and a skeleton crew of security, so a large, widespread signal like that could only belong to—"

"Soldiers!" Otto blurts, pressing her finger to the window. "There are soldiers over there! By the corner of that building!"

I look to where she's pointing, and sure enough, in the distance, two soldiers in camo-patterned helmets and uniforms are cautiously stalking forward across the courtyard, their automatic rifles angled at the ground in a low, ready position. Two more soldiers appear from the alley between two buildings approximately thirty meters away from the base of the Security Station, and those four soldiers are soon followed by two more pairs. The eight soldiers quickly fan out and then hold their positions. They slowly and methodically turn in every direction as they survey the open expanse of the courtyard. The soldier leading the squad calls something back over his shoulder, and the empty space behind the eight men suddenly bursts alive with activity as nearly a hundred armed soldiers come streaming out from the line of buildings to the left.

"Wow!" exclaims Otto.

George sighs with relief. "Blackstone Technologies works very closely with the government's armed forces. Select groups often train here to test the latest weaponry before it's deployed in the field. Whatever is going on here, I'm sure they'll sort it out."

"I'm glad to know you have so much faith in the military," I mutter. "But those soldiers are on alert. They already know this is more than just a power outage, and they'll be assuming it's some kind of attack until they can prove that it's not. If the computer sends armed Drones to engage with those troops down there, somebody is going to die."

"Why would the computer kill United Alliance troops?" asks George. "That doesn't make any sense."

"It already tried to kill *us* with Drones, so I don't reckon the computer is thinking sensibly at all right now, George." I turn and stride back along the path. "I don't know about you two, but I don't want to be caught in the cross fire if the shooting starts, and I don't want to be trapped up here if the robots win. We need to go, and we need to go now."

With George and Otto right behind me, I skirt back around the silver tube and through the open door of the elevator. After George presses his thumb to the plate and jabs the ground-floor button, we stand in tense silence as the lift descends. With a gentle jolt and a quiet ping, the elevator door slides open.

"Don't move!" shouts a voice as three gun barrels are shoved toward our faces. Otto shrieks, and George drops his case of tools with a clattering thud as I slowly raise my hands. Standing in front of us are three large camo-uniformed soldiers wearing black visors and combat face masks. "Two more students and a technician," says the soldier in the center. "Just like the blonde girl said. Stand down." The soldiers all lower their rifles as the one who gave the orders points at George. "You. I need you to shut down all three of these wall displays," he says, motioning at one of the huge floor-to-ceiling screens. "We need a clear line of sight to outside."

George slowly picks up his case and nods. "Yep, I can do that," he mutters. The soldiers, clearly on edge, watch George like a hawk as he steps out of the elevator and disappears around the side of the silver tube.

"You two," the soldier says, pointing at us, "go join your classmates."

Otto and I walk out of the lift and around the elevator shaft to see Brent, Brody, Margaux, and Ryan standing inside the circular desk with three people who I've never seen before.

"Professor!" screeches Otto. She breaks into a run and embraces a tweed-suited old man, almost knocking him over and bumping into George, who's kneeling by the emergency-power compartment in the floor.

"Now, now, Miss Otto," the old man says, peeling her away from his waist. "Thank you for the sentiment, but let us behave with the appropriate decorum, shall we?"

Professor Francis doesn't look very different from how I imagined him. The mousy brown-haired boy must be Dean, and the weary-looking guy with the red tie, thick sand-colored hair, and blood-spattered shirt has to be Percy, the tour guide. I bet he wishes more than anything that he'd called in sick this morning.

"Sorry, Professor. I'm just glad you're alive. All of you." Otto's words are laden with relief as she smiles at Dean and Percy.

Percy smiles back, but it's forced. There's no joy in his eyes at all, just upturned lips marred by trauma. Dean doesn't even seem to notice Otto. His twitchy eyes are vacant and distant, flitting past the edges of people's faces as he sniffs and wipes at his blood-smeared nose.

"Where are Jennifer and Amy?" asks Otto.

"Unfortunately, we haven't seen Miss Cheng or Miss Dee as of yet," the Professor says, slowly shaking his head. "We can only hope that they have found somewhere safe to hide until this tragedy is over."

I assume that he and Otto are talking about two more students. That's all I need, two more kids to babysit. I'm starting to feel like I'm getting the short end of this deal. If they are hiding, I hope they continue to.

As per the soldier's request, George twists the key in the hole in the floor, and every display shuts off at once, leaving only the tinted sun outside to dimly light our tired faces. The middle soldier in the group of three throws a brisk nod of thanks at George, and all of them move in a silent group toward the far glass wall near the front doors. There's an awkward moment of silence. No one seems to know what to say. At least, not until Otto slings a satchel up over her head and does her best to look enthusiastic. "I got our phones and slates if . . . if anyone wants them?"

Margaux perks up immediately and pushes in between Dean and Brent, jabbing her hand into the satchel like a hungry horse nuzzling its food bag. "I need to call my mom and my dad and my mom's lawyers and my dad's lawyers and my manicurist and my hairstylist and DirtDish.com and anyone else who will listen. After I've sued this place for everything it's worth . . . ," Margaux says, wrenching a diamond-encrusted phone from the pouch, "I'll be rich, and they'll be sorry."

"You're already rich," says Ryan.

"Then I'll be richer," Margaux says, stabbing at the phone with her finger. The screen lights up, but the momentary flash of joy on Margaux's face quickly disappears. "No signal! What do you mean, no signal?"

"They don't work, Margaux," says Otto. "Communications are being jammed. Look." Otto holds up her computer slate, and the holographic lines, bumps, and charts spring up from its surface again. Margaux looks at them, bewildered, either unable or just too frustrated to make any sense of them. Her eyes crease and fill with tears. She's clearly emotionally exhausted, and something as meaningless as a disconnected phone has turned out to be her breaking point.

"Well, if it doesn't work . . . ," Margaux says, waving her phone right in Otto's face, "then what freaking use is it?" With an exasperated shriek, Margaux hurls her phone clear across the room. It streaks toward the far glass wall in a tumbling blur and smacks square into one of the soldiers' helmets with a dull thud. All of them turn, but only the middle soldier of the three holds up a hand and speaks.

"Miss, please calm down. I know this must be a traumatic experience for you, but I'm confident that once a sweep of the facility has been completed and cleared of any hostile forces, you'll all be free to go. Trust me; everything is going to be alright."

Margaux whimpers and covers her mouth with her hands. Tears spill down her cheeks. Brent steps forward and tries to console her with a hug. Everyone in the group looks at the two in their embrace. Compassion and a shared understanding for Margaux's sorrow show clearly on everyone's faces, except for that of strangely dead-eyed Dean, who's gazing into nowhere, and Otto, who's looking up at me, her frightened eyes wide with concern. I quickly look down at the computer slate resting on the palms of her hands and immediately see why. An enormous holographic power spike is jutting from the surface of the slate, and it's moving very fast, skittering in a curving trajectory, heading directly toward the small red dot in the center.

The small, red dot . . . exactly where *we* are all standing.

There's no time to warn the others as I spin and lunge at Otto.

As a flash of light illuminates the room and we fall toward the floor, the only thought searing through my mind is one of undiluted fear. Fear that the soldier's comforting words were not only wrong . . . but could also be the last words that any of us would ever hear.

CHAPTER TWELVE

The blast punches into the room like a thunderclap, rupturing the front windows into glittering powder. The explosion itself doesn't kill the three soldiers, not really. Neither do the spraying fragments of glass. It's the air that does it. The invisible, expanding sphere of superheated gases hits the men like a concrete wall, sending their bodies flying backward as their internal organs are pelted into tattered meat by the shrapnel of their own shattered bones.

The shock wave reaches us in a violent rush of glass, concrete, wood, and metal. The base of the desk stays mostly intact—that's what saves us—but parts of it fly off. A decent-size chunk catches me in the head as people tumble and splay all around me. Mouths are screwed into contorted shapes, hands and arms shield faces, and ears are thumped into deafness, but for that second, for that brief, destructive point in time, the only things that exist are the brutal noise and the percussive force. I don't think or feel anything. There's no fear, no confusion, no questions.

But when the broken pieces are settling, and the chaos fades, I know that those three things will fill every bewildered corner of our reeling minds.

There's moaning and labored movement. "Wha . . . what happened?" asks a muted voice. I only barely hear it through the high-pitched tones warbling in my damaged ears, but it sounds like George. I rub my eyes and survey the room.

Dust and debris are strewn all over the tangle of people scattered around me. Otto is lying facedown beside me; her glasses, remarkably unbroken, are just a half a meter from her mop of frizzy brown hair. I push myself up onto my knees and press my palm to the side of my skull. There's blood matted in my hair, but the dull throbbing warning tone in the back of my mind tells me that it's not too bad. I crawl to Otto, move a broken section of desk from her legs, and turn her over onto her back. She groans and winces, her computer slate still safely cradled in the crook of her elbow.

Looking around, I can see that everyone in our little group seems to be intact. No appendages missing, no eyeballs hanging out of faces, no ears or noses sliced off. Ryan pushes up onto his elbows and looks in my direction. I should run; this is my chance to ditch everyone and go it alone, but something won't let me. Something inside me is making me stay, holding me like a magnet to these people. Despite what I think or what I want to feel, I just can't deny the intensely uncomfortable fact that . . . I'm beginning to care what happens to them.

"Help me get everyone out of here!" I shout. Ryan seems to get the message through the ringing he's undoubtedly hearing, because he nods and rolls onto one knee, tugging at the shirt of a groaning Brody who's lying on his side nearby. I snatch Otto's glasses from the floor, wipe their dusty lenses on my equally dusty shirt, and slide them onto her nose. "C'mon, Bit," I say, grabbing her under her arms. "We gotta go."

Her eyes focus on mine, and she hooks an arm around my shoulder. "Infinity . . . ," she says croakily, "you called me 'Bit.'"

"Yeah, well . . . just shut up and move, would ya?"

I hoist her up, and she's understandably a little shaky on her feet. She absentmindedly slips her slate into her satchel; then, still clearly in a daze, she crouches to retrieve two more slates from the floor. Ryan and Brody are helping the others, and soon Percy is up, the look on his face so serious that it could be a stone carving. The Professor is on all fours, muttering about his glasses as he searches through splinters of desk, and that weird Dean kid just sits there, his blank, twitchy expression from before the explosion completely unchanged.

"What the hell was that?" Brent squeaks as he scrambles to his feet.

"I don't know," I reply. "But if it happens again, we had better not be here."

Ryan moves to look over the top of the desk. "Those three men, the soldiers . . . are they . . . ?"

I slowly shake my head. With little more than a solemn look, he turns away to clear a section of fallen ceiling panel from the chest of a prone, shallow-breathing George, who seems to be more than a little freaked out. I don't blame him. I bet this is the last thing the mild-mannered technician expected to happen when he pulled on his coveralls this morning. Ryan, on the other hand, seems more jaded than the others. I imagine he's experienced more actual life outside the golden walls of luxury than the rest of these privileged teenagers, but it's still disturbing how quickly someone can become accustomed to death.

"Why is this happening to me?" Margaux screeches as she pushes up from the floor, dust-darkened tracks of tears lining her face.

"We need to go!" I shout, pointing at the gaping rectangular hole in the front of the building where the windows used to be.

"Toward the explosion?" asks Brent.

"Do you see any other way out of here?"

Brent looks pissed off, but after a quick scan of the two remaining glass walls, he knows there's nothing to argue about. He takes Margaux's hand, and they start toward the breach, but I reach out and hiss at them to stop. "Wait!"

Everyone freezes.

The ringing in my own ears has faded enough to hear the rat-tat-tat of automatic gunfire outside. Soldiers very rarely shoot at nothing, so whoever or whatever caused this must be in somebody's sights, and it isn't very long until a strange noise piques my interest. It's a thudding sound, like heavy footsteps. And it's heading in this direction.

Frowning with curiosity, I peer over what remains of the top of the desk, waiting to see whatever is making the weird tromping noise. "What is that?" I ask, glancing back at the group.

Dean is standing now, his eyes still vacant, but everyone else, including Otto, is rooted to the spot, staring wide-eyed toward the approaching sound, all of them wearing the same expression, like kittens cowering from a wild dog. It's then that I realize . . . they all *know* that sound. It's a sound that has paralyzed them with fear, a sound that's getting louder and closer with every weighted thud. It's so close now that I can feel each pounding beat shuddering through the floor. I turn back toward the gaping hole in the side of the building to see two huge, bulbous, army-green-colored legs step into view outside the empty window frame.

Even though I can only see it from the chest down, I still can't believe my eyes. It's a robot, and—oh my—what a robot it is.

I thought I had studied them all, but right now, I'm at a loss for words. I have no idea what kind of machine that is. I can hear the spacking sound of bullets hitting it all over, but for all the damage they're doing, the soldiers might as well be firing peashooters. It could be a R.A.M., I suppose, but . . . they don't make them that big. Do they?

Almost as if it were a choreographed maneuver, everyone except me and that Dean kid jerks at the knees, ducking down behind the desk at the same time. Percy tugs the weirdly dazed boy down by his sleeve and bats at the air, signaling me to drop out of sight, too. Wary, and yet still intrigued, I slowly lower behind the desk and peek out through a small hole in its base. I've ducked just in the nick of time; a laser beam suddenly streams into the room, spreading into a bright-green fan through the floating particles of dust. It's projecting from the center of the robot's chest, flitting over the debris as if it's searching for something. Is the robot looking for us? Maybe it's scanning for Otto's slate? That power spike was heading straight for us, after all. If it fires another grenade or missile into this room, we're done for . . . it's over. And there's nothing I can do except keep quiet and hope like hell that doesn't happen.

Through the hole, I nervously watch the laser as it moves across the floor and over the body of a fallen soldier. It travels up the legs of his tattered uniform and over his hips, dipping into the gouges torn into the sunken curve of his blast-bared stomach. It sweeps across his blood-soaked chest and head, then switches direction and roves along his arm. The soldier's corpse is apparently no more important to the robot's scanner than the meaningless debris strewn around him. Suddenly the green fan of light snaps to a halt and begins to close, shrinking down and changing color from green to yellow before finally tightening into a bright-red beam, right in the center of the wide silver band wrapped around the dead soldier's wrist.

His command module. The robot has found what it's looking for.

The laser cuts off, and all of a sudden, there's a new sound, horrible and unlike anything I've ever heard before. It's a high-pitched squeal at first, but elevates quickly. Even with my palms pressed hard against my ears, the noise becomes so loud that it drills into my skull, filling my head and the whole room with a wailing scream. All around me everyone is doing the same, holding the sides of their heads as if they're going to explode. Even Dean is wincing. The scream begins to crackle, and I can smell the ozone tang of electricity burning the air. Then, with a violently powerful, droning roar, the remaining glass walls of the room come alive with reflected light as an astonishing eruption of power is unleashed from the robot's arm.

It takes everything I have to keep my eyes glued to the hole in the desk as I witness the soldier's entire body being shredded into oblivion by the incredible force of the robot's weapon. Pieces of the floor shatter and fly as his body is transformed from a human corpse into nothing more than a thick smear of human ingredients.

The brutal storm of gunfire thankfully ends, and I can hear my adrenalized heart pulsing in the depths of my ears. My breaths have become quick snorts, and my wide eyes are mirrored on the faces of everyone in the group. All of us are still grinding our hands into our ears.

That's when I see it out of the corner of my eye: the glint of silver that makes my stomach tighten and lurch.

Wrapped around the tour guide's left wrist . . . is another command module.

I hear the robot's laser snap on, and I quickly peer through the hole in the desk. There, flitting across the floor, is an eerie green line of light . . . and it's headed directly for us.

"Your wristband! Take it off!" I hiss. Percy's hands drop from his ears, and his brow furrows in confusion.

"The robot is tracking the command modules!" I whisper-shout, jabbing my finger at his wrist. "Get rid of it! Now!"

Percy looks down at the silver band, and his eyes widen.

I quickly turn back and spy through the hole. The laser is now shining directly on the other side of the desk. I look over at Percy and growl at him through gritted teeth. "Hurry!" He immediately presses his thumb to the black stone on the band and whispers the word "Disconnect." The wristband detaches and drops into his palm.

"George!" rasps Otto. "George has a module, too!"

I look over at George. He's still lying there with a board resting on his leg, his eyes blinking slowly behind his glasses as he stares at the ceiling. Something obviously isn't right with him. Otto scrambles across the floor toward him, lifts his hand, and hurriedly begins whispering to the deathly pale man.

"Take this thing off, George," she insists. "You need to do it right now."

Between shallow breaths he slowly nods, touches the stone, and faintly mumbles into it. With a soft click, it comes away from his wrist, and, in a panic, Otto tosses it to Percy as a thin beam of glowing green shines directly through the hole in the desk. It stops dead center on the two thick silver bands grasped in Percy's palm and instantly turns bright red. The hellish, high-pitched squeal of the robot's weapon fills the room again, and Margaux shrieks as Brody, Ryan, and the Professor scramble away from Percy like he has the plague.

"Throw them!" I yell over the noise. "Throw them now!"

Percy quickly stands and thrusts his hand high above his head. He's panting like a dog on a hot summer's day, terror contorting the edges of his eyes.

"Throw them!" bellows Ryan as the laser spreads green over the top of the desk and begins moving upward over Percy's chest. But Percy doesn't move. He's frozen, petrified solid as the glowing green line dips in and out of the creases in his face. The sound of the robot's weapon screeching gets louder as the fan of light narrows into yellow on Percy's forearm. Like a possum blinded into paralysis by an oncoming car, Percy doesn't move at all. In a few seconds, the top half of his body is going to be raw hamburger.

"Throw them!" I scream, but even I can't hear myself over the intensity of the piercing noise.

The laser reaches Percy's palm and sharpens into a beam as it turns a bright shade of scarlet red.

I have no idea how much time is left before Percy is turned into a bloody heap of remains, but I have to move . . . *now*. I leap up from the floor and lunge at his hand, and in one fluid movement, I snatch the modules from his palm, spin, and fling them wildly. The modules whip through the air and tumble all the way across the room. Purely by chance, my throw couldn't be better; they clink against the leg of the robot and clatter on the path at its feet like a hand-delivered sacrifice. I dive at the ground and peer through the hole as the laser thankfully skims back across the floor, finds the modules, and immediately cuts off. The tense muscles in my shoulders grip my bones tightly as the sound of the screaming weapon wanes back into the blissful relative quiet of Percy's heavy breathing and Margaux's puppy-dog whimpers. With a surprisingly quick movement for such a massive machine, the robot lifts one of its huge legs and brings its foot pounding down on the wristbands with a loud, ground-shaking thump.

I watch as the seemingly satisfied giant robot slowly trudges off toward the shouts of the soldiers in the courtyard, no doubt drawn to the high number of modules gathered there. I can hear Brody gulp with relief. Percy leans his head back toward the ceiling and lets out a long guttural groan as he buckles onto his knees beside George.

George's face is ashen. His chest has stopped moving.

I crawl over beside him, lift the board and two cracked computer slates from his leg, and there, sticking out of a blood-soaked rip in his coveralls, is the point of the screwdriver he slipped into his pocket barely twenty minutes ago. It's skewered right through his leg, and judging by the amount of blood, it must have torn his femoral artery in two. I look into his blank, sunken eyes, and I know that he's gone. With a wound like that . . . he didn't stand a chance.

I get to my feet and look toward the breach. "George is dead. Let's go."

"Oh my god," whispers Otto.

"Where do we go to?" asks Ryan.

"Anyplace where we won't end up like this," I say, pointing down at George's body.

"I'm not going out there with that thing!" squawks Margaux.

"It's heading away from us," I reply. "If we hurry, it won't even see us."

Ryan steps forward. "I'm with you," he says. "We can't stay here, and . . . most of the time, it kinda seems like you know what you're doing."

I don't really know what to make of that backhanded compliment, so I just decide to ignore it.

"I'm afraid I must agree," the Professor says shakily as he adjusts his glasses on his nose. "We must at least attempt to get out of harm's way."

Everyone stands, cautiously eyeing our exit point. I stride over the debris, sidle through an access gap in the broken desk, and begin scanning the floor for the soldiers' rifles. Two of them are intact, but the other has been rendered in half by the robot's weapon, its barrel lying beside a furrow filled with the unrecognizable remains of that unfortunate soldier. When this is over, his family will probably be presented with a Ziploc bag instead of a coffin.

I pick up one of the rifles, check its magazine and chamber, then sling it onto my back.

"Ah, Miss Brogan?" says the Professor. "*That* is a dangerous weapon; perhaps it would best be left alone."

It takes me a second to realize that he's talking to *me*. Miss Brogan? *Really?* Major Brogan gave Finn *his* last name? Figures, I guess. The few memories of hers that I saw showed that he loved her like a daughter, while I was only ever treated as a killer. Just like before, I feel the hate boiling my guts. I take a deep breath and try to calm the fire.

"It's OK, old man . . . ," I say as I walk to the second rifle and kick it up into my palm. "I've had lots of training." I look over at Ryan. "How's the shoulder?"

"It's a little tender, but it's OK," he says, flexing and rolling his arm. I throw the rifle at him, and he catches it with one hand.

"Do you know how to use that thing?" I ask.

"I've been kicked out of nine military schools," he says as he checks the weapon with practiced movements. "I can dismantle it blindfolded, if you like."

"This is unacceptable," trumpets the Professor. "I can't have students walking around with loaded guns!"

"School's out," I say, staring at the thin, gray-haired, tweed-jacket-wearing old nuisance. "And if you try to take this rifle away from me, I'll shoot you myself."

Of course, I don't mean it; he's a harmless old man, but judging by his incredulous expression, the Professor is more than slightly taken aback. "I see a good many detentions in your future, young lady," he huffs.

"Well, let's make sure you live long enough to punish me, then, shall we?"

With a flick of my head, I signal Ryan to join me as I approach the blasted-out window.

"What's the plan?" he whispers.

"All I need you to do is point and shoot if you have to."

"I can do that. Not that it'll do any good against that not-so-jolly green giant."

"No. But you could probably take out a Combat Drone if you hit it in the face mask a few times." He gives me a serious nod, and it feels good to have a battle comrade again. It reminds me of all the missions I've been on in the past with my *actual* mission partner, except, unlike him, Ryan actually speaks and doesn't have a creepy combat mask permanently fixed to his face all the ti—

BOOM!

Another explosion, more shouting, and more bursts from the robot's hellish weapon, all coming from the direction of the courtyard. I look back at the rest of the group. They stand in a nervous pack a few meters behind us.

"Go to the right," I tell Ryan. "Take them with you. I'll stay here until you're safely around the side of that white building on the corner."

"Then what?" he asks.

"We know that the robot is scanning for wristbands, and it's heading for the soldiers' power signals in the central courtyard. We can use that distraction to go around the outside of Dome One to your school bus. I'm assuming there's a bus?"

"Of course there's a bus," Ryan says, giving me a strange look. "You really don't remember anything about this morning, do you?"

"Keep your mind on the task," I hiss.

Ryan frowns. "Fine, I'll lead the others to the corner, but then we have to find a way to warn the soldiers about the command modules."

"No, we don't."

Ryan's eyes narrow into a look of deep disapproval.

"This is what those men out there signed up for," I whisper. "It's their job to protect the citizens of the United Alliance. Now take *those* citizens . . . ," I say, pointing at the group, "and help the soldiers fulfill their duty. Get them around that corner. If that robot comes back this way, I'll distract it until you're out of sight; then I'll catch up with you."

"It's a good plan. I can help lead the way out," Percy says from behind us.

Ryan glances back at the bunch of bedraggled people, then leans out of the breach, squinting toward the screeching foghorn of the robot's weapon emanating from the courtyard. "Percy can take them, and I can—"

I cut Ryan off before he can finish his stupid thought. "Don't run out there to warn them . . . Heroes die."

Ryan lets out an exasperated sigh. "OK, OK. I hear you." He throws an angry glare in my direction before turning to the group. "Everyone, follow me!"

There's no argument as the still visibly stunned cluster shuffles forward. Margaux, in particular, is an absolute mess. With our rifles at the ready, Ryan and I step down onto the patch of grass by the path just outside the window frame. Otto's frightened gaze meets my stoic mission face. I throw her a confident nod, and she tries her best to smile back. I elbow Ryan in the side to get his attention and swat at the air mouthing, "Go, go, go." He motions at the group to follow as he and Percy take off, leading them toward the corner of the white-stone building forty meters away. They've only gone a few meters when Otto breaks away from the pack and comes running back toward me.

"What are you doing?" I whisper. "Get out of here."

She looks me in the eyes with stony conviction. "If you're thinking about running off to find Richard Blackstone without me, you can forget about it. We had a deal."

"I'm coming to the bus. I swear."

"What about the mission? We've come too far to stop now. I can't believe you're just gonna drop this."

"I'm not dropping anything, and I didn't forget our deal. I promised that I'd help get everyone to safety. I keep my promises; you'd better keep yours." I grunt and push her away. "Go, get out of here. When the others are in sight of the bus, we'll double back."

"I'm trusting you," Otto whispers, her eyes narrow with suspicion.

"Go. I'll be right behind you. I promise."

Otto turns and jogs off toward the corner, glancing back at me on every other step. I shake my head and crouch beside the Security Station with the rifle at my shoulder, staring through the gap in a freshly pockmarked U-shaped tree and wondering how the hell I got so soft. I can see the inactive service Drone we saw before. It's still standing frozen in the same place, but now one of its arms has been shot off, and its torso is riddled with bullets. The giant R.A.M. has moved out of sight around the black angular structure on the corner, but I can still hear it firing in sporadic bursts, and I can clearly see some of the horrific damage that it's done.

It's not a pretty sight in the courtyard.

There are wide gouges scorched into buildings, smoke billows out of shattered windows, and pieces of camouflaged bodies lie among swaths of blood and scattered rifles. I turn away, angered and sickened. A simple infiltration and assassination—that's all I wanted—but this whole day is turning out to be a twisted nightmare.

I look back to check on the group. Everyone has made it around the corner except for Professor Francis, who's dragging a stumbling Dean behind him. Otto catches up with them and tries to help by shoving Dean along with her shoulder. In a few more seconds, they'll make it, and I can get the hell out of . . .

STOMP . . .

The shudder of a heavy footstep makes me jump in my skin.

STOMP . . .

I should have run the moment I heard it.

STOMP . . .

That would have been the smart thing to do, Infinity.

STOMP . . .

Obviously, I'm not as smart as I think.

STOMP.

Because I just *had* to turn back and look, didn't I?

There, standing at the corner of the building near the courtyard and towering at least nine meters high . . . is the R.A.M. Through the gap in the tree, I can see its huge, domed head with a pure-black strip sitting atop its massive rounded chest and shoulders . . . and it's looking this way.

I'm about to turn and run for my life when movement to my left catches my eye and sends my already-peaking adrenaline levels skyrocketing. The reason why the robot is coming back has emerged from behind the tree, and he's limping along the path barely ten paces from me.

It's a soldier. A solitary, wounded soldier.

He's bleeding badly from multiple wounds to his upper body, and the toe cap of one of his boots has been blown clean off. He sways off balance and reaches for the trunk of the tree to steady himself. Behind him, I can see a trail of bloody prints leading to a door in the adjacent building. The huge robot moves again.

STOMP . . . STOMP . . . STOMP . . .

The soldier's wristband is drawing the R.A.M. to him like a fly to dead meat, which is exactly what we're both gonna be if we don't . . .

THUD!

The R.A.M. walks straight into the side of a building. With its head wildly rotating left and right, it raises one of its huge hands and scrapes it along the wall, almost like it's trying to feel where to go next. I watch it closely; its movements are strange and clumsy. Its head swivels, and the plain black strip where its eyes should be pivots in this direction, but it doesn't stop. Instead, it skims right past where the soldier and I are standing. Then it occurs to me: the reason why the R.A.M. is scanning for command modules is because . . . the stupid bucket of bolts can't see! It must be firing blind at the power signals!

I don't know why that robot is blind, and I don't care; an advantage like that could give me the fighting chance I need to get this soldier to safety. I look at the insignia on his arm and read the name tag on his chest.

"Corporal Roth! We need to go!"

Seemingly oblivious to the walking death machine behind him, the soldier shakily raises his black visor with a bloodied hand, and a brutal truth is suddenly revealed. His eyelids are fluttering over a hollow stare glazed with panicked desperation. He's looking right at me, but I can tell that he isn't really seeing me.

Everything looks very different to someone in the final stages of shock.

I once saw a man try to scrape his own intestines back into his belly and seal it closed with mud because of shock. "Mother," the soldier rasps. "Take me home."

Corporal Roth's mind has abandoned him.

Twenty meters away, the R.A.M. has stopped altogether. Desperately hoping it stays that way, I seize the moment and step toward the Corporal, but as soon as I do . . . that dreaded green laser beam snaps on. It fans out from the robot's chest and begins scanning the wall of a nearby building. The jittering green line moves toward Corporal Roth, getting closer and closer with every passing second. When that laser finds his wristband, he's dead—and I'll be caught in the cross fire. I can't let that happen.

"Your command module!" I shout. "Take it off! Throw it away!"

"Help me," he whispers.

He's not listening to me at all, and the laser scanner is only ten meters away.

With my rifle dangling from my shoulder, I run at the Corporal and grab at the command module on his wrist. "Mother," he murmurs. He wraps an arm around me, and his legs buckle. He's heavy. Grunting to hold him up, I pull at the wristband, struggling but awkwardly failing to pull the thumb of his other hand toward the diamond-shaped black stone. Out of the corner of my eye, I can see the laser coming closer, the bright-green line roving across the wall barely five meters away.

"Help me, please," he sobs. Any second now, that R.A.M. is going to fire and kill us both. I'm desperate. This isn't working, and time is running out.

I know what I have to do.

I heave the Corporal off me and kick him hard in the chest. He stumbles away, falling backward, bewilderment and confusion creasing the edges of his eyes as he flumps heavily onto his back, groaning. With a jagged lump in my throat, I pull the rifle to my shoulder. Every fiber in my being screams out for me to close my eyes, but I grit my teeth, knowing that only my careful aim can provide mercy to that poor, suffering man. I hold my breath . . . and squeeze the trigger. With a loud bang, the rifle kicks in my arms, and my bullet finds its mark.

Right through the center of Corporal Roth's command module.

He screams out in pain, pulls his wrist to his chest, and I look toward the laser . . . It's still coming. The shot didn't deactivate the module. The laser line touches his boot. I raise my rifle again, hoping his hand will fall away from his body and I can get a second shot, but he holds it close, right over his heart. I can't fire again without killing him. But that doesn't matter now. It's too late to help him. The laser flickers across his body.

Yellow.

It narrows into a focused beam directly on his wrist.

Red.

The robot's weapon begins screaming, and I do the only thing I can. I turn . . . and I run.

I'm halfway to the corner of the white-stone building when the crackling squeal becomes a deafening roar. The terrifying noise only lasts for a few seconds. I don't dare look back.

The only sound I hear is my heart beating in time with my frantic footsteps. All I can smell is electricity and burning meat. The only thing I feel is overwhelming guilt . . . and all I can see in my mind is the image of Corporal Roth's sky-blue eyes pleading to be saved.

I failed him.

I make it to the corner of the building, panting at the air. I can't see properly. Everything is swimming in my field of vision; colors are merging and dripping into each other like oil in water. I have no idea what's happening. I panic and collapse against the wall, sliding down to the ground, blinking hard, willing my eyes to work again. Only after I feel the warm, wet droplets rolling down my face do I realize . . . that I'm crying. I've only ever cried once before. I was five years old. And on that day, I swore that I would never show that kind of weakness again, but everything I try to do on this mission from hell is ending in failure. And I hate it.

"Infinity?" Otto says, kneeling down beside me. She takes my hand. "We saw what happened. Are you OK?"

I know the definition of embarrassment, but I've never felt it before. Now, here I am, sitting on the ground, blubbing like a child. I feel like someone has cut my guts open and hung them in the town square for everyone to laugh at. I've seen soldiers die many times before. I've killed enemy soldiers myself. But I've never felt *anything* like this before. Why is *this* time different?

I want to shout "I'm fine!" and throw Otto's hand away, but when the words seep from my lips, they're quiet and feeble, and all I do is grip her fingers tighter. Finn is somehow infecting me and making me lose control. She's the one making me soft. She's the one making me care. She's the one forcing me to *feel*. It's the only thing that makes any sense. I detest her with a seething rage, especially now, but as much as I hate her for doing this to me, I can't get the image of Corporal Roth out of my goddamned head.

"Ryan," I say croakily. He steps forward and kneels beside me.

"Yes. I'm here," he replies.

"You were right . . . ," I murmur. "We have to warn them all."

Both Ryan and Otto help me to my feet as I sniff back whatever is dribbling from my nose and try to regain my composure.

"So, the bitch has feelings after all." My head snaps toward the insult, and my narrowed eyes zero in on Brent's scowling face.

"Mr. Fairchild!" exclaims the Professor.

"For now, I'll forget I heard that," I say, staring Brent down.

"I won't forget that I said it," he replies as he turns away and hugs Margaux to his chest.

"Hey!" barks Ryan. "If it's all the same to you guys, I'd like to get the hell out of here! So can someone tell me what we do next?"

"Mr. Blake?" the Professor says, looking in Percy's direction.

"I . . . ah . . . ," Percy stammers. He looks drained. This day has wrung his mind dry, and it shows.

I look out past the group. We're standing on a wide pathway that skirts the outer walls of a row of buildings. Trees and gardens line the edge of the path. Beyond them, lush, green grass spreads out in a flat expanse for at least a kilometer all around before the ground sweeps up into rolling hills in the distance. I can only just make out the shape of the dark curve of Dome One through the canopies of the trees. It looks to be about four hundred meters away.

"Percy. Are there any fences or barriers between here and Dome One?"

Visibly relieved at being asked a question he can answer, Percy shakes his head. "No. The only fences we have to worry about are at the three guard posts on the drive to the main road. But they have electrified gates that can only be opened by someone in the"—Percy's face drops—"in the Security Station."

"That doesn't matter. The bus will go right through those gates."

"Awesome," whispers Brody.

"OK, is everyone ready?" I say as I walk to the head of the group.

"Ah . . . I have a question," says Brent. "Who put you in charge?"

"I did," I reply. "Now move it."

I start jogging down the path, checking the nearest alleyway on my left for danger as I go. Halfway down, I see that it's blocked by a high wall. I glance over my shoulder, and sure enough, everyone, including a clearly fuming Brent, has begun following behind me. Major Brogan taught me a long time ago that sometimes all you need to do is act like you're in charge for people to put you in charge. In this case, he was right on the money.

Ryan and Percy catch up with me at the front of the pack, and the three of us run abreast. "What about the soldiers in the courtyard?" Ryan asks.

"I'm checking the alleyways for access," I reply. "I'll stick with you guys until I find a clear route, and then I'll cut through and find someone to warn. You carry on around the dome."

Ryan nods, and we jog on, both of our heads now flicking to the left as we pass each narrow passage between the buildings. With the light breeze rustling the leaves above me and the sunlight dappling the paving stones beneath my feet, this could easily be a pleasant jog through a park on a warm summer afternoon. Unfortunately, the two sweaty, dirt-smeared, blood-spattered guys running beside me completely destroy that illusion.

We carry on at a steady pace, and soon part of the massive outer wall of the dome comes into view through the thinning green canopy overhead. "We're almost there." I glance back, and the rest of the group isn't far behind. Even the old Professor is keeping in step, jogging right beside a red-faced Brody, who is very impressively plodding along despite piggybacking a gormless-looking Dean. Seriously, what the hell is wrong with that kid? A wet sack of potatoes has more personality.

Percy, Ryan, and I arrive at the end of the row of buildings and wait for the others to catch up. Beside the last building is a thicket of densely packed plants. I turn to Percy. "Can I push through here?"

Wheezing and gulping from running, he shakes his head and shrugs his shoulders. He doesn't have a clue.

"I'm gonna try. You get going," I say, pointing across the 150-meter expanse of grass between us and the visible edge of the dome's rounded black wall. Ryan nods. I look back at the group. Everyone is gathered, hands on hips, catching their collective breath.

"I'll be waiting for you outside the bus," Otto whispers with a knowing look. "Be careful, Infinity."

"You're Infinity?" gasps the Professor. "So that murderous hacker was looking for *you*?"

I don't know what he's talking about, so all I can do is stare blankly.

The Professor looks bewildered and shocked and confused all at once. "Someone took control of that monstrous robot and killed poor Miss Cole and all the others . . . because of you?"

I stand there in silence, frowning at the Professor as he turns and barks at Otto. "What is going on here? I demand an explanation!"

"Later, Professor, I promise," Otto says, dragging him away by the arm.

Ryan looks over at me. "You watch your back."

I smile and nod. "Don't get killed."

He returns my smile, then addresses the group, "C'mon, everyone; we're almost home free."

They move off at a cautious pace, with Ryan and Percy leading the way. I can still hear Professor Francis muttering my name as I turn, step up onto the edge of the concrete planter, and push my fingers into the thicket. I have to force my shoes into the tiny spaces between the roots of the plants and lean my shoulders sideways, pushing forward with all my might just to make any kind of decent headway. If I had one wish right now, it would be for my favorite black-handled knife to magically appear in my hand so I could clear away these damned plants that are catching and scratching against me. *Actually, if I had one wish, it would be for Richard Blackstone to be dead, so stop wasting time with the daydreaming, Infinity; get to the courtyard, and warn the first soldier you see.*

With my useless flights of fancy firmly put in their place, I carry on grunting and heaving at the sinewy vegetation until I can finally make out the pattern of paving stones through the tangle. I'm almost halfway through this wretched mess of weeds when a calm computerized voice suddenly speaks from somewhere on the other side of the garden.

"Combat Drones have been dispatched to eliminate unauthorized intruders. I repeat, Combat Drones have been dispatched to eliminate unauthorized intruders. Due to unresolved system malfunctions, all Drones are operating at a diminished capacity, so to avoid accidental

harm, all authorized staff are advised to remain in your nearest emergency shelter. I do apologize for any inconvenience and hope to resolve this conflict in the most efficient way possible. Thank you for your patience, and . . . have a spectacular day."

That was Onix. I've never heard anyone tell me they're going to murder me in such a polite manner. It sure doesn't make it any easier to take.

Despite the warning, I carry on. I'm pushing at a clump of weird, prickly shrubbery when there's a scream in the distance. I freeze. That high-pitched, annoying scream is one that, lately, I've become all too familiar with.

Margaux.

Suddenly much more alert and concerned, I look back down the very roughly hewn track that I've barely carved between the plants, straining my ears in the direction of Margaux's frightened shriek.

Rat-tat-tat! At the sound of Ryan's rifle, I nervously clutch a handful of branches. *Rat-tat-tat!*

On his second salvo, my body twitches, and I immediately think of Otto. I quickly lurch back the way I came, angrily grunting at the trees and thick tufts of tall grass in the way as I scramble as fast as I can back through the garden.

I emerge, stumbling out of the thicket onto the path at the exact moment I hear Ryan bellow an ominous command: *"Everybody . . . ruuun!"*

There, about a hundred meters away, I see the whole group running back across the grass toward me, fleeing in outright panic. And the reason why becomes blatantly clear: beyond them, emerging from a large, rectangular hole in the sheer-black side of the dome are ten scarlet-faced, gun-toting Crimson-Class Combat Drones.

Ryan is holding his position, his rifle at the ready, one knee down on the grass. He's already dropped one of the androids; I see it lying, deactivated, beside the wall of the dome. Ryan's rifle flares with a rapid burst of rounds, and another Drone's head jerks, its mask snapping from red to black as it falls facedown onto the ground. Even with a bad shoulder, he's a very good shot. Ryan springs to his feet, turns, and starts sprinting for his life as the rest of the Drones raise their semiautomatic rifles in unison . . . and open fire.

The sound of bullets whizzing past me kicks my reflexes into high gear, and I take off, bolting across the grass toward the dome. I swing my rifle around into my arms as I go, pumping my legs against the ground, my eyes focused on the silver-hooded robots trudging in a haphazard formation across the field. I notice that a couple of them, strangely, aren't even walking in the right direction. As I get closer, I see that only half of the Drones' rifles are pointing toward the group; the rest are *way* off target. With every missed shot they fire, it becomes more and more apparent that the Drones are behaving a lot like the R.A.M. was. They definitely seem to sense movement from this general direction, but they're shooting like they're wearing blindfolds. It's another lucky break, but those are still bullets that they're firing, and the more they pull those triggers, the greater the odds are that someone is gonna get shot.

The thought has barely entered my mind when it's proven to be true. A Drone's gun barrel flashes, and a split second later, a patch of red blooms like a flower on the leg of Brent's trousers. He drops, dragging Margaux by the hand down onto the soft, green grass. Ryan sees them fall, but the others are oblivious, far too busy escaping to notice. I come to a skidding halt as Otto, Percy, Brody, Dean, and the Professor hurriedly approach. I point back the way I came, shouting, "Go through the garden!" as they all barrel past in a frantic bustle.

With bullets whizzing past my head, I dive onto the grass and prop my chin on my rifle. I line the sights, take a breath, and, with a slow exhale, squeeze the trigger three times. Far across the field, the face mask of one Drone cracks into shards. It does a clumsy half spin before thudding to the ground. I take aim at another and shoot again.

I hit a Drone twice in the mask; it doesn't go down, but my shots aren't entirely wasted as it veers to the left, walking out in front of another android, obscuring its line of fire.

I glance back. Otto and the others have almost made it to the garden.

I look over at Ryan. He's thrown his rifle down and grabbed Brent by his arm. He drags Brent's wrist over the back of his neck, lifts him over his shoulder into a fireman's carry, and hoists him from the ground. Ryan starts running as fast as he's able, but he doesn't get very far. A slight trip becomes a stumble into a toppling loss of balance; he and Brent both fall, tumbling headlong onto the grass.

Seven Drones are still standing, but only the four closest are pointing their weapons in the right direction. That's the good news. The bad news is, the closer they get, the more their guns seem to be zeroing in on Ryan, Brent, and Margaux. I need to buy them some time. I take aim at the nearest one and breathe in through my nose, slowly breathe out, and then gently squeeze . . .

Rat-tat-tat-tat-tat-tat-tat-tat-tat!

I quickly look up from my rifle. I haven't pulled my trigger, but the Drone I had in my sights is suddenly being pelted with bullets. A line of holes dots up its torso and head, shattering its face mask into pieces. The android drops onto its knees and falls flat on the ground as the next Drone in line is immediately hit by the continuous barrage of gunfire. Pockmarks speck up across its chest and crack through its forehead. Its whole body freezes like someone's flicked an off switch, and it falls onto its back with a heavy thud. Two down, just like that. I look across the field to my right, and I can hardly believe my eyes. With her skirt stretched tight across her wide stance and Ryan's rifle dug into her hip is a wailing, wild-haired, teeth-bared, android-annihilating Margaux, the flaring weapon kicking in her white-knuckled hands as she peppers a third Drone with a hail of bullets and drops it like a ton of bricks. An amused smile creeps across my lips. *Give 'em hell, Blondie.*

Margaux is still rage-yelling at the top of her lungs when the gun, its ammo spent, begins clicking like a castanet. Ryan, having already hoisted Brent onto his shoulders again, is halfway back to the garden when Margaux throws the empty weapon to the ground, turns on her heels, and sprints after them.

There are only four functioning Drones left. If I can take them out, then the path to the bus will be clear. I take aim at the first one, but my grand plan is instantly shattered: ten more Drones walk out of the door-shaped holes in the side of the dome.

Even if I could take them all out before my ammo is gone, they'll probably just keep coming. I don't want to admit it, but I have no other choice. This battle isn't worth fighting. We'll have to find another way. I spring up from my position, sling my rifle onto my back, and take off across the field.

The Drones keep firing, and I keep running, bullets zipping past me on both sides. The Drones are terrible shots from this distance, but even a bad shot can get lucky, and more than a couple come a little too close for my liking. I keep my pace at full throttle all the way back to the garden.

When I arrive, Ryan and a deeply concerned Margaux are crouching next to Brent beside the concrete planter. All the others have started making their way through the brush. I can see the back of Brody about a meter in, swearing and pushing at Dean to move. Ryan has ripped a strip off Brent's trouser leg and is busy tying it around his wound as Brent grits his teeth, wincing as he grips Margaux's hand. I'd be lying if I didn't admit that it brightens my mood a little to see him in pain.

"How is it?" I ask between breaths.

"It's bad," Brent growls.

"Shut up," Ryan says, pulling the knot tight. "It's not that bad. The bullet took a bite out of his thigh, but he'll be OK."

"I'm bleeding!" Brent groans.

"That's generally what happens when you get shot," Ryan says, wiping his bloody hands on his trousers.

Brent glowers up at me, and flecks of spittle spray from his lips. "I bet you're loving this, aren't you?"

I'm about to tell him just how right he is when another shot zips by. I look back at the Drones. They're about forty meters out. They're tromping blindly in our general direction, but they're still closing in fast.

"Get in there, quick!"

With one eye on the Drones, Ryan pulls Brent to his feet and unceremoniously stuffs him headfirst into the tangled makeshift path the others have forged through the garden.

Margaux follows, then Ryan. The Drones are barely twenty-five meters away. Two bullets pit a tree beside the path, and another zings past so close to my head that I feel the air move against my cheek. Time to go.

I lunge onto the edge of the planter and shove my way into the thicket behind Ryan, awkwardly maneuvering my rifle as it catches on stray vines and branches.

I can hear the dull, thudding footsteps of the Drones getting closer. They're nearly at the path. I push on behind Ryan without looking back, and it doesn't take long before he shoves the last few strands of vegetation aside and stumbles out of the brush. I emerge right behind him into a recessed alcove formed by two curved bench seats, almost identical to the one we crawled into when we exited the vents on the opposite side of the courtyard.

Everyone is perched on the seats in silence, anxious fear painted on all their faces. I look back into the thicket and can just make out glints of silver between the matted fronds and branches as the Drones on the other side of the garden tromp and wander blindly, searching for movement. Even though it seems that we'll be relatively safe where we are, the androids are way too close for comfort. We need to move on.

I walk through the alcove, crouch in the gap between the benches, and quietly push aside the thick leaves of a nearby flax plant. To the right, I see a wide, curving staircase leading up to a row of buildings at the top end of the courtyard. I slowly scan over a wide-open space of empty paving stones, and as I turn my head to the left, my body suddenly seizes with fright. Barely a meter away is the unmistakable triangular muzzle of a Hellion 90 triple-barreled, fully automatic shotgun . . . and it's pointing directly at my head.

CHAPTER THIRTEEN

"Hold it right there," orders a quiet, graveled voice.

A lone soldier is standing just to my left. I carefully stand, raise my hands, and whisper an appropriate lie in my best frightened-schoolgirl voice: "I'm a civilian."

"Come out here," he whispers. "Slowly."

I walk a few steps out into the courtyard and look over at the uniformed man. His eyes scan me up and down from beneath his raised visor. "Remove the weapon and hand it to me."

I pull the strap up over my head and offer up my rifle. The soldier steps forward, carefully takes it, and slings it over his shoulder. "There are more of us," I say, calmly turning to face him.

The soldier lowers his gun, I lower my hands, and he calls toward the nook. "You can come out now."

The trembling voice of Professor Francis issues from the bushes. "Is it safe?"

"Yes," replies the soldier. "Please come out of there."

There are shuffling sounds behind me as the sorriest-looking, most ragtag bunch of people I've ever seen emerges in a tight group out of the nook and into the courtyard. Everyone is dirty, bloody, scratched up, and clearly exhausted. Maybe it's mostly due to his "poor me" demeanor, but Brent looks especially rough as he limps pathetically, his arm slung over Margaux's shoulder for support. The same goes for Dean, still gormless, propped up and being half-dragged along by Brody. The soldier looks over all of us. "My name is Private Carter. If you'll follow me, we'll get you cleaned up and have a medic take a look at your wounds."

There are quiet sighs and looks of relief on some faces, but not on Ryan's. His expression flicks to one of high alert. "The command modules!" he blurts at the soldier. "The R.A.M. is tracking the command modules!"

Private Carter nods. "It's OK; we know. As soon as we realized that, we ditched them all into an open space and it blew every single one to pieces."

"Where is that infernal machine?" the Professor asks, nervously scanning the area. "Did you defeat it?"

"No, but don't worry," replies the soldier. "Without the modules to hone in on, it stopped moving. Now it's just standing there."

Margaux raises her hand. "Excuse me, sir, but . . . there are robots with guns—"

The soldier raises his hand, stopping Margaux short. "Your shots alerted us to the situation. A sniper is being positioned on the roof to take the rogue androids out. I was sent to retrieve you from the alcove."

"You knew we were in there?" Otto says, frowning at the soldier.

He nods. "We were watching from the window of the command post upstairs. Saw you all duck into the garden."

"Then what was with the gun pointing?" I ask.

"Sorry about that. Just making sure you didn't mistake me for a robot and put me down, too."

Private Carter nods toward me. "You can shoot, and you . . . ," he says, pointing his finger at Margaux. "Remind me never to get on your bad side."

"If you don't mind, Mr. Carter . . . ," pipes up Professor Francis. "I would appreciate it if you didn't encourage my students' abhorrent behavior. I find your cavalier attitude very disconcerting; this is a tragedy of monumental proportions. Many innocent people, including my colleague Miss Cole, four of my students, as well as your very own men, and a Blackstone employee have all been killed."

Private Carter nods. "I apologize; I didn't mean any disrespect. You're right, of course. I'm not very good at dealing with civilians."

The Professor gives Private Carter a teacherly glower. "In fact, two of my students are still missing. Their names are Jennifer Cheng and Amelia Dee."

"I'm sorry, sir. I haven't seen them, but squads are still sweeping the complex. I'm sure they'll find your missing students."

Brody thrusts a hand in the air, but the soldier's easygoing mood has shifted, and he waves it down. "Please, there will be time for more questions later. We're getting everything under control, but the main computer is still malfunctioning and communications are down, so, as a precaution, please follow me to the temporary command post. I'm sure that as soon as the medic has checked you out and we've cleared Dome One, we can send you all home."

Private Carter turns and heads off down a lamppost-lined path along a row of the very same buildings that, only a few minutes ago, we were running behind in the opposite direction. As everyone begins following Private Carter, I decide to lag in the back. I stare at Otto; she catches my loaded look and hangs back, too, as the others file past. We let them walk on a little before following at a distance. I scan past the group, farther down into the courtyard. The abstract sculpture we saw before is about fifty meters away, and beyond that, in the distance between some trees, I can make out the shape of the stationary R.A.M. It looks like there are soldiers moving around it, most likely trying to secure it while they scrape what's left of their fallen comrades into body bags. Otto taps my arm. "Everyone is safe with the soldiers now," she whispers. "Do you think we can slip away somehow?"

I nod. "Yeah, but we'll have to wait for the right moment."

"They're gonna come looking for us as soon as they find out we're gone," says Otto.

"That's why we'll have to move fast and stay out of sight," I reply. "We'll head deeper into the compound, lose them any way we can, and hope like hell that Richard Blackstone hasn't been evacuated."

"If he was even here to begin with," says Otto.

"Well, I guess we're gonna find out," I reply.

"Stop dillydallying, you two!" Professor Francis shouts. Up ahead, Private Carter is standing beside a doorway in one of the buildings, and everyone is filing in past him.

"I'm ready to go whenever you are. I'll follow your lead," Otto whispers with a determined nod, and we quicken our pace toward Private Carter.

The door is a fire exit just off to the side of the building's main entrance. The cracked glass and bent frame are obvious signs that it's been kicked in. We sidle past Private Carter and follow the echoes of the others' footsteps up four flights of narrow stairs, through a stairwell door, and into a large, open-plan office. Desks have been pushed aside, cubicle walls have clearly been moved into particular positions to serve new purposes, and there are soldiers everywhere—more than thirty at a quick count. Some are organizing weapons and equipment, others are helping the wounded to and from a partitioned section in the corner, and some are hovering around a desk that has been pushed up against the windows overlooking the courtyard. Light from outside is filtering in, but the room has that distinctive dimly lit look you get from an office devoid of electricity.

Among all the activity, the desk is definitely the center of importance. A thick power or data cable of some kind is snaking out a window, and I can see the light of computer screens in the spaces between the murmuring soldiers.

Private Carter and another soldier carrying a sniper rifle emerge from the stairwell door, brush past me and Otto, navigate around the rest of our little group, and walk toward the desk. Private Carter unslings my rifle and props it against a cubicle wall.

"The civilians have been retrieved, sir, and Private Sekula here has dispatched the rogue Drones with sniper fire. He told me it was like shooting fish in a barrel," he says, jabbing a thumb at the smiling man standing beside him.

One of the men hunched over the desk straightens and addresses the two soldiers. They're standing in the way of his face, but I can hear his voice. "Good job, Sekula," he says. "Get back on the roof just in case any more of those robots wander this way." The soldiers salute the commanding officer, and as they move off to their respective duties, my eyes go wide.

The Commander is tall and solidly built. He has olive skin, thick, black, neatly side-parted hair, and a macho, yet distinguished, moustache. He's also divorced, forty-six years old next November, drinks expensive tequila, and smokes Cuban cigars. The reason I know all this is because that man is Captain Javier Delgado, Covert Field Operations Supervisor, security-clearance-level nine, and . . . the commanding officer on thirteen of my previous missions. This is not good. I'm on a personal, unsanctioned mission. If he sees my face, there are going to be some serious questions coming my way—questions I'd most likely be answering in a military prison cell.

Captain Delgado looks over at our little band of misfits, and I quickly sidestep behind Otto. "What are you doing?" she whispers. I don't reply; instead, I grab her arms so she doesn't move and peek around the side of her frizzy brown hair.

Captain Delgado leaves the soldiers at the desk and joins our group. He nods at Percy and then extends a greeting to the Professor, grasping the old man's hand and shaking it firmly. "For a moment, I thought we lost you at the Security Station. I'm glad to see you made it out safely." The Captain scans the front row, and I quickly duck down out of sight behind Otto's back, only barely avoiding being spotted. "I see a few new faces," says Captain Delgado.

"Oh yes, these are some of the other students that I mentioned," replies the Professor. "Everyone, this is Captain Delgado. He and his men rescued us when the power failed and the second dome collapsed."

"The dome collapsed?" Brody blurts.

"'Disintegrated' is probably a better word," says Percy.

"We found these three wading through chest-deep black sand," Captain Delgado says, waving a finger at the Professor, Percy, and Dean. "How is the young man doing?" he asks, frowning in Dean's direction. "Any improvement?"

"Sadly, no," replies the Professor. "The neural device that linked him to that infernal robot seems to have done quite some damage to his mind. I don't know how I'm going to explain any of this to their parents."

"Well, I can tell you right now that you won't," says the Captain. "I'm very sorry about what happened in Dome Two, Professor, but the waiver you all signed is ironclad. None of you can speak a word about anything that has happened here. Ever."

"B-but . . . ," stammers the Professor. "I have to tell them *something*."

Captain Delgado puts his fists on his hips and clears his throat. "You can tell them that this was a tragic industrial accident. A computer malfunction caused an explosion that sadly resulted in the deaths of three students and a teacher, and rendered a boy catatonic from the trauma of witnessing said tragedy. That's what you will say. That's all any of you will be permitted to say."

"*Four* of my students were killed, not three!" barks the Professor. "And those children have very wealthy and powerful parents who . . ."

"Who are not nearly as wealthy or as powerful as Blackstone Technologies," Captain Delgado says, leaving the Professor gaping at him like a fish on dry land. "Look, Professor, I've lost eleven good soldiers today. It makes me wanna tear a new one in whoever's responsible, but I know my place. And my lips are staying zipped."

The Professor doesn't say a word, but he must be fuming, because Captain Delgado sighs and does his best to look consolatory. "Professor, I don't know why on god's green earth anyone would authorize a school field trip to a classified research facility, but it happened, and people died. None of this is your fault, but the truth is you'll probably lose your job. On the bright side, the settlement you receive from Blackstone Technologies will make you a millionaire."

Making sure to avoid being seen, I cautiously peek out from behind Otto. The "my word is law" expression on the Captain's face is all too familiar, and I know exactly how completely helpless the Professor must feel right now. I can't count how many times I've stood in front of Captain Delgado and had to bear his smug authority, but you just can't win when someone else is holding all the cards. And Professor Francis knows it.

"Apparently, the *truth* is whatever you say it is, Captain." I can't see the Professor's face from where I'm standing, but I can hear the bile coating every word.

Captain Delgado gives the Professor a patronizing smile. "Now you're getting it."

The Captain casually waves an open hand toward a far corner of the office. "We've set up a temporary infirmary. The medics can take a look at your injuries. Now, if you'll excuse me, I have some rather important issues to deal with." And with that, Captain Delgado turns and walks back toward the huddle of soldiers.

I breathe a sigh of relief as Ryan lets out an altogether different exhalation. "What a complete assho—"

"Mr. Forrester!" Professor Francis hisses, cutting Ryan short. "There is no need for that kind of language . . . but if there were, I might be inclined to agree with you wholeheartedly."

At the Professor's coaxing, everyone begins moving toward the infirmary area in the corner. I make sure to stay on the opposite side of the group as we go, as far away from the eyes of Captain Delgado as possible, which, considering that he and I are in the same room, isn't far enough for my liking. Otto, observant as ever, glances from me to Captain Delgado and back again as we all weave and bump past the sideways looks of the busy soldiers. Cubicle walls have been set up to provide a reasonably spacious separate region for the infirmary, and I do my best to nonchalantly glide behind the nearest one. Just inside the area, two office couches have been pushed together to form a waiting room of sorts. A soldier with a bandage wrapped around his forehead is dozing at the end of one couch, his helmet, combat mask, and visor resting on his lap. Further in, six desks have been pushed against the windows and far wall to act as makeshift beds. Five of the desks have soldiers lying on them with various shrapnel and blast injuries. The sixth desk is empty, and a rubber-gloved soldier is standing over it, wiping blood from its surface with a wet sponge. He looks over at us. "Need any help?" he asks.

The Professor nods at the soldier. "Yes, thank you." He guides Dean and motions at Brent to come forward, as well. A concerned-looking Margaux, a pathetically mewling Brent, a vacant Dean, and the Professor all make their way toward the medic's desk as Otto, Brody, and Ryan take a seat on the empty couch. Unsurprisingly, Otto pulls her slate from her satchel. I perch on the arm of the couch beside her, giving me just enough height to peek over the top of the cubicle wall and keep a wary eye on Captain Delgado. Percy wanders past us and flumps down beside the bandaged soldier on the other couch, absentmindedly chewing on a fingernail. Otto pulls some gum from her shirt pocket. She peels a piece, pops it into her mouth, then offers the pack around. I shake my head, but Brody and Ryan both gratefully take a strip.

"Worst field trip ever," Ryan mumbles as he unwraps his gum.

I look over at him, and we both smile ironically. "You're a pretty good shot," I say, trying to ease the tension.

Ryan raises an eyebrow and nods. "Thanks. You're not so bad yourself."

Brody is sitting beside Otto, slowly chewing as he watches her fingers tap away on her ever-present slate. "Hey. I didn't thank you for pulling me into that vent. And I'm sorry for biting you," I whisper.

Brody looks up at me and gives me a goofy grin before turning back to watch Otto. "What do you look like without your glasses?" he asks, staring gormlessly at the side of her face.

Otto does a funny little frowning double take at Brody before ignoring him completely and tugging on my skirt. "Infinity, here, take this." Otto detaches the top corners of the slate and hands one of the small, black, plastic triangles to me. I stare at the weird little thing in my palm and wonder what the hell I'm supposed to do with it.

Otto takes her plastic triangle and nestles it into her ear, so I follow suit and do the same. The back of it is soft and molds in quite comfortably. Otto slides her fingers over the top of the slate and pops off a small, rectangular section from the back. She fishes her half-chewed gum from her mouth, wads it onto the black plastic rectangle, and then hands it to me. I frown at her and shrug my shoulders. She points at the cubicle wall three meters in front of us and makes a pressing motion. I get what she wants me to do, but I'm not sure why, so I'm still frowning as I walk over and stick the rectangle to the wall.

While I'm there, I sneak a peek over the top. Across the office, I can see the side of Captain Delgado's face; he's leaning over the desk, muttering to the soldier standing beside him. The insignia on the soldier's uniform tells me his rank is Corporal, and he's a rather concerned-looking one. I scan the rest of the room, eyeballing weapons and pondering exit strategies, when a burst of static suddenly hisses through my ear. I wince and look back at Otto. She doesn't look up. She just keeps swiping and tapping at the slate. The static begins to clear, giving way to layers of rhythmical thudding sounds surrounded by overlapping whispered conversations, rustling, scraping, tapping, humming, and clicking. It's like every sound in the whole room is being channeled into my ear all at once. One by one, the sounds begin to vanish as Otto pecks at the surface of the slate. Soon only the whispers remain. One by one, those fade as well, until only one voice remains. Otto swipes her finger up, and the faint voice becomes loud and clear. It's Captain Delgado.

I give Otto an admiring look of surprise. She cocks her head, raises her eyebrows, and shrugs. I throw her a devious smile and peek back over the top of the wall. Captain Delgado's lips are moving in perfect sync with the words piping through the little plastic wedge in my ear.

"So what exactly are you saying?" he asks the Corporal beside him.

"Well, we've finally managed to manually patch into the hard-line data feed in the conduit above the cortex level, and as far as we can tell . . . something is hindering crucial computer functions," replies the soldier.

"Something? I'm going to need a better explanation than that."

"Sir, I know my way around computers, but when it comes to artificial intelligence, I'm way out of my depth. The Blackstone main computer is a lot like a human brain. You'd need an information architect with a data scalpel for this job. For all the use I am, I might as well be a plumber with a pipe wrench."

"I need communications and main power up and running right now, soldier. So I don't care if you shove a pipe wrench or a crowbar or a goddamned jackhammer in there. Do something useful before I shove my boot up in your out port."

The Corporal is visibly flustered. "We . . . ah . . . we've identified two streams of unusual neural data interlaced with the main computer feed. We may be able to disrupt them with a data spike, but we're not completely sure what will happen if . . ."

The Captain stands straight and glares at the soldier. "Stop flapping your lips, Corporal Avary, and get it done."

Captain Delgado steps away from the desk and stands at the windows overlooking the courtyard. I can tell that he's pissed off by the particular way his shoulders rise and fall as he breathes.

"You heard the Captain," Corporal Avary says as he nudges the uniformed man sitting in a chair beside him. "Do it."

The man looks up at the Corporal, his profiled features showing clear concern. "Execute the action, Private. That's an order." I hear an audible gulp, the tap of a finger against the glass of a computer slate, and . . .

Nothing happens.

Corporal Avary looks confused. He leans in, scanning the multiple screens set out on the desk and muttering to his colleagues, when, all of a sudden, the previously dark ceiling lights throughout the dim office begin blinking on one by one. Computer slates lying blank on pushed-aside desks all around the room begin flicking on, too, all with little holographic Blackstone logos twirling above their surfaces. Captain Delgado glances around the now brightly lit office, then turns his attention toward the huddled group of men with a stern—yet pleased—expression. "You got the power back on. Well done."

"Oh, y-yes, sir, of c-course," Corporal Avary stammers, nervously looking around the room at the slates booting up.

Captain Delgado pulls a walkie-talkie from his belt and barks into it. "Radio check, this is your commanding officer. Squad leaders, respond if you're receiving me, over."

"Alpha Three reading you loud and clear, Captain," replies a voice. *"Delta Six here Captain, signal is strong,"* says another. *"Omega Five squad reporting in,"* says a third voice.

The Captain nods his approval. "Looks like you got communications back as well, Corporal."

"Yes, sir, local radio comms are operational. But we still don't have a usable cellular signal or access to the network."

"Keep at it," the Captain replies as he raises the radio to his lips. "Alpha Three, report, over."

"Mechanoid is secured with containment foam, but we've still got some bodies to bag, sir."

"Carry on, Alpha. Delta Six, what's the situation? Over."

"The sweep of the buildings surrounding the courtyard is complete, sir, awaiting further orders."

"Go and help Alpha team. How about you, Omega Five?"

"We found the two missing female students hiding in an alcove in Sector B, sir. They're pretty shaken up, but they're OK, over."

"Nice one, Omega; bring 'em back to their friends at the command post."

"Sir, yes, sir. Omega out."

Captain Delgado hooks the walkie-talkie back on his belt. "Finally, I can give the Professor some good news," he murmurs to himself. My eyes go wide as a smiling Captain Delgado leaves the desk and begins striding in this direction. He's halfway across the room, sidestepping soldiers as he approaches. I quickly look around; there's nowhere left for me to hide. I can hear his footsteps getting closer. He's almost at the entrance to the makeshift infirmary. The ridiculous thought of grabbing Otto's slate and holding it up in front of my face flits across my mind when I suddenly hear a voice crackle from a walkie-talkie barely a meter from the other side of the cubicle wall.

"Captain Delgado! Come in, sir!"

The Captain's footsteps stop. "What is it, soldier?"

"We've got movement, sir. A long section of pavement is elevating out of the ground, and . . ."

"And what?" barks Captain Delgado.

"Find cover!" yells the soldier's voice.

"Delta Six, report!" yells Captain Delgado.

"Combat Drones, sir! Twenty, maybe thirty Combat Drones have risen out of the ground in a single line at the top of the courtyard."

I can hear Captain Delgado hurriedly stomping away. I peek over the top of the cubicle while Brody and Ryan, alerted by the soldier's voice, spring up from the couch and walk over to join me.

Captain Delgado rushes to the window. "I can't see a damned thing from here!" he bellows. "Delta Six, what's going on down there?"

"The Drones' faces are red; they're in Threat Mode, but they're not moving, sir. They're just standing there. What are our orders, Captain?"

"Stay where you are, Delta; if they move an inch, open fire. Come in, Omega Five."

"Yes, sir?"

"What's your position? Over."

"Coming in from Sector B, approaching courtyard."

"Send someone to escort those schoolgirls to the command post; the rest of you join Delta squad."

The Captain turns back to the men crowded around the desk. "Whatever computer magic you did before, do it again! Get those cameras back online!"

Around the desk, there's fervent muttering, and I catch a few words though my earpiece. "Initiate another data spike . . . We need to disrupt the second neural stream . . . We could make it worse . . . How could it get any worse . . . Shut up and do it . . . Just get out of my way . . ." I can hear a shuffling, a series of frantic taps on glass, and then an ominous descending hum as all the lights in the office suddenly begin to dim and flicker.

"What's going on over there?" the Captain shouts. "What's happening to the lights? Where's my camera feed?"

At the desk, there's pointing and accusations as the men try to decide who's going to tell Captain Delgado that they have no idea what the hell they're doing.

Finally Corporal Avary straightens and smooths down his uniform, clearly struggling to think of an excuse to tell Captain Delgado. He takes a breath and is about to speak when six holographic projection screens suddenly spring from the series of slates on the desk in front of the men. The Corporal looks as surprised as everyone else when, all around the office, slates on other desks begin beaming large, glowing holoscreens into midair, too. There must be at least a dozen, all of them identical blue-rimmed rectangles, and all of them fizzing with static. "You're on a roll, Corporal!" booms Captain Delgado. "Where are the pictures? Show me what's happening down there."

No sooner does the Captain say the words when the lines of static begin dipping and bending and contouring into a shape. A shape duplicated on every floating screen in the room.

"What the hell *is* that?" the Captain asks.

As if responding directly to his question, a ghostly, distorted voice suddenly whispers eerily throughout the room. *"What have you done? I tried to hold them back. I tried to give you time. What have you done?"*

At the sound of the voice, Otto leaves her slate on the couch and quickly nuzzles in beside me and Brody to peek over the wall. Percy is standing now, too, and Brent, Margaux, the Professor, the medics, and even the wounded soldiers are focused on one screen or another.

"Who are you?" Captain Delgado demands.

The shape is becoming more defined. Now I can make out the fuzzy pits of two eyes and the curve of a nose.

"I have been trying to help you," says the voice. *"But whatever you did, you've ripped me away, and I can't get back."* It's still raspy and distant, but it's undeniably female.

"Who is this? Identify yourself," orders Captain Delgado.

"Javier, please, listen to me." At the mention of his name, Captain Delgado's expression freezes. The static shape begins morphing and sharpening into three-dimensional detail until there, hovering over every slate on every desk, is the face of a strikingly beautiful woman, her long, straight, jet-black hair; deep-blue eyes; and pale-pink lips perfect against her flawless porcelain skin. I can't stop staring. I've seen that woman before; I'm sure of it. I dredge through my mind, searching everything I've seen from all the years of Finn's life that I've trawled through over the past four weeks, and suddenly it hits me. That woman was standing beside Richard Blackstone in a photograph I saw in Finn's memories. I remember now. That woman out there is Finn's mother, which obviously means that she's also my . . .

Out of nowhere, my heartbeat gets faster, my breaths shorter, my stare more intense. My thoughts are suddenly jumbled with unwanted emotions that I know are not mine. They can't be mine. I was made in a Blackstone military laboratory; that's what I've always been told. I don't *have* a mother. That was just another lie they put in Finn's head. It *has* to be! Confused, with my thoughts reeling, I force my eyes away from the woman's face, and they fall upon Captain Delgado. I always thought he was unshakable. But it's plain to see that right now, he and I are in the same sinking boat. He's stunned, his expression blank, gripping the walkie-talkie so tightly it's hissing white noise from his clawed fist. My eyes drift back to her face. A face that looks so much like my own, it's uncanny. Could she *really* be . . . ?

"Oh my god . . . Genevieve?" murmurs Captain Delgado. "After all these years, is that really you? How is this possible? What has Richard done to you?"

The woman seems to ignore the Captain's questions and turns toward him with a look of utmost seriousness. *"I don't have much time. Please, just listen. Onix has lost his mind, and he's coming for all of you. I blinded the androids, and hid you from the cameras for as long as I could, but you've pulled me away from the main data feed, and soon he'll regain full control. You need to run. Before he can fully access the Drones' combat capabilities. Go . . . Go now!"*

The holograms all around the room start to hiss and distort and flicker on and off. The woman grimaces, as if in pain, the lines in her skin marring her immaculate features.

"Gen! What's wrong? How can we help you?" shouts Captain Delgado.

"You can't help me, but you can help those children. Get them out of here. Protect the children."

"I will. I'll protect them," promises Captain Delgado.

One of the holograms on the other side of the room shimmers and pixelates before suddenly reverting to a blank glowing rectangle of hissing static again, the woman's face wiped clean away. Another reverts, then another, and another. All over the office, one by one, the holograms begin shifting back to blank screens until soon only a single image remains floating over the soldiers gathered around the central desk. The beautiful woman's face glitches and distorts as she winces and grits her teeth. *"Please, before it's too late, for the sake of all humanity, promise me that once the children are safe, you'll find a way to get to Richard . . ."*

Captain Delgado is staring at her intensely. "Richard is here, Genevieve; he's in the tower. We've got communications back; I can contact him now. He'll know how to fix all of this."

The hologram rolls and warps, and the woman glares at the Captain, her eyes full of anger. *"Listen to me . . . ,"* she says, her voice cutting in and out. *"You must find Richard and promise me, promise that you'll . . ."*

"What?" blurts Captain Delgado. "What do you want me to do?"

Her beautiful face distorts one last time, and then, as suddenly as it appeared, it vanishes, leaving only the fading whisper of her departing words drifting through the room.

"Promise that you'll kill Richard Blackstone . . . and burn this place to the ground."

CHAPTER FOURTEEN

"Get her back!" bellows Captain Delgado, his expression a crazed mixture of bewilderment and disbelief.

"S-sir?" Corporal Avary stammers. "May I ask who that woman was, and why . . . ?"

"No, you may *not* ask," Captain Delgado snaps. "That information is classified. Now shut up and get her back!"

Corporal Avary and the other soldiers clamber around the desk, poking, prodding, and swiping at the array of computer slates, fervently scanning the blank holoscreens hovering before them. "I'm sorry, sir . . . ," the Corporal says shakily, "but we don't know *how* to get her back. We don't even know where to start."

"Who *was* that?" whispers Ryan.

"I dunno, but she was nice to look at," mumbles Brody.

I take Otto by the arm and lead her back toward the couch. "Did you hear what I heard?"

She nods emphatically. "Richard Blackstone is here," she whispers. "And it seems like you're not the only one who wants him gone for good."

"Well, she'll have to get in line behind *me*."

Otto's eyes narrow behind her glasses. "Did you recognize that woman?"

"Oh yeah, she's probably my dead mother" is exactly the kind of crazy answer that would make me look insane, so I keep my mouth shut and shake my head.

"You look an awful lot like her."

I frown at Otto. "Shut up and listen. She said that Onix is coming for all of us. If that happens, it just might be the distraction we need, so be ready to go." Otto nervously bites her lip and nods.

Across the room, Captain Delgado paces away from the main desk and mumbles something into his radio. I hold my fingers against the wedge in my ear and listen in. "Lieutenant Walters, can you read me? Come in, Delta; what's happening down there?"

"*Omega squad has arrived at our position, sir,*" responds the Lieutenant. "*The two civilian girls are en route to the command post, and the robots haven't moved. Over.*"

"Alpha, drop what you're doing and join the other squads," the Captain orders before turning to a couple of soldiers standing by a stack of equipment crates. "You two, get to the transport hangar. I don't care if you have to burn it, bust it, or blow it open. We're buggin' outta here." Without question, the soldiers immediately begin unlatching crates.

"We're leaving, sir?" asks Corporal Avary.

"If you want to play target practice with those Drones out there, you're welcome to, Corporal. I can think of better ways to spend my weekend, and none of them include picking a fight with a platoon of kitchen appliances."

The two soldiers beside the crates begin stuffing what look like plastic explosives and detonators into a duffel bag. They each take a rifle from another crate, sling it over their shoulders, purposefully stride across the room, and disappear out the door leading to the stairwell. All of a sudden, the six fizzing holoscreens floating over the central desk begin to clear, flicking on with images showing various angles from cameras all around the courtyard.

Captain Delgado's attention is unsurprisingly piqued. "Finally, we can see something! Good work, men."

Corporal Avary scans the screens from left to right. "Sorry, sir, but we didn't do anything."

Suddenly, as if confirming the Corporal's admission, a very familiar computerized voice reverberates through the entire office.

"Surveillance cameras fully operational in Sector A, areas one through five. Visual capabilities restored."

Onix can see again.

The soldiers around the desk mutter and point and tap at the slates, and Corporal Avary's head pops up from the group. "The mainframe is regaining full control in this sector, sir, just like that woman said it would."

Captain Delgado glares at the displays as Onix speaks again.

"Additional Crimson-Class weapon systems currently functional and fully operational in Sector A2."

As I spy over the top of the cubicle wall, my gaze flits across the images on the holoscreens. I can see soldiers down in the courtyard taking cover behind trees and stone benches on screens one to five, but when I see the image projected on the sixth display, my eyes widen, my stomach tightens, and I whisper a stream of curses under my breath. At the top of the stairs at the far end of the courtyard, a long rectangular section has risen up from the paving stones like a huge, elongated elevator, and inside . . . stands a row of what must be thirty armed Crimson-Class Combat Drones, their red masks glowing menacingly down toward the spread of anxious soldiers. This is not good, and judging by the looks on the faces all around the room, I'm obviously not the only one thinking that.

"Attention, all authorized staff," announces Onix. "To avoid accidental harm, please remain in your emergency shelters. To all unauthorized intruders: trespassing with the intent to infiltrate this facility for the purpose of corporate sabotage is deemed a terrorist act. Pursuant to clause one eighty-seven of the international Zero Tolerance Decree, I am permitted to use any means at my disposal to nullify a threat of this magnitude. Please be advised that your termination will commence in ten . . . nine . . ."

Otto's eyes lock with mine, and she whispers, "It's happening." She quickly scoops her computer slate from the couch and presses her thumb to the screen. With a few flicks and swipes, six small holographic screens project from its surface, each one an exact miniature copy of the large ones hovering over the central desk on the other side of the room.

"Eight . . . seven . . ."

All the faces I can see—Brody's, Ryan's, Percy's, and even the previously dozing soldier with the bandaged head's—are plastered with steely-eyed anxiety.

"All units! Open fire on those Drones! Open fire!" Captain Delgado yells into his radio as Onix continues with his ominous countdown.

"Six . . . five . . . four . . ."

Through my earpiece, I can hear the soldiers' rifles echoing in the courtyard. On the holoscreens, the pictures match the sounds as the Drones are pelted with bullets. One Drone falls, then another, then two more, and then five more buckle. Judging by the multiple headshots, the soldiers clearly know the right places to aim when it comes to dealing with androids.

". . . three . . . two . . . one," counts Onix.

Even though the soldiers are making quick work of the Drones, that doesn't stop Captain Delgado from pointing and shouting orders, sending nearly every able-bodied person in the room scrambling toward the weapon crates. Soon only the Captain, Corporal Avary, and the medics are left standing at their respective stations, all eyes trained on the large displays floating over the central desk. There's commotion in every direction; ammunition is being loaded into rifles; helmets, face masks, and visors are being strapped into place; and soldiers are racing for the door. I look down at Otto's slate. The soldiers outside are still firing, and there are only about fifteen Drones left standing when Onix's voice echoes loudly through the courtyard.

"Accessing Drones' higher battle functions. Initiate Full Combat Mode."

On the screens, I see the bright red of the Drones' masks rapidly recede until only two streaks of angry scarlet eyes remain on each slick, black, oval face. In perfect unison, the remaining Drones grip their assault rifles and hunch into an aggressive stance as their shiny silver skin begins darkening into a mottled military camouflage pattern. My stomach drops. I vaguely recall a short paragraph about this in a classified file, but those robots aren't even meant to exist for another twelve months, so of course I've never seen a Crimson Drone in Full Combat Mode. I dread what's coming, hoping like hell that the soldiers finish them off before any of the Drones are able to completely switch over. Three more androids are taken down, their camouflage coloring snapping back to silver as they drop one after the other, but the rifle fire in the courtyard is sporadic and thinning in places as the soldiers are forced to reload. They've done an admirable job, impressively taking out eighteen Drones, but, unfortunately, twelve are still standing when Onix issues his final, foreboding order.

"Attack."

Like Olympic sprinters reacting to a pistol shot, the Drones burst out of the elevated compartment, weaving and dodging the soldiers' gunfire as they fan out into the courtyard.

While the blinded, partially controlled Combat Drones we encountered near the dome were slow and clumsy, these fully operational Crimson-Class androids couldn't be more frighteningly different. Their movements are lithe and smooth as they advance quickly in a coordinated pattern, hunched over, weaving from side to side like predators stalking their prey.

"Move back!" orders a Lieutenant. "Find cover!" The soldiers immediately begin backing up, firing as they go. The retreating troops are doing their best to keep their flaring weapons trained on the robots, and some bullets do find their way into the androids' thick armor, but these Drones are moving too damn fast to put down at a distance, ducking and bobbing with inhuman speed as bullets whizz past the vulnerable sensors and processors behind their face masks.

Six Drones arc around to the right; the other six curve around to the left, all of them zigzagging and sidestepping as they go. One Drone tears into a sudden sprint, and I lose sight of it on the display as it charges straight through the front window of a building. Another Drone on the left jumps at the wall of a structure and literally gallops up the side of it, gouging divots into the concrete as it climbs toward the roof. The android that crashed through the glass reappears at an upstairs window, and, having achieved a strategic high position, it raises its weapon and opens fire into the courtyard. An unfortunate soldier is immediately strafed with bullets; plumes of blood spray from the holes punching through his body armor. The Drone on the opposite roof opens fire, and a soldier clutches at his throat as blood spills between his fingers.

There's screaming and yelling as the Drones at ground level approach, attempting to flank the soldiers on both sides, conserving their ammo and picking their shots as they close in. One, then another, then three-four-five soldiers are shot in the head, chest, gut, leg, and shoulder. All of them go down. Soldiers are turning and running and diving behind anything solid they can find.

"Private Sekula!" Captain Delgado shouts into the walkie-talkie. "Do you have a line of sight on those snipers?"

"No, sir. Trees are in the way," he replies. "But maybe if I move two rooftops over."

"Jump those alleyways, gaad damn fly if you have to, soldier, but get those bastards before they kill any more of my men!" bellows Captain Delgado.

On the ground, someone lobs a high-explosive grenade toward the five Drones on the left side of the courtyard. It's an excellent throw, sailing high and far before bouncing twice and rolling right into the midst of the robots' loose grouping. With unnaturally fast, preprogrammed reactions, the Drones suddenly leap away in five different directions all at the same time, each hulking robot landing just outside the fatal blast radius of the grenade as it detonates with a percussive thud. The robots immediately resume their advance as if it never happened, quickly tromping back into their flanking formation before the highest-flung debris from the explosion even has a chance to speckle the ground.

Despite the bullets zipping toward the soldiers, another brave soul leaps to his feet, pulls the pin of a second grenade, and baseball-pitches it directly at a Drone approaching from the right.

It's a very long throw, under fire at a moving target, and his aim is absolutely superb, but he pays the high price for his courage with two rounds straight through his chest. The grenade speeds to its mark regardless, but, like a frog shooting its tongue out at a fly, the Drone incredibly snatches it from the air and whips its arm, sending the small, green sphere in an almost perfectly mirrored trajectory right back where it came from. The soldier who threw it is lying on his back and coughing up blood when the grenade reaches his position and explodes in midflight, right above his face. It's possible that he might have survived being shot, but there's no way he lived through a close-proximity blast like that.

One soldier peeks out from cover and manages to put a round right through the head of a Drone in midstride. The Drone's skin flicks back to silver, and its red eyes fade as it stumbles and slams to the ground.

A Lieutenant points and shouts an order: "Focus fire!" The soldiers' excellent training shows as every available rifle suddenly turns on the nearest Drone. It's dodging and ducking thirty meters out, but it can't escape the concentrated barrage as the android is hammered with bullets. Some of them manage to hit the sweet spot, drilling right through its mask. It teeters, then falls heavily, another silver robot corpse. The eight remaining ground-level Drones are getting closer. "Focus fire!" the Lieutenant shouts again, and rifle barrels bristle out from behind every makeshift blockade, pointing at the next closest robot. But this time, the androids are expecting it. As the soldiers peek out from cover, five are hit through their helmets by the robot snipers on the buildings and are killed instantly.

Barely a minute has passed, but this situation is already beginning to look like an unwinnable massacre, and Captain Delgado knows it. He shoves his walkie-talkie against his moustache and yells, "Fall back! I repeat, fall back! Get the hell outta there!" Almost as if they heard the Captain's order to withdraw, which—thanks to Onix—they very likely did, the Drones' behavior immediately changes as they all begin approaching faster and more directly, still bobbing and weaving, but clearly charging in to finish the job. Even the sniper robot on the left leaps from its three-story perch and runs to join its robotic brothers in the slaughter. The results speak for themselves as soldiers begin dropping with alarming frequency. From what I can see on the displays, at least ten are dead, another dozen badly wounded, and the ones that are left are pinned down behind trees, concrete planters, benches, and whatever else they can crawl to.

"Fall back to command! Move, move, move!" shouts a Lieutenant.

One soldier lobs a couple of canister grenades toward the Drones; they clatter on the paving stones and begin spewing thick gray plumes of smoke. In a retreat situation against human soldiers, a smoke screen is a very good tactic; it obscures the enemies' line of fire and makes you harder to hit as you escape, but combat robots have had thermal-vision capabilities for years, and they can see body heat right through a smoke cloud. Maybe it was panic or lack of training that made the soldier throw those canisters, because against those Drones . . . it was a very bad mistake. Now, only the *Drones* are hidden from view, the soldiers have nothing to aim at, and the casualties keep increasing as the androids keep advancing. Bullets are tearing chunks from trees, soldiers are being hit, blood is spurting, and panic is spreading as the group of nearly thirty troops that ran from the office finally appears on the displays, firing blindly into the cloud of smoke while the remaining members of Alpha, Omega, and Delta squads retreat, running, limping, ducking, and dragging wounded soldiers as they go.

I can hear the echo of voices and tromping boots in the stairwell. They get louder and louder until finally, two panic-stricken teenage girls and a soldier burst through the open door of the office.

"Jenny! Amy!" screeches Otto. The two teenagers break into a run toward us, and the pretty Asian girl nearly knocks Otto off her feet as she embraces her and sobs.

"You're alive," the girl whimpers, looking around at everyone. "We were afraid you were all dead."

Professor Francis rushes over and takes the other girl's hand. "Amelia, thank goodness you and Jennifer are both safe." The petite girl nods, her puffy, red eyes on the brink of tears beneath the fringe of her disheveled, blonde, bob haircut.

"I don't wanna spoil the moment, Professor . . . ," Ryan says, looking toward the displays at the desk, "but I don't think any of us are safe." Ryan isn't wrong. The displays tell a horrific and bloody story as almost every screen cycles through images of the bodies of fallen soldiers strewn across a wide section of the courtyard.

Otto frees herself from Jenny's hug and looks back at her slate. The holoscreens jump up from its surface again, and all of us gather around, staring at the scenes of carnage. Even Margaux, Brent, and two nearby medics make their way to the circle and crane their necks to see.

Margaux gasps. There are so many dead and injured: I count almost forty in all.

On the other side of the room, Captain Delgado grips the walkie-talkie again. "Private Sekula! Fire as soon as you're in position!" Barely three seconds after he gives the command, the head of the Drone on the rooftop across the way explodes like a sledgehammered watermelon. It doesn't even lower its gun as its silver carcass topples from the side of the building and pounds into a heap on the pavement below.

"Yes," Brody hisses quietly.

It's a small victory, but I suspect it didn't go unnoticed by the Drones at ground level, because their behavior changes dramatically again as they all quickly rush forward in a tight pack into the center of the gray smoke, a maneuver that completely obscures them from Private Sekula's gun sights. Their tactic is confirmed as their gun flares flash high above the smoke in the direction of the roof above us, and Private Sekula's voice shouts so loudly through Captain Delgado's radio that I can hear it from where we're standing.

At least some good comes from the Private's unintentional diversion, providing the soldiers on the ground a brief respite as they run for their lives. At last count, including that sniper Drone, there must have been nine robots in that smoke cloud and, at a guess, around forty battle-capable soldiers left. In any other situation, numbers like that would give the soldiers every advantage. But this is like nothing I've ever seen, and clearly it's like no firefight any of these troops have ever encountered. Even at forty against nine, they're terribly outmatched. I can only imagine what would have happened if all thirty Drones had stormed out of that elevated compartment. The troops would have been completely obliterated. That outcome is still highly likely.

I can hear the first of the retreating soldiers scrambling into the stairwell, and soon we're all going to be crammed into one room. For those Drones, killing us will be like shooting birds in a cage.

I know that I have to do something, but an unfamiliar feeling of fear is beginning to grip me, and it's muddling my thoughts. Do I grab Otto and run? If so, I may have waited too long. Once the Drones dispatch Private Sekula, they'll be here in ninety seconds. Or do I pick up a gun and fight? I'm no match for nine armed Combat Drones. Am I?

I'm still weighing up the incredibly horrible options when soldiers begin spilling into the office and the room suddenly becomes a bustling panic of shouting and groaning. All three of the already-scrambling medics spring into a higher level of action, readying their meager supplies of cotton and gauze and spray-on bandages as a stream of injured soldiers stumbles and limps toward the infirmary area.

Otto swipes the holoscreens away, strides to the cubicle wall, snatches back the small, black rectangle that was stuck there, and quickly tucks her slate in her satchel as she trots back toward me. The first of the bleeding troops are pouring into the makeshift infirmary.

"You kids, get out of the way!" shouts a medic. Everyone in our little group tries to lunge aside as we're pushed and shoved by the wounded jostling into the increasingly inadequate partitioned area.

"Everyone, gather in that corner!" Professor Francis shouts, pointing over the manic turmoil. With no other obvious option, we all do as we're told and move in a bunch toward an empty desk that has been shoved up against a far wall.

There are so many wounded filling the office that I completely lose sight of Captain Delgado in the chaos. "They don't stand a chance," I whisper in Otto's ear as we move. "And if we stay here, neither do we."

"What are we going to do?" she asks, her eyes brimming with fear.

Her fear adds fuel to my own. I don't want to admit it . . . but I'm scared. "I don't know," I whisper. It's the truth. I can't see through the fog of terror growing in my mind. I can't see a way out of this.

The group reaches the empty desk in the corner and huddles around it like frightened children, which, let's face it, most of them are.

Even *my* hands are trembling. This is not the way I thought it would end, but what can I do?

I don't feel like myself. I don't feel any fight in me. I feel like a cowering nobody. *Finn, you bitch. Stop making me weak. Your emotions are infecting me like a disease! Take them back. Let me go! I need to focus!*

I look at the windows. I can jump through them to the ground. I'd probably break my leg, but I could heal it fast, and then I'd be outta here. But what about Otto? She might not survive a three-story drop, and I can't leave her behind; I just can't. I may not have known her for very long, but she's the closest thing to a friend that I've ever had. *What do I do? What do I do?*

I look toward the door. Soldiers are barricading it with overturned desks. I look at the infirmary area. It's jam-packed with bloodied flesh, writhing bodies, and screams of agony. I look at our little group. Desperate fear is seared into their faces. I look at Otto's slate. The canisters are spewing the last of their smoke as the Drones hiding in the cloud fire skyward.

I stare blankly into the chaos unfolding all around, my breathing heavy and shaky. This has all gotten too far out of hand. My instinct to survive makes the decision for me. I need to save myself. *I'm sorry, Otto. You're on your own.*

I swallow hard and turn toward the windows, but something catches my eye through the moving bustle of military uniforms and stops me cold. There, on the other side of the room, his glare of recognition fixed on my face, is the wide-eyed, disbelieving stare of my former Mission Commander.

Covert Field Operations Supervisor, level nine . . . Captain Javier Delgado.

Captain Delgado storms across the room in a straight line. I know that I should be smashing through the glass behind me right now and leaping to safety, but I can't seem to move at all. All I can do is stare him in the eyes as he quickly strides in this direction, gruffly pushing soldiers out of his way. He doesn't look surprised anymore. He looks mad as hell.

Captain Delgado unceremoniously shoves a nearby soldier aside and stands over me, glaring down at me. "Why are you here?" he seethes.

"Oh, Captain Delgado . . . ," an oblivious Professor Francis says, interrupting from the other side of the group. "I was wondering if you could tell me . . ."

The Captain turns his bayonet stare at the Professor. "Shut up, old man." The Professor recoils, obviously offended as Captain Delgado turns back to me and grabs my face firmly in one of his large hands, studying my eyes closely.

"I say!" barks the Professor. "Unhand Miss Brogan this instant!"

"Is that who I'm looking at?" growls Captain Delgado. "Are you Finn Brogan today?"

"Hey!" shouts Ryan. He grabs at the Captain's arm, but Captain Delgado shoves him away without even looking.

"Well? Answer me!" bellows the Captain.

Everyone in the group is focused on us with half-open mouths and crinkled brows, not knowing in the least what to make of any of this.

"It can't be a coincidence that you're here," says the Captain. "The first school group allowed inside these walls and you just *happen* to be among them? I don't buy that crap. Why are you here? Who sent you? Who's your target? Did you have anything to do with that slaughter out there?"

I'm a covert Blackstone assassin who works for a secret branch of the military carrying out my own mission without authorization. If we manage to survive today, I know that Captain Delgado will report this, and either I'll be locked away for the rest of my life or they'll simply make me . . . disappear. Either way, I'm screwed. I don't know what else to do but to use the disguise that they gave me. I do my best to look timid and scared, which, considering the circumstances, isn't much of a stretch.

"Yes, I'm Finn Brogan, and I . . . I don't know what you're talking about, Captain Delgado."

Captain Delgado smiles. "I've known Finn since she was little, and she always called me 'Mr. Delgado,' just like she would right now if you were *actually* her. Maybe you should have done a little research before you tried pretending to be that kind, sweet girl, because kind and sweet, you definitely are not . . . Infinity One."

I sneer at him. "Fine. You got me. So what."

"So what? I'll tell you what. We're all gonna die if you don't get your ass down there like a good soldier and dispatch those Drones."

I stare at him, right in the eyes. "You must be out of your goddamned mind if you think you can order me to do anything anymore. I'm done with people bossing me around. I'm free from you. Free from Richard Blackstone. Free from *everyone*. I'd rather die on my own terms than be your lapdog for one more second."

Captain Delgado raises his eyebrows. "Oh, really?" Suddenly, without warning, he grips my shirt firmly with both hands. Buttons pop and tumble through the air as he forcefully rips the collar open. Stunned and confused, I grab at his wrists as Ryan and Brody both dive at him. All four of us fall hard to the floor in a grappling mass.

"Restrain these civilians!" shouts Captain Delgado as Ryan and Brody try their best to hold him down. The Captain releases one of his hands and smacks Brody in the face with the back of his fist. Brody lets go, clutching at his nose, and is immediately scooped up from the floor by a soldier and secured in a double armlock.

Out of the corner of my eye, I can see everyone in the group looking down at us in horrified fascination.

"What are you doing?" screeches Otto. "Let her go!"

The troops watching the three of us in this bizarre wrestling match look just as confused as I feel, probably fearing that the stress of the situation has caused their commanding officer to lose his grasp on sanity. That's exactly what I'm thinking when I mentally tighten the muscles in my right arm into a concentrated bundle of raw power, readying myself to fight back. Captain Delgado manages to maneuver all his weight on top of me, and my pendant cuts into the back of my neck as it tangles in his clawing fingers. In a double-action blur, my fist moves like a spring-loaded piston, knuckle-striking him twice in the side in less than half a second. Inches from my face, spittle sprays through his gritted teeth, and veins bulge from his neck as he lets out a throaty groan. I'm not surprised; I just cracked two of his ribs.

Soldiers lunge forward and grab Ryan by his legs. "Get your hands off me!" he yells, still scrabbling at Captain Delgado's camouflage pants as he's roughly dragged away.

The Captain's eyes are crazed with determination, and the olive skin of his face is turning red with effort. I dagger my fingers hard into his side; he lets out a guttural moan as an involuntary reaction curves his body away from the pain. I use it to push his bulk and roll him off me onto the floor. I'm only free for a split second when three soldiers pounce on me. I'm strong when I put my mind to it, but these men know exactly how to restrain someone properly. I struggle and try to kick, but I can't get any leverage. They haul me to my feet and restrain me securely with a sleeper hold tight around my neck and a soldier on each arm, their legs firmly wrapped around mine.

As hard as I try . . . I can't move.

"Help me up," mutters Captain Delgado, waving an outstretched hand. Two more soldiers jump forward and pull him to his feet as he groans and clutches his side. I'm snorting angrily as the Captain hobbles over to me, heaving labored breaths of his own. He looks down, gently pulls the chain of my pendant out from the top of my shirt, holds the black stone between his thumb and forefinger, and whispers ten very specific words.

"Infinity One, Emergency Combat Mode, authorization Delgado, level nine . . . activate."

CHAPTER FIFTEEN

A soft light ripples across the cracked surface of my pendant, and as Captain Delgado releases his thumb from it, I suddenly feel completely at ease.

My fear, anger, and anxiety vanish as if they never existed at all, and I immediately stop struggling.

I feel good but also quite strange. My mind is clear but simultaneously preoccupied. It's like I'm beginning to remember the hidden meaning of a forgotten song sung to a specific melody that I've never heard until this very moment.

"You can let her go now," Captain Delgado orders, and the soldiers release me. Holding his hand to his ribs, he groans as he leans forward and looks me in the eyes. "The Combat Drones in the courtyard are your targets. Your mission is to deactivate those Drones. If you survive, you'll report back to me for further instruction. Do you understand?"

I stare back at him and feel hate streak through me. I shout, *"Screw you!"* but my lips say, "Sir, yes, sir."

"Good," replies a smug-looking Captain Delgado. "Go get 'em, Infinity One."

Without another word, I turn and push the soldiers out of my way. I can hear Otto calling out to me, but I don't look back. Ryan and Brody are still being restrained. As I pass them, Ryan struggles to get free, but his throat is wedged tightly in the crook of a soldier's elbow. "Infinity?" he hisses though his teeth. "Infinity! What has he done to you?"

I don't reply. There are far more pressing issues to deal with than chitchat with civilians. I march on, fully aware of what I'm doing, while a separate me is watching the world through the windows of my own eyes. I feel in control, but my body seems to be moving on its own, and all I can think about is fulfilling my mission.

I want it badly, more than I've wanted anything in my life. In fact, I more than want it . . . I *need* it.

I stride over to the weapon crates, and a soldier holds up a hand to stop me. I glower at him as Captain Delgado shouts from the other side of the room. "Let her take whatever she wants!"

The soldier looks extremely confused, but he obediently stands aside. I push past him and start popping latches. There isn't much left inside the crates—most of the guns are lying next to dead bodies out there in the courtyard—so it's little more than a jumble of a few hastily strewn short-range weapons, ammo, and combat clothing. I pick through the mess and choose a Hellion 90 shotgun with a fully loaded explosive scatter-shell magazine. I attach a strap, sling the weapon onto my back, and make sure it's secured tightly to my body. I also find two fully loaded Talons, twenty-shot automatic pistols, and their holsters. As I buckle one to each leg, something surprising catches my eye at the bottom of a crate. It's a magna-band.

Anyone outside Covert Operations would probably think it was nothing more than a sturdy, army-green wristwatch, but a magna-band is actually a powerful, specific frequency magnetic emitter, and half of a very specialized assassin's weapon. I immediately grab for it, hoping that its accompanying component is somewhere nearby. I latch the band around my right wrist and splay my fingers as wide as I can. A dim blue light illuminates on the side, and a rectangular object shaped like a king-size candy bar suddenly comes flying out of an ammo bag and slaps firmly into the palm of my hand.

A smile creeps onto my lips. It's a Jack-knife, an assassin's slang for an extendable, synthetic-diamond-edged, close-combat weapon. I test it by flicking its switch to the first setting. With barely a sound, rigid sections snap-fold out from the handle into a twenty-centimeter-long, matte-black throwing knife. I flick it to its second setting, and the blade snaps into a one-meter sword. If you swing it hard enough, this thing can cut through titanium. Satisfied, I retract the blade and tuck the Jack-knife handle into the waistband of my skirt.

"Do you need body armor?" a nearby soldier asks. My silence is the answer to his question. The clumsy gear the soldiers are wearing would just hinder my movements, but I do pick up a combat mask and press it to my face. It snugly covers my ears and the bridge of my nose down to my chin. The black visor covering my eyes activates and flickers on with distracting readouts of my vital signs and other useless combat information. I raise it and, with a quick yank, snap it off entirely and toss it in a weapon crate. I press my fingertips into the two notches on the front of the mask, and as the metamorphic adhesive molds to my skin, I feel the cool mix of oxygenated stimulants releasing from the microjets inside. I inhale the vapor, and my already-excellent vision suddenly sharpens even further as every edge and color of every object I look at is chemically honed into detailed clarity.

Feeling instantly more alert, I fish an ammo belt out of another crate and sling it across my chest. I hook one smoke canister and four high-explosive grenades to the belt and walk toward the central desk, snatching an automatic rifle from another soldier's hands as I go. I pull it to my shoulder, and Corporal Avary hastily leaps out of the way as I scan the holoscreens through the gun sights.

The displays show the smoke outside is clearing; the Drones' cover is dissipating. It's useless now, and the robots seem to know it. Three of the androids make a sudden dash for the building where Private Sekula is positioned, and he impressively manages to rupture one of their heads as the other two leap at the side of the structure and begin to climb. When they reach the top, he'll be dead. But that's the least of my concerns as I watch the five remaining Drones on the ground barreling out of the haze at full speed, heading straight for the command post. They are my first priority. I pull the trigger.

With a string of loud bangs, the rifle kicks repeatedly in my arms as I shoot straight through the holoscreens, shattering the courtyard-facing windows into a fine lattice of cracks. I throw the smoking rifle aside. It clatters on the floor as I vault onto the central desk and jump, tucking my knees toward my chest as I cannonball at the glass and bust through the window in a shower of glittering fragments. My clothes ruffle against my body as I drop three full stories. As the ground speeds up to meet me, I quickly thrust a hand out, catch a lamppost, and spiral two full revolutions around it before my shoes tap lightly on the paving stones and I'm off, arms blading through the air as I sprint across the courtyard and out into the open. With a quick glance to my right, I see the Drones approaching. They're about thirty meters away, but swerving quickly toward the stairwell door that leads up to the command post. I need to draw them toward *me*.

Midstride, I whip a pistol from its thigh holster, spear my arm in their direction, and drum my finger on the trigger. The gun flares and jolts in my palm as I sprint in a wide, curving arc. Even though I'm tearing across the courtyard at full speed, firing one-handed at moving targets, my adrenalized mind is processing everything at quadruple the normal rate.

My heartbeat is steady and strong, my breathing is measured and controlled, my limbs feel like tightly coiled ropes of pumping muscle, and my senses are sharp and crystal clear as my gun-holding hand rises and falls in time with my footsteps to maintain an unwavering line. I instinctively know how much lead to give my shots to compensate for my forward momentum. It pays off as I hear fifteen of my twenty bullets hit their marks. One even spacks an android square in the face, but the ballistic glass easily deflects the small-caliber-pistol round. I knew a handgun wouldn't do any damage to the androids, but my little attention-getting barrage serves its intended purpose as all five Drones skid to a halt, turn their rifles in my direction, and open fire.

I throw the empty pistol away, pull the smoke canister from the ammo belt, and hurl it toward the five robots as I bound into the air, tucking into a side flip as bullets whizz past me. I straighten my body, then roll in midair. When I hit the ground, I pump my limbs against the paving stones like pistons, springing like a cat into a two-meter-high sideways arc. I land in a low crouch right where I wanted to be, obscured from the Drones' line of fire by the trunk of a large oak tree fifteen meters in front of me. The smoke grenade begins spewing thick gray clouds, and I listen carefully to the thuds of the Drones' footsteps as they advance on my position, trudging right into the center of the dense fog. The Drones will round that tree in no time, but this will only work if I wait for the perfect moment. I keep my head down and wait, tuning my ears to the sound of their steps.

Thud . . . thud . . . thud . . . thud . . . NOW!

I quickly hold down all four safety levers on the high-explosive grenades with one hand, thread my fingers through the pins with the other, and pull them all at the same time. The pins clink on the ground as all four timed fuses begin hissing on the ammo belt.

I have seven seconds.

I bolt into a sprint and jump. It's a huge tree, but I easily go sailing six meters into the air and land dead center on one of the oak's thick lower limbs. I know that they're tracking me; I can hear the Drones' footsteps slowing to a halt beneath the canopy on the opposite side. I deftly jump from limb to limb, and as I circle around the trunk, rifles flare from the gray cloud and bullets begin taking chunks out of the wood all around me. My quick movements through the leaves and branches are making me a hard target to hit, even with the robots scanning my body heat. I can't see them at all through the billowing fog below, but that's OK; I know exactly where they are . . . and they're right where I want them. I hear the rapid clicking of one, then two, then a third rifle as the last of their ammo is spent. The satisfying clatter of empty weapons being cast aside greets my ears as I dance through the massive tree, leaping from side to side, using the thickest limbs to take the brunt of the diminished gunfire. With the grenades fizzing on my chest, I bob and weave through the branches.

Even though I'm evading the bullets the best I can, the warning bells chiming insistently in my head and the warm blood oozing from my side and trickling down my leg tell me that I've been shot at least twice. From the chiming, I'm guessing that one wound is pretty bad, but I'm not dead yet, so I keep going, knowing full well that the three unarmed androids of the group might decide to climb this tree and pull me down so the other two can finish me off. I can't let that happen.

It's time to end this.

I dart onto a sturdy branch hanging over the smoke, sprint halfway along it, snatch two grenades into the palm of each hand, and dive headfirst as high and far as I can. Time seems to stretch out like a rubber band. I can hear the high-pitched, spiraling turbulence of the bullet trails speeding by as I javelin through the air, my arrow-straight legs drifting skyward as my whole body inverts completely vertically upside down. Floating directly above the Drones, I can't help but smile. With their sharp robotic eyes and superfast reflexes, they can pluck a grenade from midair and toss it aside, or leap away to safety the instant they see one coming. I saw them do exactly that. But what can they do if *four* grenades, primed to explode and hidden by smoke, are dropped right on their preprogrammed heads? I guess I'm about to find out.

Even though every slice of the last seven seconds was slowed to a crawl by my hyper-racing mind, my timing is still perfect as I thrust both arms toward the swirling fog below and release. The grenades vanish into the gray, and, an instant later, four hazy globes of light erupt like flashes of lightning in a storm cloud. A loud, pounding rhythm shocks the air as I tuck myself into a ball and let momentum take me hurtling through the outer edge of the canopy. I burst from the foliage twelve meters above the ground.

I pull the shotgun up over my head and into my arms as I arc through the air all the way down to the ground below. I hit the paving stones, roll to my feet, and spin back toward the cloud with the wooden stock of the Hellion wedged tightly against my shoulder, quietly snorting quickened breaths as I point all three barrels in the direction of the Drones.

Thanks to the explosions, the hissing smoke canister has skittered clear across the courtyard, and the bulk of the haze has been spread thin. There are no heavy footsteps and no sounds of movement—just my breathing and the leaves overhead rustling in the warm afternoon breeze. As the fog clears further, I'm finally able to see the fruits of my labor. A Drone with its arm blown clean off is sitting with its back against the trunk of the tree, and the other four are lying on the ground in varying contorted positions. All have reverted back to their silver color, and all have been deactivated.

My job here is done, but my mission isn't over. There are still two more functioning Drones on top of one of these buildings somewhere, and I need to take them down. I turn and jog, one hand holding my shotgun, the other pressed against the hole leaking blood from my side. In my mind, I knit the flesh closed, and a sharp piece of bullet fragment oozes out of the wound between my fingers. The injury on my leg is a meaty slice. It's deep, but will be relatively easy to heal. I concentrate and feel the gash closing as I scan the building fronts for the climbing gouges left by the other two . . .

THUD, THUD, THUD, THUD, THUD, THUD, STOMP!

I look back over my shoulder, and my eyes go wide as I see the one-armed Drone in midjump, flying straight for me, its glitching skin undulating in mottled waves of silver, green, and brown. It lands with a heavy thump, very nearly right on top of me. I try to bring the Hellion up to the Drone's face mask, but I've been caught off guard, and I'm not nearly fast enough. The Drone's forearm becomes a swiping blur as it brutally backhand pummels me. My left arm takes the full force of the blow, and I hear the bone crack as it slams into my side, snapping at least three of my ribs in the process. Injury tones clang loudly in my head as I go sailing through the air. I hit the ground hard, and the wind is punched from my lungs as my shotgun clatters away from me, tumbling end over end before coming to rest upright against a stone bench seat two meters away.

Even though I've trained myself to convert pain into sound, I can feel the agonizing, undiluted sensations stabbing searing holes in my mental veil, just like my broken ribs are stabbing into my left lung. The damaged Drone is walking toward me. I try to get up, but my body won't let me as the sharp edges of my cracked bones skewer through the muscles I need to move. I grit my teeth, pull the Jack-knife from my waistband, and flick it to the second setting. It snaps open into a one-meter blade, but I quickly realize that I can't stand, and I can't swing it hard enough to do any real damage to the robot. I don't even have the leverage for a feeble stab at the damn thing. A combat sword is useless to me.

The Drone is six meters away.

I look over at the shotgun resting against the bench. It's so close, but it's not close enough.

The Drone is four meters away.

I have only one chance left, and it's a slim one. I flick the Jack-knife to the first setting, and it snaps back into a dagger.

The Drone is three meters away.

I turn my head and glare at the shotgun.

The Drone is two meters away.

Breathing through the pain, I curl my arm tightly.

The Drone is one meter away.

The robot's huge shadow falls across my body, and I whip my hand out to the side as hard as I can, praying for a miracle as the knife spins away from my fingertips.

THOCK!

My prayers are answered as the blade wedges tightly into the wooden stock of the gun. I splay my fingers as wide as I can. Pulled by the knife, the shotgun clacks on the ground and begins sliding across the paving toward my outstretched hand. The Drone bends down and clutches the wrist of my broken arm. I hear my bones cracking and grating as its grip tightens, and genuine pain burns through the barriers in my mind like white-hot splinters. I screech in agony through my clenched jaw and try to pull away from the robot, but its grasp is like a hydraulic vise. With one last, desperate effort, I jerk my body, and my left shoulder pops completely out of its socket as I reach for the Jack-knife. My fingertips find the knife handle, and I wrench it to me, fumbling for a handhold on the gun as the Drone holds me high in the air like a carcass of meat. The dripping stump of its right arm begins swiping at the air as if the Drone is trying to grab me with a limb that isn't there.

Screaming at the top of my one functioning lung, I swing the Hellion up under the Drone's chin; my finger finds the trigger, and the shotgun kicks like a horse against my arm as all three barrels roar with a deafening BOOM! An intense burst of light and heat erupts beside my face as the android's head is completely obliterated in a shower of golden sparks and fire. My ears ring with damage as the Drone and I collapse to the ground. I roll onto the pavement, coughing up blood as warning tones throb and bellow in my head.

I focus my mind on repairs, and I can't help but groan as the sharp tips of broken rib bones extract themselves from the holes torn in my lung and move back into their proper places. I mentally seal up the internal wounds. With my rib cage repaired and my lungs patched, I sit up and join the breaks and fractures in my left arm and wrist as the warning tones gradually fade into the back of my head.

I pop my shoulder back into its socket, push off the ground, step over the headless Drone, and take off toward the row of buildings. I'm running under the high leaves of another tree when there's a sudden cracking of branches overhead. I look up and see a dark silhouette just in time to dive out of the way as Private Sekula comes crashing through the leaves and slams into the ground right where I was standing. His arm is bent completely the wrong way, his eyes are wide, and his jaw is opening and closing as blood pours in torrents down the sides of his face like a storm drain overflowing from a heavy rain. He stops moving, and blood gurgles in his throat as his eyelids lower, hooding his distant, dead stare.

I leap over Private Sekula's body and dash out into the open, but more movement from overhead catches the corner of my eye, and I come skidding to a sudden halt. A large shadow skims across the ground, and a two-meter-tall Combat Drone drops out of the sky, cracking the paving stones with a shuddering thud. It slowly straightens and turns its head toward me. It's standing four meters away and doesn't have a weapon, but that changes in an instant as silver bayonets flick out like oversize switchblades from each of its camo-colored forearms.

I quickly raise the Hellion, clicking it to cycle-fire mode with my thumb as I aim and pull the trigger. The triple barrels rage one after the other, spewing sparking fire at the Drone, which shields its face with its arms as it launches itself sideways. The Hellion's spray of explosive pellets erupts along the Drone's limbs, and one of its arms comes away at the elbow as it dives into an evasive roll. There's another heavy thud right behind me.

The second Drone!

I spin around, and the other Drone lunges, reaching toward me with its huge, four-fingered hands. I leap backward and swing the shotgun around, yanking at the trigger, shooting blindly in a blazing half circle of percussive fire. I manage to score a hit on its torso, tearing a bowling ball–size hole from its side as it continues to tromp forward. The top half of the robot flops grotesquely as I hit the ground, roll backward onto one knee, and unload my last five shells at its staggering body. Flashing pockets of light erupt all over the android as the explosive pellets rip its skin and mask apart, exposing two red-globe eyes set in a smashed open frame of jagged ballistic glass.

I throw the empty Hellion aside, whip my second pistol from its holster, flick it to fully automatic, and pull the trigger hard. The gun blazes into action, thrumming loudly in my hand as bullets rain into the robot's face. The Drone's head vibrates with every impact as the rapid stream of shots bombards its vulnerable components. Circuits fizz and burn, and its robotic eyes explode, spattering orange fluid from the open cavity of its shattered mask as its silver body finally drops heavily onto the paving stones, deactivated.

I hardly have time to breathe when I hear footsteps tromping behind me. I quickly turn as the last active android pounces toward me, bayonets first. I kick my leg in a fast sweep and spin up from the ground, splaying my fingers wide as I launch myself toward the Drone. The Jack-knife leaps from my waistband into my palm and snaps into a sword as my body twists through the air. The Drone's right arm swipes, and a bayonet misses the top of my head by a hair's breadth as my blade becomes a blur of force and momentum, slicing the android's body completely in half at the waist as I emerge, spinning through the gap between its severed torso and legs, showered in a liquid curtain of artificial orange blood.

With my arms spread like wings, I land in a lunging crouch and see, lying on the ground by my shoe, a cracked, palm-size segment of the face mask that I blasted from that Drone. It's smeared and scratched, but . . . beneath the blemishes, among the scrapes and damage are my own eyes, mirrored in its glossy black surface, staring back at me like a stranger's. That's when something stirs inside of me. I slowly lower my arms and reach down for the fragment. I gently pick it up and stare at it, transfixed at the empty, soulless reflection of my own eyes. I look deeper, and a wave of emotion ripples through me. The angry expression of my reflection softens; it suddenly feels like a cloud is moving away from the sun, like I'm waking up from a daydream.

I feel like me again. What did Captain Delgado make me do? I turn and survey the carnage. The courtyard looks like a war zone. There are blast marks and blood, bullet holes, and Drone parts everywhere I look. That bastard is a control freak, and we are nothing but cannon fodder to him. I wipe a smudge from the mask fragment, and when I hold it up to my face again, I see eyes that I recognize. Captain Delgado won't be doing that to me ever again. I tuck the souvenir into my breast pocket and snap the Jack-knife shut.

All of a sudden, a weird electric-crackling sound bursts out of nowhere. I frown, confused as the static noise abruptly clears, breaking into whooping and laughing and raucous cheering blasting into my left ear. I wince at it, momentarily surprised before remembering the little plastic wedge.

"Infinity? Can you hear me?" Otto's voice whispers over the sounds of celebration in the background.

"Yes . . . I can hear you," I reply.

"Who are you talking to?" says Brody's voice. "Is that Infinity?"

"Where is she?" I hear Ryan ask. "Bit, let me see the screens."

"Stop crowding me!" hisses Otto. There's a fumbling, then a shuffling sound, before Otto's annoyed voice pipes into my ear again.

"Sorry, I'm back. Just had to crawl under a table for a little privacy," she says. There's a beat of silence, and then a quiet gasp. "Infinity . . . you destroyed all the Drones? How?"

"You weren't watching?" I ask.

"No. The moment you jumped out the window, they crammed us all into a tiny conference room. They even tried to confiscate my slate, but I gave them Dean's instead. I regained access to the security cameras the first chance I had, but I didn't see what happened; none of us did."

At Otto's mention of the cameras, I suddenly remember that Captain Delgado is undoubtedly watching me right this second. The fact that I'm just standing here, talking to Otto instead of escaping, hopefully means that he thinks I'm still under his control. If that's the case, I need to keep it that way. With no clear plan of what to do next, I decide to maintain the charade and do what would be expected of me. The Captain ordered me to return to the command post, so, hoping that a bright idea of how to get out of this mess pops into my head soon, I begin walking back the way I came.

"Did you hear the soldiers celebrating?" asks Otto.

"What? Oh yeah, I did," I reply.

"It seems you made quite an impression," she whispers. "I'm kinda sorry I missed the show."

"It's not like I had any choice," I growl. "Captain Delgado made me do it."

"I *knew* he did something to you. One second, you were fighting him to the floor, the next, you were calling him 'sir' and jumping out a window. What did he say to you?" asks Otto.

"That may be difficult to explain," I murmur.

"Oh. Well . . . it looked like a posthypnotic suggestion to me," Otto whispers.

"OK, maybe not so hard to explain then. Captain Delgado was my commanding officer. He must have implanted some kind of behavioral modification in my subconscious."

"What *is* it with these guys and mind control? That is not good, Infinity," Otto says, stating the glaringly obvious. "If he did it once, you can bet that he'll try to do it again."

I look in the direction of the command post. Anger instantly begins boiling up inside me, and my fingernails dig into my palms.

"The next time he tries . . . I'll cut his tongue from his head."

I take a breath and try to temper my seething hatred into a more manageable, smoldering contempt. "What's the situation up there, Otto? Tell me what's happening."

"They're making final preparations to leave. I heard Captain Delgado say that the men he sent to the hangar are returning soon with two transports to fly us out."

"I'm not leaving," I reply. "After everything I've been through today, I'm gonna see this through to the end. The Drones have been taken care of, so there's nothing else standing in my way."

"*We* are gonna see this through to the end," says Otto. "I didn't come all this way just to give up now, either."

I smile and nod. "OK, then. I'm coming to get you."

"Alright," she replies. "The door to the conference room is at the far end of the office, behind the weapon crates, but there's a whole roomful of . . ."

Otto's voice suddenly goes quiet, and the wedge hisses in my ear.

"Hello? Otto? Come in. Can you read me?"

There's no answer.

"Otto?" I say louder, glaring in the direction of the command post, but there's nothing but a static crackling sound. "Hello? Otto?"

Sensing trouble, I quicken my pace across the courtyard, but I've only gone about a meter when Otto speaks again.

"Sorry, I'm still here, Infinity . . . I've just picked up a strange signal."

"What do you mean, 'strange'?" I ask.

"My slate has detected some kind of low-frequency vibration. It's registering like a weak earth tremor, but it's repeating in sequence. Maybe if I try this . . ."

I can hear Otto tapping on the slate, and, a few seconds later, her excited voice chirps from the earpiece. "Infinity! The vibration is encoded! I'm deciphering it now . . ."

I hear a finger tap, and a man's voice hisses into my ear.

"Attention. As conventional methods of communications have been jammed, I'm hoping you're the capable girl I suspect you are and have discovered this seismic transmission. If you're receiving this, please, you must follow my instructions. The main computer is malfunctioning. It has already managed to dispatch a heavily armed mechanoid to your location at the Security Station, and it's only a matter of time before it gains control of more. There's a hatch that leads to my laboratory beside the koi pond in Sector B, near the Japanese pagoda. It's the only place you'll be safe. Get out of the Security Station now! Get to the hatch! I hope you receive this message in time. Attention. As conventional methods of communications have been jammed, I'm hoping you're the capable girl I suspect you are . . ."

Otto shuts the message off. "It's a cycling vibration, repeating the message over and over in a loop, and it sounds like whoever sent it has been watching us somehow. Do you recognize the voice?"

"No," I reply as I step over smeared trails of blood and walk through the open door that leads to the command post.

"The attached time code indicates the message was sent nearly forty-five minutes ago," says Otto. "Just before the Security Station exploded. There was so much interference from the data hives and command modules back then that my slate didn't pick it up, but localized radio transmissions are working now, so why hasn't he tried to reestablish contact? Who do you think it is? One of the security staff? Maybe we should tell Captain Delgado? They might need help."

"I don't know who sent the message, and I don't care," I reply between breaths. "All I care about is getting you out of there and hunting down Richard Blackstone."

"OK, but there's a roomful of armed soldiers right next door," warns Otto. "You can't just walk in and demand that they let me go."

I arrive at the entrance to the command post, grip the Jack-knife handle tightly, and whisper my reply.

"Why the hell not?"

CHAPTER SIXTEEN

"Keep quiet, and be ready to move."

"OK," whispers Otto. "Good luck."

I rest my thumb on the Jack-knife switch, take a deep breath, and knock on the door to the command post. The barricade that was stacked against it must have been removed for the evacuation, because the door swings open almost immediately. The first face that I see is Private Carter's. There's blood spattered on his uniform, and his arm is in a sling, but he's holding the door wide open and smiling like an idiot.

On my guard, I walk through the doorway into the office. Every able-bodied soldier suddenly stands and begins applauding. Keeping up my brainwashed pretense, I don't acknowledge them at all as I scan the room for Captain Delgado. He's standing beside the central desk with his shirt unbuttoned, and I can see stabilizing bandages wrapped around his midriff.

Grinning soldiers stand aside, clearing a path to the Captain as I pass, and as I cross the room, I can hear some of them whispering as they watch me with curious fascination. "Incredible," says one. "I didn't know they trained operatives that young," says another. "Maybe she's a robot, too?" I hear someone murmur. "She should be dead; she can't be human," whispers someone else.

I come to a halt in front of Captain Delgado, tuck my Jack-knife back into my waistband, and salute. He looks down his nose at me but doesn't return the gesture, most likely because raising his arm would hurt like a bastard from the injury I gave him. Instead, he gives me a simple nod. I snap my hand back to my side and stare blankly at him over the top of my face mask.

"Nicely done, Infinity One. See what a difference a little subliminal implantation can make?" Each word is hissed through gritted teeth. His broken ribs are clearly making it uncomfortable for him to speak.

"I was watching you out there," he says, reaching toward me. It takes all the self-control I can muster to stay still as he slides his fingers into my breast pocket and pulls out the fragment of the Drone's mask. "What's this? Collecting scalps, Infinity One?"

I'm not sure if he expects an answer, so I decide to just keep my mouth shut. He tosses the fragment onto a nearby desk, and as he studies me with an expression of deep suspicion, I realize my mistake. I shouldn't have kept the fragment. Choosing to take a souvenir may have given me away. Captain Delgado tries to lean forward to take a closer look into my eyes but winces and clutches his side, choosing instead to take my chin in his hand and turn my face up toward him. "I warned you," he whispers. "I told you I'd find a way to twist your brain to my way of thinking. Do you have any problem with that?"

I know what he's trying to do, but I won't take the bait. I don't react. I just stare gormlessly at him and say, "No, sir."

Captain Delgado's gaze lingers on me. Finally he releases my chin, and relief washes over me as he addresses Corporal Avary. "Add those seven tin soldiers she took out to the overall tally; what does that give us?"

Corporal Avary taps at a slate. "Well, according to your intel, sir, fifty prototype Crimson-Class Combat Drones have been constructed to date, so, including those last seven . . . all fifty have been deactivated and accounted for."

"Good," replies Captain Delgado. "What can you tell me about the main computer? It hasn't said a word since the attack, and I don't like it."

A nearby soldier slides a computer slate with a pulsing blue stripe and scrolling lines of green code toward Corporal Avary. He studies it for a moment, then turns to the Captain. "Like I mentioned before, sir, artificial intelligence is a little out of my league, but . . . as far as I can tell, the situation hasn't changed. The computer is still in defense mode, so it's probably safe to assume that it continues to view us a threat."

Captain Delgado's eyes narrow. "In my experience, if the enemy isn't talking, they're dreaming up new ways to kill you. It's time to leave. Where the hell are my transports?"

A young soldier beside the desk points toward the windows on the opposite side of the room. "Incoming, sir."

I turn and see two dark shapes moving in the blue sky, heading in this direction. They disappear from view behind the canopies of the trees outside, and, less than half a minute later, I can hear the deep, rolling hum of propulsion engines roving over the top of the building.

The sound gets considerably louder as the transports slowly descend into the courtyard. Treetops flurry, and tepid air from the aircrafts' thrusters wafts into the office through the smashed-open window frame. Landing legs fold out, and a stone bench is crushed beneath one of their large hydraulic feet as the two military-gray Gryphon VTL 400s settle on the paving outside. The blue flames jetting from their thrusters cut out, and there's a loud chorus of high-pitched whines and grumbling stutters as the transports' turbines begin winding down. As the cargo doors in their bellies open and lower to the ground, Captain Delgado turns and speaks to the whole room.

"Attention. It's gonna be a tight fit, so if it has a heartbeat, load it on those war birds. We'll be back to retrieve our fallen as soon as we can. That's all; now move out."

They obediently do as they're told. Soon there's a groaning, limping line of bloodied bandages and war-torn uniforms making a slow but relatively orderly exit through the door into the stairwell. This is good. It won't be long before this place is cleared out, which will make Otto's extraction a whole lot easier than I had expected. All I have to do is wait for the right moment, so in the meantime I stand and observe, making sure to maintain my blank look. I keep my trap shut and limit my movements to slow, zombielike head turns.

Corporal Avary and his team take apart the array of computer slates and pack the components into a number of army-green satchels. They sling the bags on their backs and head toward the exit. The office is almost empty. There are only a few soldiers left when Captain Delgado motions to one of them standing beside a door on the far wall. "Bring the civilians out."

The soldier opens the door, and I can see what Otto meant when she said the conference room was small. With ten people packed into it, the room is definitely cramped, so much so that most of the group is sitting on top of a table with their legs dangling over the edge. The soldier motions for them to come out. As they're shuffling off the table and filing into the office, they all look understandably exhausted. Ryan, Brody, Brent, and Margaux are the first to emerge. From the moment Ryan sees me, his eyes are fixed on me. The girls that Otto called "Jennifer" and "Amy" exit next, and are followed by the visibly drained Percy and Professor Francis. Finally I see Otto crawl out from under the table. Just like Ryan, as soon as she sees me, her stare is glued on me. I give her the slightest nod, and she returns the tiniest hint of a smile.

"What the hell?" mutters Captain Delgado.

My eyes flick toward the Captain, and he's glowering down at me with a look of bewildered anger. "I knew it," he growls. "You sneaky little . . ."

Captain Delgado grunts with pain as he whips his sidearm from the holster on his hip and jabs the muzzle against my left temple. "Secure this girl!"

The soldier by the wall immediately pulls his rifle to his shoulder and keeps me in his sights as he sidles around the group, sidesteps a stack of weapon crates, and strides toward me. There are sounds of movement and the clacking of guns being cocked, and out of the corner of my eye I can see at least two more soldiers on the other side of the room training their weapons on me.

Captain Delgado cringes with discomfort as he reaches with his free hand and pinches the finger holes on the nose of my face mask. The adhesive releases from my skin, and he pulls the mask away from my face. He drops it at my feet and jabs at my head with the gun. I don't react at all. I just carry on staring blankly at him. His eyes narrow. "I don't know how you're overriding my command, Infinity One, but don't insult my intelligence. You can drop the act."

I let out a resentful sigh and raise my hands as my brain-dead expression furrows into an angry stare. If I'm fast enough, I might be able to take the Captain hostage and bargain my way out the door. A knife held to his throat will do the job just fine. My eyes lock with Captain Delgado's, and as I hold his enraged gaze, I hope that he doesn't notice the fingers of my right hand slowly stretching wider. He pushes the pistol hard, tilting my head at an angle.

"Don't even think about it," he growls, eyeballing the Jack-knife tucked into my waistband. "You move, and I swear I'll blow your goddamned brains out. Private, take her weapon." The nearest soldier lowers his rifle, steps forward, and reaches toward the black handle.

"I wouldn't do that if I were you," I mutter.

The burly soldier's eyes go wide, and his hand slowly withdraws.

"Take the damn thing!" barks Captain Delgado.

The soldier's hand creeps forward again. His gaze jumps back and forth from my face to the handle, and his expression is a comical mix of fear and reluctant obedience. His fingers are trembling, and he actually gulps. The poor guy looks like he's been commanded to put his hand in a bear trap.

"Captain Delgado?" says a voice. Professor Francis steps out from the school group and sidles around the stack of weapon crates.

The Captain doesn't acknowledge him; in fact, he doesn't dare take his eyes *or* his gun off me for a second. "Private, ignore the high school teacher and take that weapon right now, or I'll throw your worthless ass in the nearest military prison and drop the key in the ocean."

The soldier gingerly extends a hand but freezes once more as the Professor butts in. "Captain, today's tragic events are rigorously testing my sanity. But I do not think that I'm alone in that regard. All of our lives have been completely turned upside down. I may not understand the intricacies of your personal relationship with Miss Brogan, but she appears to have saved all of our lives, and—"

"Shut your mouth, you pompous old bastard," hisses Captain Delgado. Professor Francis flinches like he's been stung by a bee.

"And you . . . ," the Captain grunts at the embarrassed soldier. "You're bloody useless. Now raise your damn rifle, and if she tries anything . . . shoot her. Did everybody hear that order?"

All around the room, there's a chorus of "Sir, yes, sir."

The burly soldier hurriedly raises his rifle, and Captain Delgado groans loudly as he leans forward and pulls the Jack-knife from my waistband. He slides it into his pocket and then he reaches over, flicks open the latch of the magna-band, and pulls it from my wrist. He stuffs that into his pocket, too, then he lowers his gun and looks over at Otto and the rest of the group.

"All of you. It's time to go," says the Captain.

Margaux sighs with relief, and Amy looks like she's about to cry.

"Thank heavens," mutters Percy as Brody smiles dopily beside him. Ryan takes the Dean kid by the arm and pulls him along as everyone begins wearily moving toward the stairwell door.

"You," the Captain grunts at me. "I'd like to strap you to the roof of one of those transports and fly through a hailstorm for what you did to me. But for now, I'll make sure I find you a comfy little spot shackled to a floor rail next to the piss bucket. Now put your hands behind your head and move."

I grudgingly do as he says and fall in behind the group as the big twitchy soldier prods me in the back with his rifle. Otto glances over her shoulder at me, a look of concern creasing her brow. This is not exactly going to plan.

Including the soldier behind me, there are five men pointing rifles directly at me. I may be hard to kill, but I'm not invincible, and judging by the hair-trigger intensity on all these soldiers' faces, making a move now in this confined space would most likely get both me and half the school group killed. Two soldiers position themselves between me and the group, and three stay behind me, with Captain Delgado bringing up the rear. All of them cautiously keep a reasonable distance as I walk down the stairwell like a death row prisoner.

So this is what happens when you decide to infiltrate a top-secret research facility with nothing but a computer geek and the flimsiest revenge plan in history. I'd like to say that I'll learn from this experience, but, after the Captain is finished with me, I doubt I'll remember my own name—let alone all the mistakes I recklessly made today.

Ryan was right. This *is* the worst field trip ever.

Our bizarre procession trudges on in silence, and it isn't long before I'm led down three flights of stairs and out the exit into the warm afternoon sunshine. The air is saturated with the pleasant, savory-sweet aroma of aviation fuel. Otto and the others are standing nearby, observing the soldiers boarding the two transports. The priming, high-pitched whine of their idling engines is already quite loud, so the soldier beside the ramp of the nearest transport is guiding us toward the open ramp that leads up into the second aircraft's cargo hold. A couple of medics and the last of the wounded are making their way up the ramp as the school group approaches the transport. With my hands still behind my head, I'm prodded in the back with a rifle as Captain Delgado strides ahead, glaring at me with contempt as he passes.

As I grudgingly shuffle forward, a shiny glint of light catches the corner of my eye, and I turn to look back down the courtyard toward Dome One. In the distance are what appear to be six large, metallic platforms. They're steadily rising from the ground in front of that tall angular sculpture. As they continue to rise, I quickly realize that they're not platforms at all; they look more like boxes, or some kind of huge, rectangular containers. They elevate higher and higher, until soon they're so tall that they completely obscure the sculpture altogether. It's difficult to tell from here, but I'd guess each one must be at least eight or nine meters high. My eyes widen, and my mouth goes completely dry. There's only one thing I've seen today that would fit in a box that size.

"Sir!" shouts one of the soldiers. He points in the direction of the containers, and as soon as Captain Delgado sees them, he wrenches his walkie-talkie from his belt and bellows into it, the pain of his broken ribs instantly forgotten. "Fire up those engines; I want those birds airborne in sixty seconds!" His order is immediately carried out as both of the transports' four turbine engines suddenly throttle up into a steady roar.

The sides of the silver containers begin folding down in sections, and as they fully collapse to the paving, my already-racing heart begins hammering in my chest. There was no warning from Onix this time. Maybe he learned that it isn't wise to tell your enemies what's coming? Or maybe he did politely announce the impending arrival of those hellish creations, and we simply didn't hear it over the sound of the engines. I guess it doesn't matter now, because sending *six* Remote

Articulated Mechanoids to kill us is going to be like squashing an ant . . . with a sledgehammer.

And only two minutes ago, I honestly thought this day couldn't get any worse.

"Go, go, go!" shouts the Captain. Otto glances over her shoulder at me with a look of abject terror as the school group breaks into a run toward the transport.

"Sir, what about the prisoner?" yells the soldier standing directly behind me.

"Priorities have changed, wouldn't you say?" replies Captain Delgado. "Leave her, and get on that transport!"

My five guards don't need to be told twice as they all turn on their boot heels and run toward the cargo door. With the threat of being shot in the back removed, I drop my arms as Captain Delgado glares at me with narrowed eyes, looking me up and down like he's trying to decide what the hell to do with me. I have no doubt that the thought of leaving me here with those six robots is at the forefront of his mind, but as he draws his gun, I suddenly realize that he may be considering a more swift and final solution.

My breathing quickens, and adrenaline courses through me as I stare right at him, almost daring him to do it. *Go ahead, you bastard. Kill me. I can see in your eyes that you want to, so just get it over and done with. What are you waiting for?* I ball my fists and tense my muscles, wondering if I'm fast enough to cross the distance between us before he shoots me in the forehead. But Captain Delgado doesn't pull the trigger. Instead, he lets out a frustrated snort, and, to my surprise, he walks right up to me. He jabs the gun in my side and drags me by the arm as he hurriedly strides off across the courtyard. "For Finn's sake, I'm pulling you out of the fire, but you're still in the frying pan, Infinity One. I'm your only way out of here, so don't try any funny business."

He's right. He *is* my only way out of here, but that means leaving behind the only chance I might ever have to get to Richard Blackstone.

I need to weigh my options. I glance to the left, knowing that there are paths winding among the buildings that lead to the rest of the facility. Somewhere farther in, Richard Blackstone may still be here somewhere, hiding like a rat in a maze they say he never leaves. But without Otto's help, it could take hours to find him, and by then, Captain Delgado will be back with more soldiers and more firepower. I look toward the transport. If I get on board, I'll most likely be thrown in a military prison or have my brain fried to a crisp. That would not be ideal. I look to the right. Six of the most advanced robotic killing machines in the world are booting up. They still haven't moved, but when they do, they'll tear this whole place apart to eliminate any threat, and I think it's safe to say that would include me. So . . . I can either stay to be hunted down like an animal or be marched off to a prison for a lobotomy.

Wow. My options *really* suck.

The school group has already disappeared into the transport's cargo hold, and Captain Delgado and I have nearly reached the ramp. The time to make my decision ends the moment I set foot on that aircraft, but . . . I suddenly realize there is *another* choice. A choice I've already considered once today.

I can run.

I can forget Richard Blackstone and run. I could take my chances out there in the big, bad world and hope like hell that stupid bitch, Finn, doesn't wake up and march my body back into the arms of the authorities. If Otto was telling the truth, and I could make it back to her in time, maybe she could erase Finn before that happens? That's a whole lot of "mights" and "maybes," but what other choice do I have?

I can easily disarm the Captain and duck around the side of the transport. I could make it to the buildings on the other side of the courtyard before the R.A.M.s fully activate. He wouldn't dare risk coming after me. Not with the threat of those mechanoids hanging in the balance. After that, if I keep up a good pace, I could probably find a town somewhere around here before nightfall.

OK. My mind is made up. I have to run. It's my only chance at freedom . . . and I have to do it now.

A few paces from the edge of the ramp, I thrust my arm forward, breaking Captain Delgado's grip and knocking the barrel of the pistol away from my side in one slick maneuver. Caught by surprise, the Captain pulls the trigger, and the gun flares, but the sound of the shot is completely drowned out by the roaring engines, and the soldiers trudging up the ramp have their backs to us. No one is alerted. I easily twist the pistol from Captain Delgado's hand and elbow him hard in his broken ribs. He doubles over and drops to the ground. I dart away and skirt around the transparent heat curtain attached to the side of the ramp. I immediately regret my rash decision when I'm blasted square in the face by the scorching downdraft of the turbines. Luckily, the engines aren't directly overhead, or I would've been incinerated, but it still feels like I've stepped into a furnace. My clothes whip violently as the jet wash burns my eyes and throat. I hold my hand up to shield my face, and I stumble, dropping the pistol as I turn and run, half-blinded, out into the open, a route I most definitely did *not* want to take.

I have no choice but to carry on running as fast as I can in any direction—it doesn't matter where anymore, just as long as it's away from Captain Delgado. I keep going, rapidly blinking my eyes in a desperate attempt to clear them. It seems to help a little, and I must have covered at least thirty meters when my shoulder suddenly jolts and blood sprays onto the paving in front of me.

I've been shot.

I grab the wound tightly and keep moving. I feel another impact, and blood bursts out from my stomach and speckles the ground. I zigzag, trying to make myself a harder target to hit, but it does no good as another bullet brutally punches through my left thigh. My leg buckles underneath me, and I reach out as I hit the ground hard, scraping the skin from the palms of my hands as I slide to an abrupt stop, facedown on the paving. Warnings throb through my head. I'm bleeding badly, but I'm thankful that whoever shot me has terrible aim. I roll onto my back and glare toward the transport. My vision is still poor, but I can make out blurry shapes of frantic movement on the cargo ramp. I screw my eyes shut and will them to heal. I can feel the damaged film on the surface of my eyes sealing over, and when I open them, the blurred shapes sharpen into focus, and I immediately see why I wasn't shot straight through the heart.

Swaying violently from side to side, trying to wrench a rifle from a soldier's hands . . . is Ryan.

Otto leaps from the cargo hold onto the ramp and joins the fight as she swiftly whacks the soldier on the back of the head with a computer slate. The soldier fends her off, and she falls awkwardly onto her bottom. Ryan saved my life, but when those R.A.M.s wake up, I'll be the closest target, and all his effort will be for nothing. I turn to check on the line of robots and immediately feel nauseous. All six pairs of white-circle eyes have turned an angry shade of bright red. If they're anything like the Combat Drones, it'll only be a matter of seconds before they fully activate. I need to move. Thankfully, my friends are buying me some time. I focus on closing my gunshot wounds, but I've lost a lot of blood today, and it's getting harder and harder to heal the damage, especially when it's this bad . . . Wait a second. Did I just call Ryan and Otto my . . . *friends*? Is that really what they are now?

They're trying to keep me alive, so to my complete surprise, the answer to my question is . . . *yes*. They are my friends.

Well, I'll be damned.

Suddenly much more concerned for their safety than I thought I ever could be, I look back toward the transport. Three unarmed soldiers have run down onto the ramp. One of them assists Captain Delgado, helping him up from the ground, as another roughly pulls Otto into a choke hold and drags her out of sight. Ryan head-butts the man he's fighting, and the soldier reels from the blow as Ryan pulls the rifle from his grip. The soldier tumbles onto the ramp, clutching his nose as another soldier runs forward and sucker-punches Ryan in the side of the head.

Ryan drops to one knee, but as his assailant steps over him, Ryan swings the butt of the rifle, catching the man in the groin. The soldier buckles at the knees and drops as yet another man appears from the cargo hold and strides angrily toward Ryan. Even though he's putting up a hell of a fight, Ryan is eventually going to be beaten to a bloody pulp by those men. And it's all because of me. I have to try and help him. Maybe if I can stand, he'll see that I'm OK and surrender. My shoulder is fixed, and the holes in my stomach and leg are almost closed, but my internal injuries still need some time to heal, so my body protests fiercely as I drag myself up onto one knee. I raise a hand toward the transport to show Ryan that I'm alright, but his eyes are focused on his enemies, not me. The angry-looking soldier steps over his fallen comrade and is only a couple of meters away when Ryan hauls himself to his feet and pulls the rifle to his shoulder.

No. Ryan. Put the gun down.

Regulation requires rifles to be stowed for takeoff, so the soldiers standing on the ramp are empty-handed. They glare at Ryan, motioning at him to lower his weapon as he waves the barrel back and forth at them.

That's when I feel the vibrations.

I turn to look back down the courtyard, and my stomach churns. The R.A.M.s. are awake and approaching, marching in a synchronized line like six giant, red-eyed monsters, and I'm not the only one who's noticed them.

Captain Delgado is standing at the top of the ramp, shouting and gesturing wildly to someone inside. The turbines throttle up, and the transport suddenly begins to lift off with Ryan and the soldiers still standing on the open cargo door. All of them sway unsteadily as the transport rises. The aircraft leans; Ryan loses his balance and staggers. He fumbles with the rifle; it slips from his grasp and clatters at his feet. Captain Delgado lunges and pulls a pistol from a nearby soldier's hip. He raises the gun, and as easily as someone would swat a fly, he pulls the trigger . . . and shoots Ryan square in the chest. Ryan twists from the impact and topples backward off the edge of the ramp.

"NOOOOO!" My scream is lost in the roar of the engines.

Clawing at the air, Ryan plummets from the transport and hits the ground hard. His head slumps to the side, and his lifeless eyes stare into nowhere. The other transport takes off, following right behind Captain Delgado's. As I watch both transports climb above the buildings, seething rage boils through my veins. I vow that one day, I'll personally gut Javier Delgado and force him to watch as I make him choke on his own intestines.

My gaze falls on Ryan's body, and I quietly whisper, "I'm sorry."

The pain of futile remorse grips my heart as I watch the transports leave. Ryan was so close to making it out of here. He could've been on that transport, but now, because of me, he's dead. I try to console myself with the knowledge that Otto is finally safe. And if I'm ever going to make Captain Delgado suffer, I need to save my own skin, too. I grit my teeth and turn my hate into the fuel I need to carry on. I look toward the mechanoids. They're still far enough away for me to make a safe escape, and I'm about to make a run for it when I pause.

The R.A.M.s have stopped walking.

They're all just standing there in a line with their domed heads swiveled upward. All of a sudden, like fingers creeping toward the sky, I notice five small missiles rising up over the left shoulder of one of the mechanoids. Five more rise over the shoulder of the next robot, then the next in line, and the next one after that, until soon the shoulders of all six R.A.M.s are bristling with them.

I feel pathetic and useless, tortured by my inability to stop this from happening, but there really is nothing I can do. Before today, I'd never felt what it's like to know someone you care for is moments away from dying. It feels like a fist is squeezing my insides and forcing them up into my throat. *It hurts.*

First Ryan, and now you.

You don't deserve to die like this, Bettina.

I'll never be able to tell you how truly sorry I am.

I watch helplessly as the missiles ignite and begin launching, one after the other, in rapid succession. The gut-wrenching sight fills my eyes as the missiles hiss and wind through the air like serpents, weaving a white lattice of smoke trails as they climb higher and higher into the clear blue sky.

Please . . . forgive me.

CHAPTER SEVENTEEN

All hell will be breaking loose inside the cockpits of those transports. Missile-lock alerts will be blaring, displays will be flashing, panic will be spreading among the passengers like wildfire, and the pilots' nerves will be stretched to breaking point as they're forced to choose from a very short list of split-second, life-or-death decisions.

The first of the missiles has nearly reached the lower transport when multiple glowing red globes of light begin shooting out of the aircraft's undercarriage. The pilot has activated the antimissile countermeasures. The red flares are designed to draw heat-seeking missiles away from the engines, and I can tell by the missiles' vapor trails that the distraction appears to be working as one, then another, then four more projectiles begin swerving toward the lines of drifting red lights.

There are multiple flashes, and I momentarily lose sight of both aircraft behind a swath of fiery orange and yellow. The transports are already quite high, so there's a two-second delay before the resounding bass beats of the explosions echo loudly throughout the courtyard. A glimmer of hope ripples through me as I spot Otto's transport emerging from high above the darkening, smoky stains of the explosions. It tilts to the left and begins curving through the air, inexplicably heading back the way it came as it shoots its own strings of flares out behind it. A group of heat-seekers takes the bait, and half a dozen bulbs of fire burst harmlessly in the sky far below the aircraft.

The other transport roves into view as it breaks through the blackened cloudbursts of the first detonations. The smoke trails over the aircraft's fuselage like a ghostly veil as it veers wildly to the right. I see the blue flames at the mouths of its turbines burn brighter as the pilot attempts to gain altitude. The shock waves of the first explosions took out a good number of the other missiles, but, unfortunately, they weren't nearly good enough. It would only take one to bring that transport down, and the heat from its engines at full burn is drawing three missiles toward it like hungry piranhas to a bleeding carcass.

Otto's transport makes a sharp turn as more lines of flares spit from its undercarriage. Seven missiles veer toward the flares. Four explode, but the other three are merely knocked off course by the blasts. Their vapor trails twist and turn erratically for a couple of seconds before, to my horror, the tumbling missiles correct themselves and continue their deadly purpose, curving back toward their target. I see the glowing engines of Otto's transport go out completely. Either the engines are malfunctioning, or that pilot is attempting some kind of desperate survival maneuver. It appears to be the latter as the Gryphon drops like a stone and more flares begin spouting out from behind it.

The evasion technique seems to work as the persistent missiles lock onto the flares, speed in . . . and explode in a line of raging fireballs. Otto's transport is buffeted by the shock waves, but it's in one piece. Its engines flare back to life, but only for a moment before they cut out again. They fire up once more, burn for an instant, and then are extinguished again. Something is wrong. Otto's transport is losing altitude fast.

Both Gryphons are in dire trouble. I quickly look toward the other transport. Its engines are now at full power, and it's speeding away with the three missiles still in pursuit. Two more lines of flares eject from the transport's belly, but it's too little, too late. The three missiles chasing it are far too close now to choose a warm appetizer over the piping-hot main course of the turbines. The curving trails of the heat-seekers become arrow straight as they speed past the flares and close in on their target. Everyone on that aircraft is as good as dead.

I'm sure even they know it by now.

No sooner does the morbid thought cross my mind than blooms of fire open up in the sky. The transport violently rocks and jolts as it suffers three successive direct impacts. All I can do is pray for the occupants' deaths to be quick and painless, and by the time the gruesome rhythm of the explosions reaches the ground, the burning shell of the aircraft is already falling out of the sky.

Otto's Gryphon is still dropping, its engines firing in sporadic bursts as it tilts and sways through the air.

The other transport continues plummeting toward the ground, but . . . it's not falling the way I thought it would. Somehow, its turbines must still be functioning, because the transport is being propelled on a strange, twisting trajectory. A thick trail of billowing black smoke spews out from behind it as it zigzags through the air like a leaf caught in the wind. It's coming down fast, and the closer the falling aircraft gets, the more it dawns on me that the wreckage might actually crash-land . . . right here in the courtyard! There's no way of telling exactly where it will hit, but when it does, I sure as hell don't want to be underneath it. I quickly turn and take off toward the row of buildings behind me as the labored whine of the transport's engines gets louder and louder directly overhead. It's coming down, and it's coming down *fast*.

Functioning on little more than pure adrenaline, I run for my life, vaulting over bench seats and dodging around tree trunks and lampposts. Panting at the air, I sprint along the line of buildings, heading for the only structure I know of with an open door . . . The command post. I'm nearly at the entrance to the stairwell when I look into the sky and spot Otto's transport. It's low, and it's coming down over the buildings farther into the facility. I hope like hell that they're able to land safely.

The other transport has curved around and is coming in fast, right into the courtyard, just like I feared it would. It's close enough that I can see that the bottom half of the Gryphon is almost completely gone, but three out of four turbines are still attached to the upper half of the crippled aircraft. Anyone in its cargo hold that survived the explosions would have fallen to their deaths, but I'm still amazed the whole thing wasn't completely blown to smithereens with the initial strike. It's moments from hitting the ground when suddenly the two front turbines roar to life. The nose of the transport pulls up at the last instant.

It's so close to the ground that it roves in between two trees as a huge swath of black smoke pours down behind it, dousing everything in its wake with a blanket of billowing darkness. I'm less than fifteen meters from the stairwell door when I suddenly skid to stop and stare in stunned disbelief. Incredibly, through the shattered glass of the Gryphon's cockpit, I can see a man struggling with the controls. There's no mistaking what he's trying to do. He's not trying to land the transport safely, oh no. If he were, he would've chosen anywhere else to attempt it. I only caught a glimpse of his face for a split second, but it was long enough to tell me exactly where he's aiming that wreck.

Directly at the line of six robots.

The part of their programming that controls self-preservation must have suddenly kicked in, because all of them turn and break into a run. Three go to their left, and three lunge to their right as fresh sets of missiles launch from all of their shoulders. Heat-seekers fill the air, winding and spiraling in every direction. Some curve and head for the runaway transport, but, with the target so close, many shoot straight up and out to the sides before correcting their course, veering in wide, out-of-control arcs. One of the errant projectiles spirals and then loops around, hitting one of the R.A.M.s square in the center of its own head. The detonation rips open the green dome like a tin can, and the giant robot drops to the ground like a marionette that's had its strings suddenly sliced away.

There's no time for celebration as missiles slam into the sides of buildings, weave upward, or head straight down into the ground. Some curve toward the transport and hit trees or benches, and some streak out of view into the black fog that's steadily spreading across the courtyard. There are so many explosions that it feels like the fabric of reality is being torn apart around me. I dive at the ground, screaming as fireballs erupt in every conceivable direction. The noise is astonishing. It's like an earthquake and a thunderstorm have combined and are raging into real life.

Glass is shattering, walls are toppling, chunks of stone and concrete are raining down around me, and as the transport is hit by a barrage of missiles, it's completely obliterated in a drumming pattern of colossal detonations. The first in a series of rolling shock waves scoops me from the ground and slams me against something hard as each successive wave punches every bit of my body in quick and brutal succession. I'm speared in my shoulder and leg by flying scraps of metal as thick, burning globules of concentrated aviation gel spatter the crumbling facades of the buildings like napalm.

The shroud of black smoke engulfs me. I cough and retch inside the mire of choking darkness, desperately waving my hands. The only light I can see is coming from the patches of burning fuel and debris scattered throughout the courtyard, and the only sounds I can hear are the crackling of fire . . . and the heavy tromping of approaching footsteps.

The R.A.M.s are heading in this direction. I need to move. I run my trembling fingers down my thigh and touch the sharp edge of metal sticking out of my leg. I grasp it tightly and quickly pull it out. A warm spray of blood squirts against my hand. I slap my palm against the open wound and will it to heal. The footsteps are coming closer;

I need to hurry. I can feel the cut starting to close, but it takes every ounce of my concentration as each microscopic repair taxes my mental discipline to the limit. I'm on the brink of bursting a blood vessel in my brain when I finally stop the bleeding and only barely manage to close the skin.

I reach across and pull the shrapnel from my shoulder. Even though the warning tones tell me it's not as bad as the gash in my leg, I still don't think I'm quite strong enough to heal it. I quickly tear a strip off the sleeve of my shirt, wrap it as tightly as I can around the cut in my shoulder, and, holding one end of the makeshift bandage in my teeth, manage to tie a temporary knot.

The footsteps sound like they're almost on top of me, so I try to stand. There's movement, and I'm instantly gripped with terror. Through the oily black smoke, I can see the shadowy outline of three giant robots, the hazy glow of their bloodred eyes swiveling from side to side as their thunderous stomps shake the ground. My internal voice screams at me to get up and move. I grit my teeth, haul myself to my feet, and begin limping along the line of buildings. Tripping over fragments of dislodged paving and rubble, I reach the stairwell door that leads to the command post. I could climb the stairs, and I might be safe for a while, but I don't go in. I shamble on past the door as the pounding vibrations of the robots' footsteps spur me on, and while the thought of avoiding being crushed beneath one of their massive feet is all the incentive I need to keep going, that's not the reason why I carry on.

I need to know if Otto is still alive.

I'm sure there's enough cover between here and the buildings at the far end of the courtyard to stay out of the R.A.M.s' direct sight lines. The patches of burning fuel will hopefully disguise my body heat; so as long as I'm quick and I stay in the smoke, I think I can make it. I find the right part of my foot to put weight on so I can move faster, and I'm covering ground at a decent pace when my plan immediately begins to come apart at the seams. The black smoke I was relying on to hide me is thinning fast. It's too late to turn back now. I can see the shape of a tree up ahead. As I change direction and head toward it, my worst fears come to life as a voice suddenly booms out from the darkness behind me. It's a deep, emotionless, robotic voice. It's exactly the way I'd expect a robot designed for killing would speak, but inside it, I can hear something else: it's as if two overlapping voices are saying the same bone-chilling words at exactly the same time.

"INTRUDER DETECTED."

I'd know that other voice anywhere. It is Onix's. It's like his calm, polite tone has been wrapped in the other voice, folded into the guttural bass of those synthesized war machines. Onix's virtual insanity is going to bring this whole place down, and if I don't double my efforts, I'll be taken down right along with it.

Bolstered by the overwhelming desire not to die, I stubbornly deny the injury to my leg and quicken my pace even more, picking up speed as I near the misty edge of the dank fog. I glance back and see the hazy contours of the three mechanoids' heads and shoulders, their soulless red eyes ringed with murky halos of scarlet.

With a growing sense of terror rising in my gut, I limp out into the open. There's no proper cover between here and the tree, which is nearly twenty excruciating meters away.

A nightmarish scream cuts through the air.

It's the terrifying, high-pitched, ramping-up wail of the R.A.M.s' weapons preparing to unleash hell. I've felt fear before. I've never admitted it to anyone, but every mission I've ever been sent on has frightened me. I learned to control it, and even harness it and use it to make me stronger. But what I'm feeling now is pure, undiluted, and utterly overwhelming. Even the warning tones of my injuries fade behind the sounds of my heart beating in my chest, my throat, and my ears. The mild afternoon breeze feels cold on my lips as each breath is strained through my clenched teeth, the desperate rasp of every inhale vocalized with mewling, involuntary whimpers.

I'm not afraid.

I'm absolutely scared to death.

My damaged leg is forgotten as I break into a scrambling, unwieldy sprint. The sound of the wailing guns begins to crackle with arcing electricity, and I know what comes next. I know that I've run out of time. I don't look back; what would the point of that be? I don't want the last thing I see to be those dead, red, glaring eyes. Tears of effort and dismay trail down my face as I grunt and stumble toward the tree.

It's so close . . . but I fear it's just not close enough.

The sound of blaring foghorns shocks the air as the robots' weapons open fire behind me. I scream as I dive toward the ground and roll as the paving beside me erupts into a storm of dust and stone shrapnel. The burst of gunfire cuts off, and, filled to bursting with terrified panic, I try to push myself up. When my left hand hits the ground, it sounds like I've slapped the paving with a wet sponge. I look down and see why.

My left hand is . . . gone.

Rational thought leaves me completely. The tattered, fleshy stump at the end of my arm simply doesn't make any sense. It can't be real, so I tell myself that it isn't as I scramble to my feet and desperately hobble to the tree. I collapse against the trunk, and the deafening foghorns blast again. My long, agonized scream is completely drowned out by the brutal sound of the R.A.M.s' guns as pulverized wood chips and dust fill the air and thick, leafy branches thud on the paving all around me. I'm convinced that my eyes must be playing tricks on me when the entire massive shadow cast by the wide canopy of the tree suddenly begins to creep along the ground.

A loud, slow creaking sound is soon followed by a jarring racket of snapping and splintering, and as I look up, I realize with horror that the large tree is tilting over. A meter above my head, the bark cracks, and then suddenly the trunk ruptures into a ragged line of fractures as the bulk of the tree begins toppling toward me. Scrambling and stumbling away from what's left of the trunk, I only barely avoid being crushed as two-thirds of the tree comes crashing down around me.

A ton of solid wood and leafy canopy hitting the ground sounds exactly like a giant wave breaking on a rocky shore, and I'm smothered in the outer edge of it. I shuffle on my elbows out from underneath the fallen tree. I'm completely exposed, and I can hear the thudding footsteps tromping closer. Dazed, I roll onto my back, and my defensive reflexes kick in as I raise my hand to shield my face. But no shade covers my eyes—instead, a steady trickle of blood splashes on my cheek as I stare at the empty space where my hand used to be. I feel sick. I lower my arm and see the towering robot come into view. It's joined by another, then a third, fourth, and fifth, all of them standing in a line like gigantic, green statues.

"INTRUDER DETECTED," booms the center robot. It raises its massive arm toward me, and the metal rails of its weapon fizz with blue sparks as its wailing death-scream screeches through the air.

So this is how it ends. I expected to feel some kind of emotion when I finally came face-to-face with the moment of my own death. Fear? Anger? Sorrow? Even rage would be appropriate. But what I'm feeling can really only be described as intensely . . . *annoyed.*

Suddenly every surface of everything around me lights up with spots of dazzling blue light. They're everywhere: on the ground, on the fallen tree, on my body, and all over the five huge mechanoids. They look like scattered, indigo-colored laser beams reflecting off a mirror ball. As the lights dance across the R.A.M.s, the one in the center starts to swing its massive arm from side to side like it's trying to swat a fly. The rest of the robots begin acting strangely, too. Their domed heads swivel and tilt in every direction as missiles extend and retract haphazardly over their shoulders. One mechanoid turns and clunks into its neighbor as another giant robot just stands there staring upward, its glowing red eyes pulsing as if hypnotized.

I don't know what's happening, but this may be my only chance to escape. I try to roll onto my knees so I can stand. The pain-suppressing properties of adrenaline are wearing thin as fresh warning tones sear through my mind and skewers of genuine agony begin stabbing up and down my left forearm. I feel dizzy. The loss of blood and the loud clanging in my head, mixed with the continuous screaming of the R.A.M.'s weapon, are taking a brutal toll. I'm weak and confused and disoriented. I feel so cold, but . . . my skin is also strangely warm at the same time.

I'm trying to push myself up off the ground when I notice the whining sound of the robot's gun is changing. It's getting deeper and louder as my skin gets hotter and hotter. My vision fades in and out of darkness as I struggle to stay conscious. The wail of the mechanoid's gun is engulfed inside a deafening roar, and I collapse onto my stomach as a scorching wind suddenly whips at my body. I fear that I've finally lost my mind. Either it's that or the gates of hell are opening up to receive me. I've never believed in it before, but . . . after all I've done, I wouldn't be surprised if one of the deepest, darkest pits in the bowels of damnation has been reserved especially for me.

I take a deep breath and try to shake off my ridiculous thoughts. My vision clears, and my eyes regain their focus on reality. There, less than nine meters away, I see the actual source of all this light and noise. A pure-black transport has landed in the courtyard. It's much smaller and sleeker than the Gryphon 400s. On the nose of it, where a set of landing lights should be, is a rotating array of sparkling lenses, casting beams of blue light in every direction. A door slides open on the side of the transport, and three or four people wearing black uniforms leap out and come running toward me. I struggle to keep my eyes open, but they feel like lead, and I'm fighting a losing battle.

Everything goes dark.

Someone grabs me underneath my arms. Two more sets of hands cradle my legs, and I'm lifted off the ground. There's shouting. I can't make out the words over the noise, but the intense feeling of annoyance washes over me again, and this time it's mixed with equal parts of worry and anger. I'm jostled as I'm carried and lifted. I'm laid down on a cool surface, straps are tightened across my torso, and there's a sting in my thigh. I feel a sudden burst of energy, and when I open my eyes, there are people in gold visors and black combat masks all around me.

The transport lifts off, and through the open door, I can see the ground moving away. One of the people flips up their visor and removes their face mask. It's a pretty young woman; she may even be younger than me. She motions to someone, and they pass her two microphone headsets. She quickly puts one on, slips the other onto my head, and speaks. Her voice sounds tinny through the earphones, but I can hear her very clearly. "Welcome aboard, Commander. I'm Caitlin, but everyone calls me 'Gazelle.' It looks like we got to you just in time. It's an honor to finally meet you face-to-face."

Commander? I'm no one's Commander; she must have mistaken me for someone else. I ignore her and turn toward the door, breathing deeply to clear my head, and as the transport turns, I can see the little blue dots of light still dancing over the mechanoids below.

A male voice pipes in through the earphones. "The electronic scrambler will lose effectiveness once we hit the fifty-meter mark. If those R.A.M.s start shooting, everybody hold on to something."

Someone grabs my left wrist and plunges the stump into biting coldness. I look down; the girl named Gazelle has stuck it in a container of pink gel. I inhale sharply as the warning tones and pain intensify for a fleeting moment . . . Then they're gone. She removes the container, pulls an aerosol can from a med bag, and sprays the nub at the end of my wrist with a thick coating of liquid bandage.

The transport swings around, and someone shouts through the headset, "Missiles incoming!" Out the door, I can see the heat-seekers climbing toward us as the aircraft veers wildly to the right. I notice the flickering blue dots of the electronic scrambler in the vapor trails of some of the missiles, and suddenly a few of them begin changing course, curving away in wildly different directions.

The transport drops through the air, and my stomach feels like it's floating. Explosions shake the fuselage, and the aircraft soon begins to climb again. "That was close," says a voice.

A few seconds later, I hear an announcement that immediately grabs my attention. "I have a visual on a Gryphon." I look over and see a man leaning out the opposite door of the transport, pressing the "Magnify" button in the side of his visor. "It appears to have initiated an emergency landing," he says, "but it seems to be in pretty good shape."

"Copy that; I'm bringing her around. Point me in the right direction," says the pilot.

"It touched down where Dome Two *used* to be," replies the man beside the door.

"What do you mean 'used to be'?" asks Gazelle as she peers out the open door.

"The dome is gone," says another voice. "I can't see anyone outside the Gryphon, but there might be survivors trapped inside."

"OK, I see it," says the pilot. "I'm gonna land as close as I can. Keep it quick, please, you guys. Those R.A.M.s are probably on their way."

Different voices join in a chorus of "Copy that," and I lean toward the door as the transport descends.

Below us, I see wide-sweeping staircases, paths, and gently curving ramps all connecting multiple levels between twenty or so buildings. There are sharp, angular, modern structures, just like in the courtyard, but among those there are also buildings with ancient Greek and Roman columns, a stylized take on a Japanese pagoda, a medieval-looking castle turret, and even a pyramid that resembles a contemporary

Mayan temple. Tall silver towers support the monorail track that winds unobtrusively throughout the sector; beneath it, the paths are lined with cherry-blossom trees, artistically shaped sand gardens, and flowing water features. It's all really quite beautiful, but as our transport roves overhead, the unmistakable focal point gapes toward the sky like a hole in the earth.

A huge, dark-gray circle spanning at least a 150 meters wide sits on a plateau directly in the center of everything, and there, with two-thirds of its fuselage lying inside that circle, is Otto's transport. Our aircraft descends, and as we get closer to the ground, I notice what look like human figures standing motionless on some of the paths connecting the buildings. No, they're not people. They're service Drones, frozen in place like someone flicked a switch and stopped time, just like the one we saw outside the Security Station. The collapsed dome and those inactive androids clearly mean the power is still out in this sector. Judging from recent robot experience, I'm going to say that's a very good thing, because as scattered throughout the sector as those service Drones are, I can't look anywhere without spotting one underneath a tree or standing beside a building.

Our transport turns 180 degrees and touches down on a slab of white stone beside the outer edge of the disc. It looks flat and dark and solid, but Otto's partially submerged transport tells me that the quantum grains must be nearly chest deep. There's a flurry of movement as black uniforms leap out the side doors and begin running toward Otto's transport. The girl stays by my side. She's smiling down at me, but that weird flood of angry, annoyed concern washes over me like before.

And this time, I realize where it's coming from. If I wasn't so messed up, I would've figured out why I was feeling these weird emotions sooner.

I look toward the cockpit and see him climbing out of the copilot's seat. Hunching under the low ceiling and dressed all in black, he makes his way toward me and kneels beside Gazelle. His ever-present combat mask and visor are hiding his face, as usual. In fact, when I think about it, I've only seen his eyes once in the entire two years that I've known him.

"She's pretty banged up, but I think she's gonna be OK," says Gazelle. "She lost her left hand."

He looks down at the stump and then raises his own hand. The metallic sheen on the fingers has been worn away by combat, but as far as cybernetic prosthetics are concerned, it suits him. I remember the mission in the jungles of Sudan when he lost his real arm—chopped off at the elbow by a warlord with a machete. I was the one saving his life that time, but, to this day, it boggles my mind that in the middle of all that chaos, he still managed to save that stupid friendship bracelet of his. Pulled it off his own severed limb like it was the most precious thing in the world. Call me a cynic, but a robotic arm just doesn't look quite as cool with a brightly colored braid of twine tied around the wrist. He rests his cold metal hand on my arm, and I can feel a warm glow of emotion emanating toward me.

"Hi, Zero," I whisper. "It's good to see you, too."

CHAPTER EIGHTEEN

A voice shouting in the earphones snaps me out of our little reunion. "Hello! Can anyone hear me?"

The rescue team has reached the downed transport, and a ripple of anger shudders through me as I hear Captain Delgado's muted voice reply from inside it. "Yes, I can hear you! We have multiple casualties, the cargo door is blocked, and the side hatch won't budge!"

I get up on one elbow and squint toward the transport. "My friend is in there," I rasp.

Zero puts a hand on my shoulder and gently pushes me back down, but I resist. "I need to see if she's OK."

Zero reaches up and jabs at a control panel on the roof, and a series of three holographic displays flicker on inside the cabin, each one showing a live feed being broadcast from the visors of the members of the rescue team. Each screen is labeled along the bottom with details about each team member. Their age, sex, pulse rate, adrenaline level, GPS coordinates, and code name.

On the display, I see the first-person view of the team member whose code name is "Jackdaw." He makes his way around to the right of the crippled transport, climbs up over it, and arrives at the badly dented hatch. "Mantis, what's it like in there?" he asks.

I quickly look at the screen labeled with the same code name. The writing says Mantis is a fifteen-year-old girl, and, through her visor, I see her placing her hands on the hull of the transport. Suddenly the picture starts to change, morphing into strange pulsating lines of rainbow colors that make little sense to me. They clearly mean something to Mantis, though, because she quickly and quietly begins whispering a tally of numbers. "The good news is there are twenty-three survivors," Mantis says in a soft, almost meek voice. "The bad news is nine of them are in critical condition."

"And the worst news?" asks Jackdaw.

"I can see ten bodies with no blood movement at all. They're dead. It's a mess in there, Jack."

The one she called "Jack" shouts at the side of the transport, "Get back from the door! I'm gonna cut through!" I'm wondering how he's going to do that without any tools when he grabs his index finger and twists it until the fingernail has been rotated right around to the opposite side of where it's supposed to be. He peels an unusually rubbery pad of skin from his fingertip, and underneath, instead of flesh and bone, there's a metal point tipped with a tiny, crystalline lens. He points his weird finger at the side of the transport, and suddenly there's a spot of intensely bright light. Red-hot molten metal begins bubbling and smoking at the edges of the semicircular line that he's carving around the damaged door latch. He stops cutting, folds the skin over the lens, twists his finger back the way it was, and pounds on the latch with the heel of his palm. The cut section drops into the transport, and he grips the edge of the hole and pulls. The hatch jolts open, but only a crack. He pulls again, but it doesn't budge. The hinges must be warped on the inside. He looks over his shoulder at a teammate standing at the ready just behind him. "Bulldog, I need a hand with this."

I watch through the visor feed as the eighteen-year-old girl with the code name "Bulldog" climbs up to the hatch. She reaches into the gap and wrenches open the door so forcefully it slams against the side of the transport with a loud, echoing thud. Bulldog is unbelievably strong.

"Who are you guys?" I ask Gazelle.

She smiles down at me and says, "We're the Saviors."

On Bulldog's visor feed the first person that comes into view is . . . Captain Delgado. His face is sweaty and bloody, but not nearly as bloody as I'd like it to be. Bulldog offers a hand; the Captain gladly takes it and begins climbing out of the open hatch. I'm staring intently at the visor feeds, hoping to see Otto's frizzy hair or big doe eyes and freckled nose, when the pilot suddenly shouts over his shoulder, "Here they come!"

The three holoscreens cut out and are replaced by a single, large one, and displayed on that screen, tromping down the wide staircase at the top of the sector, are the five hulking Remote Articulated Mechanoids. They're hundreds of meters away, but the rising streaks of smoke spreading in splayed lines from their shoulders are unmistakable. Five robots launching five missiles each means twenty-five high-explosive missiles are heading in this direction.

Zero signals to the pilot to take off, and then he extends three fingers and sweeps them into the side of his downturned fist. I know Zero's hand signals. He's just volunteered us to be a flying target.

Gazelle nods and immediately barks into her headset. "Evacuate, and sit safe down there. We'll be back after the fireworks."

On the screen, I watch everything on the ground speed away as the trails of the missiles begin curving up toward us. Zero quickly makes his way to the copilot seat and flicks a couple of switches in the roof of the cockpit. Two holoscreens pop up in front of his face with words written across them. One screen says, "SCRAMBLER ACTIVATED," and the other says, "MAIN GUN ONLINE, MISSILE LAUNCHER READY."

The transport veers sharply. I can see the little blue lights sparkling over the white of the missiles' vapor, and soon a dozen or so heat-seekers begin winding and darting out of control. Gazelle leaps at the wall and slams her fist against a large, red button. Two clamps holding a hinge-mounted rotary gun pop open, and she swings the cluster of barrels out the side door. As the transport comes around, Gazelle clutches the trigger, and the cabin is filled with light and the clinking spray of bullet casings as the rotary machine gun blazes to life, raining fire down toward the R.A.M.s.

Zero waves his fingers through the gun-control holoscreen in front of him, and a glowing line of sparks pours out of the top of the transport toward the robots.

On the ground, I can see dust being thrown high into the air as both streams of large-caliber-machine-gun fire cut thick swaths into the staircase. Two of the R.A.M.s are engulfed inside a cloud of pulverized stone, and yet a whole new set of fresh missiles puff out from inside the haze and spread into the air like the fanning tail of a peacock. The three mechanoids on the right quickly begin tromping sideways across the stairs, firing missiles from their shoulders as the other two bulky, green robots emerge from the dust on the left.

Zero stabs three fingers through the missile-control screen. A "Lock-on" signal flashes red, and as he pulls his hand out of the hologram, three dark lines suddenly streak away from our transport. The pilot gains altitude to put some distance between us and the more than twenty new heat-seekers speeding our way. Zero's missiles hit the staircase with a resounding explosion, and the two R.A.M.s disappear from view inside a massive plume of fire.

The blue beams of the scrambler dance through the smoky air. It seems to be working, as a dozen or so projectiles twirl and loop wildly. Even at this height and through the noise of the engines, I can hear the thuds of the errant missiles exploding on the ground below. But not all of them have been thrown off course. There are still maybe ten or twelve in the sky . . . and they're closing in fast.

Zero flicks another switch, and those familiar lines of red flares begin shooting out behind us. The pilot swings the transport around wildly, and my eyes are glued to the screen in front of me as heat-seekers dip and turn toward us. Explosions rock the air, and I hold on to the straps across my body as tightly as I can as the turbines throttle into full burn and the pilot nosedives the transport. The outside camera must be motion tracking the missiles, because the view on the display follows them no matter which way the aircraft is heading, and, right now, we're heading for the ground.

I can hear the pilot's rapid breathing hissing through my earphones. He's panicking, and it shows in the way he's flying as the transport pulls up barely ten meters from the paving below us, missing the top of a cherry tree by an arm's length. There are still missiles on our tail. Zero releases more flares as the pilot only just manages to veer out of the way of a silver tower and fly *underneath* a section of monorail track.

Plumes of fire erupt behind us, and there's a screeching metallic whine. I look out the side door to see the silver tower we so narrowly missed is now toppling in a burning wake of detonations . . . and it's bringing a large part of the monorail track right down with it.

The pilot swerves to avoid a huge falling slab of concrete and takes the transport dangerously low as we go hurtling along a wide-open promenade lined with cherry-blossom trees. Large chunks of the monorail track tumble and thud heavily behind us as we recklessly skim only a few meters above the path. We're so close to the ground that the transport barrels straight through an inactive service Drone, completely obliterating it into a flying jumble of silver limbs and orange fluid.

The pilot strains back on the control stick, the transport rises into the air, and as we go higher, something below catches my eye. Tiny, twinkling lights have illuminated the canopies of the cherry-blossom trees at the far end of the promenade. I watch as the next trees light up, then the next. Trees bordering both sides of the wide path are lighting up one after another, the gentle glow filtering through their petals, making each treetop look like a pink cloud in the fading afternoon sun.

For a fleeting moment, I feel almost . . . serene.

BOOM!

The jarring percussion and the shuddering fuselage snap me back to harsh reality as another missile hits the new spray of flares spitting out behind the transport. Two more explosions rock the aircraft as the pilot brings us around. Clinging to handholds in the roof, Gazelle glares, narrow eyed, at the display floating in the middle of the cabin and lets out a huge sigh of relief. Those heat-seekers don't give up easily, but it looks like somehow we survived them all.

As the transport slows and hovers high above the dark circle, Zero gives the pilot a thumbs-up, and I look out the door toward the staircase at the top of the sector. Those R.A.M.s are at least ten meters tall, so, even from way up here, I can clearly see two of them lying in a large, blackened crater of rubble. I can tell by the red pinpoints of light swiveling on their heads and their jerkily twitching limbs that they're still active, but one of them is missing a leg, and the other has been completely blown in half. It's a small victory, but we've still got the other three to deal with, and, to my horror . . . I can see them moving in the direction of Otto's transport.

There's a panicked line of people hurriedly filing away from the wreck and heading downhill toward the buildings. I strain my eyes out the side door and see a group of soldiers with their rifles helping some of the wounded. I spot Margaux and Percy propping up a limping Brent. I see the Professor tottering alongside the girl named Jennifer . . . but I don't see Otto.

I hold on to hope, trying to ignore the fact that some people down there are lying on the ground in a carefully arranged row off to the side of the transport. None of them are moving, no one is tending to them, and the only glances they receive as the survivors pass by are fleeting and solemn. I quickly scan the line, and my stomach seizes when I see a school uniform. I glare toward the body, and as our transport slowly descends, I breathe a sigh of relief. It isn't Otto; it's Jennifer's friend Amy. Otto is still alive and inside that transport . . . She just has to be, and any second now, she's gonna be climbing through that hatch.

Please be OK, Bettina.

As the pilot takes us down toward the plateau, Gazelle suddenly barks into her headset, "There are three, I repeat, three mechs approaching from the north. They'll be on top of you in a matter of minutes."

"The Gryphon came down hard," Jack replies. "We've still got some live ones inside the transport, wedged in pretty tight. Bulldog is working as fast as she can, and I'm trying to cut them out, but today's training session drained my battery dead. Can you give us any more time?"

"You need to hurry!" shouts Gazelle.

"We bloody well know that!" replies Bulldog.

"No, you don't understand!" bellows Gazelle. "Get out of there now! The dome!"

"What about the dome?" grunts Bulldog. "There is no sodding do—Oh my god."

Gazelle reaches up and jabs at the control panel, and the single display switches back to the three holoscreens showing the live visor feeds from the rescue team. Every screen shows a slightly different angle of exactly the same thing. A gigantic dark convex wall is rising from the far side of the massive circle, curving into the sky like a colossal black wave. It's growing bigger and reaching higher with every passing second, and I watch as it extends up and over, forming the crown of the dome, and then begins steadily curving directly down toward the crippled transport. I don't know what will happen when that wall comes down on that aircraft, but two-thirds of the transport is lying inside the boundary, and by the way the rescue team is suddenly scrambling, I'm guessing it's probably not going to be good. But what makes it a thousand times worse and fills me with gut-wrenching dread is the fact that . . . Otto is still inside.

The pilot tilts the nose of the transport, and we drop toward the plateau. He levels out just above the landing area and deftly touches down a few meters away from the edge of the massive circle. Bulldog and Mantis run toward the open side door, and Gazelle greets them with an angry glare as she bellows at their combat masks, "Where the hell is Jack?"

"He's still in there!" shouts Bulldog.

I look at the visor feeds. Two screens show Gazelle's infuriated expression as she angrily stares out the door, but on the third one I can see the caved-in side of the cargo hold inside the transport and Jackdaw's hands gripping a metal bar as he feverishly tries to lever a twisted piece of fuselage off the leg of that Dean kid. Dean is either dead or unconscious, because his eyes are closed and he isn't moving.

"Get the hell out of here!" Jack screams.

"No!" screeches a reply. My heart lifts. I'd know that mule-stubborn voice anywhere.

Jack turns, and through his visor feed I see her lying on her side with her arm shoulder deep in a gap between two buckled struts of framework. "I've almost got it!" she shrieks.

"Your life is not worth a damned computer slate!" barks Jack, but Otto seems to ignore him completely as she continues grunting and huffing with the most determined look I've ever seen on anyone's face in my life.

I look out the side door at the reforming dome. The huge, dark curve is descending directly over the wrecked transport. Otto is running out of time. I have to do something; I have to get her out of there. I pull at the straps across my stomach and chest, but they're difficult to unfasten with only one hand.

"Jack, you've got fifteen seconds at the most!" yells Gazelle.

"So do we," says the pilot. I look out the front windows and see the three lumbering mechanoids rounding the curve of the almost fully formed dome. They're closer than a hundred meters away and getting closer with every massive stride. Zero brings up the gun-control screen and stabs his fingers at it. The bass hum of the roof-mounted rotary machine gun vibrates through the cabin as a thick line of glowing orange streaks winds through the air, brutally pelting the R.A.M.s with a maelstrom of bullets.

Sparks burst across their huge, green bodies with every impact, but the furious gunfire isn't slowing them down at all. They just keep moving forward; the raging stream of bullets may as well be a stream of water, for all the good it's doing.

"Missiles! Fire the missiles!" yells the pilot.

Zero makes a sign with one hand, signaling, "No. Too close."

"Get out of that transport now!" Gazelle shouts into her headset. "Or we're leaving without you!"

The wall of the dome has closed in on every side of the wreck now, and as it touches down on top of the transport, its hull slowly begins to crumple like it's made of paper.

Through Jack's visor, I see him finally give up trying to free Dean as he throws the metal bar aside and lunges at Otto.

Bulldog and Mantis leap into the cabin, disrupting the visor feeds into a pixelated haze of flickering colors. I watch in horror as all of the R.A.M.s raise their weaponized arms toward us . . . and open fire.

The pilot throttles up the transport and lifts off, but we're only a couple of meters in the air when there's a huge burst of yellow fire and an almighty bang. We've been hit. Red lights flash, and warning alerts ring out from the cockpit as one of the turbines sheers away from the hull and tumbles onto the paving outside in a rolling fireball. The transport tips wildly, and Bulldog and Mantis are thrown out the side door as the aircraft flips completely upside down before hitting the ground with a brutal, crunching thud.

I hold on for all I'm worth as the inside of the transport becomes something akin to an industrial tumble dryer. Gazelle is tossed from wall to wall like a rag doll, and my hair is strewn wildly over my face and into my eyes, causing the gut-churning blur of light and colors and noise to be even more disorienting than it already was.

I don't know how, but I manage to reach out and grab Gazelle by the arm. I pull her toward me, and she digs her fingers under the strap across my chest. We desperately hold on to each other as the transport violently rolls over and over and over again. Gazelle is about the same size as me, but she's so much heavier than I ever would've expected. It feels like her legs are encased in metal armor, and each time the transport lands on its underside, they bash painfully against me.

Just when it seems this ride will never end, the fuselage suddenly slams to an abrupt stop. The transport is lying sideways with the door above me open to the sky. Gazelle drops away from me, scrambles to her knees, and calls toward the cockpit. "Commander Zero! Kestrel! Are you OK?" The pilot is slumped to the side and seems to be unconscious, but I hear a groan from Zero and see his visor and mask appear over the back of his seat. That groan was the most I've ever heard him say.

Through the dented, misshapen door above me, I see that thick, black smoke has begun rising from somewhere outside the aircraft. This thing could go up in flames or even explode. We need to get out. Gazelle looks pretty beaten up; there's a cut trickling blood down her forehead, and her eye is starting to swell, but I'm betting she's as eager to get out of here as I am when she ignores the latches on my body straps, pulls a knife from a sheath on her thigh, and slices right through them. The previously rounded hull of the transport has been beaten into a vaguely rectangular shape, and what used to be the side door nearest me now opens to the sandy surface of the ground. I drop beside Gazelle as Zero points, then motions, to the sky-facing exit.

Gazelle nods, then turns to me. "Get on my back, and hold on tight."

I frown at her, confused. I know that Zero ordered her to get me to safety, but Gazelle climbing out with me on her back is gonna take more time and effort than we can spare. Even with one hand, I'm sure it will be faster if I just do it myself. I'm about to argue my case when Gazelle shuffles backward into me, slings my arms around her neck . . . and jumps.

My head snaps back as we launch straight up through the open door and go sailing what must be at least five meters high into the air. I'm taken completely by surprise, and I immediately follow Gazelle's instructions and squeeze my arms and legs tightly around her. Gazelle and I fall back to earth together and land with a muted thud on the sand in the middle of a Japanese Zen garden. Suddenly it all makes sense. That's why her legs felt so strange. She has cybernetic prosthetics, too. All of Zero's team must have them. Who the hell are these guys? And why don't I know anything about them?

Without warning, Gazelle breaks into a run, and I gasp from the sudden acceleration. Now I know why she was given her code name. I thought I was fast, but she would easily leave me in the dust. Her speed is absolutely extraordinary. The wind rushes past my ears as the ground streaks by. "Running" is probably not the right word to describe how she moves: it's more like a series of long, lunging strides, but even with my weight on her back, we're traveling extraordinarily faster than anyone should be able to run; at a guess, we must be going well over sixty kilometers an hour. With a little sideways leap, Gazelle digs her boots into the sand and slides until she comes to a stop. In just a few seconds, she's taken me almost 150 meters from the transport.

I climb off her back and wearily sit on the soft sand. She gives me a little nod. A spray of sand puffs high into the air as she takes off back toward the wreck, the forceful thuds of her footsteps pounding the ground as she covers the distance in ten powerful strides. She leaps onto the side of the transport and clambers through the opening.

The first group of survivors has reached the bottom of the hill and is heading toward me. I look past them toward the hilltop and the huge, black crown of Dome Two, hoping with all my heart to see any sign of that headstrong, frizzy-haired, brave-to-the-point-of-crazy little computer geek, and to my absolute, almost disbelieving relief . . . I do. Running down the hill, with Brody at her side, is none other than the unstoppable Bettina Otto.

The ascending hillside stretches out before me up to the plateau, and there they are, leaping and weaving over the scars and divots that were gouged into the manicured landscaping by our transport's rocky descent. Jack, Mantis, and Bulldog are following close behind them, but my joy turns sour as I see the three R.A.M.s suddenly appear at the top of the incline. Their weapons aren't raised; they aren't walking down the slope. They're just standing there, looking down at the bedraggled line of soldiers and civilians as they flee.

Margaux, Brent, the Professor, Percy, and Jennifer are the first to reach the edge of the sand garden. Brent stumbles and collapses to the ground as Margaux crouches and mewls beside him. Professor Francis spots me, and his face brightens as he leaves the others where they are and hurries toward me. Out of breath but smiling, he kneels beside me.

"Miss Brogan, I'm very pleased to see that you're . . ." His voice trails away, and his expression drops as he sees my bandaged left wrist. "Your . . . hand," he says shakily.

I don't want to look at it or even be reminded of it. I move the stump out of sight behind my leg.

Professor Francis sits cross-legged on the sand beside me and whispers, "I'm so sorry."

"Me, too," I reply sadly. For the second time today, I feel like I might cry.

A group of soldiers helping some of their wounded comrades stumbles onto the edge of the sand garden. The able-bodied ones eye me suspiciously as they gently ease the injured onto the ground. I stare at them blankly, feeling too weak to even react, but angry energy suddenly surges through me again as Captain Delgado steps out from behind one of his troops. He slowly walks over to where the Professor and I are sitting, looks down at me, and shakes his head.

"Harder to kill than a cockroach," he growls.

"Yes, you are," I reply.

He lets out an amused snort and glances at the stump at the end of my wrist. "I hope that hurt like hell."

Professor Francis glares up at Captain Delgado. "You, sir, are, without a shadow of a doubt, the most scurrilous, reprehensible, despicable, murderous . . ." The Professor stops midinsult, springs to his feet, prods the Captain in the chest, and blurts, "You, sir, are a complete and utter . . . ARSE!"

Captain Delgado is equal parts amused and surprised. I have to admit, so am I. "Feel better, Professor?" he asks with a condescending smirk. The Professor's face is turning a peculiar shade of pink as the Captain turns and starts walking back toward the soldiers that have gathered in a small group at the far end of the garden.

The Professor quickly crouches down beside me again. "Miss Otto informed Mr. Blake and me of the message she received about the sanctuary beneath the pond. That is where we will go, and believe me when I say . . . Captain Arse will most certainly *not* be joining us."

I grin at the Professor, and he gives me a determined nod as Captain Delgado addresses his troops behind us.

"Everyone on your feet; there's no time to rest! Those big, green bastards aren't gonna wait around for us to catch our breath, so . . ."

The Captain's little speech is cut short as five wide-eyed soldiers suddenly raise their rifles in my direction. The Captain quickly raises his hands. "Whoa, hold on, men! Don't waste your ammo. She's clearly no longer a threat; she's as weak as a kitten, and . . ."

Professor Francis ducks to the side, and I shield my face with my arm as the soldiers open fire.

I splay across the sand as the soldiers keep shooting. I peek over the top of my arm, wondering what the hell is going on, and I can see them advancing toward me, but they're not firing *at* me. They're aiming *over* me.

I quickly turn my head and see exactly why.

On the other side of the promenade, climbing over the huge, crumbled sections of broken monorail track like silver-skinned, scarlet-masked spiders, are more than twenty service Drones.

I look to the left down the wide, curving promenade and see more of them emerging from in between buildings, stepping out from behind cherry-blossom trees, and climbing over the wreckage of a toppled monorail support tower. The Drones are walking slowly toward the sand garden like a gathering throng of sleepwalking zombies, and the soldiers are taking them out left and right. Bullet-riddled, orange-goop-leaking Drones are dropping and crumpling to the ground in every direction, but there are far too many, and the soldiers don't have nearly enough ammo to keep them all at bay. But that inevitable truth seems to be far from their minds as they keep firing, walking shoulder to shoulder in a line toward the crowd of silver androids. The soldiers very nearly tread right on top of me and the Professor as they walk around us.

I grab the Professor's arm and yell over the gunfire, "Get out of here!"

He clutches his hand over mine and shouts, "I refuse to leave you behind again!"

"Infinity!"

I turn and see Otto in the distance at the bottom of the hill, running and waving at me as Brody huffs and puffs alongside her.

Despite the army of Drones getting closer and closer behind me, I can't help smiling. But just as quickly as it came, my smile vanishes as I notice something very strange happening up on the plateau.

The R.A.M.s appear to be shrinking.

I squint my eyes at them, trying to make sense of what I'm seeing, when I suddenly realize what the mechanoids are actually doing. They're not shrinking . . . They're curling. As they double over, I can see their arms bowing out to the sides as parts of their armor shift and reposition. Their legs bend sharply at the knees and tuck into their torsos as their domed heads lean right down and touch the ground. The black rectangles with their glowing red eyes swivel to face forward, and the transformation is complete. Like giant armadillos, those three nine-meter-high robots have very quickly and very intentionally become three massive, heavy, green, people-crushing boulders.

They tip from the edge of the plateau, and even from here, I can hear the rumble getting louder and louder as the three giant, rolling spheres begin barreling down the hillside toward us. Soldiers are firing at Drones, and there's yelling and shrieking and pointing at the hill as people try to scramble out of the paths of the oncoming R.A.M.s.

I desperately wave at Otto to get out of the way. She looks over her shoulder at the approaching R.A.M.s and thankfully takes my advice as she swerves to her left and begins running toward the wide-open path of the promenade. Brody stays with her all the way, shoving Drones aside as they both sprint as fast as they can toward the line of cherry-blossom trees.

"Run, Professor!" I screech. "Get to the pond!"

He seems to ignore me completely as he jumps to his feet and tries to pull me up. Knowing that I need to move, too, if I want to survive, I accept his help and haul myself to my feet.

Through all the chaos, I look over at the transport; Zero is standing by the smoking wreck with the pilot slung over his shoulder. He motions to Gazelle and juts his arm toward me. Gazelle nods, breaks into a run, and, three seconds later, skids to a stop beside me and the Professor. Gazelle wrenches the Professor's hands from me and shoves him flat on his bottom in the sand.

"Sorry," she says, looking down at him. "But I have my orders." Facing me, Gazelle grabs my wrists, ducks down, and with a practiced pirouette, her head pops up in front of mine with my arms secured firmly around her neck. I don't even have time to protest as she lunges into a sprint, so I grip her waist with my legs and hold on tight as the wind rushes through my hair.

I look back over my shoulder and see two of the R.A.M.s hurtle down the bottom of the hill, one behind the other, and steamroller right through the sand garden. The able-bodied and wounded soldiers alike are scattering in all directions. Some troops are firing, and some are beating Drones aside using their empty guns as clubs, but some just aren't fast enough to avoid the R.A.M.s and disappear beneath the giant, armored boulders. I lose sight of the Professor and everyone else from the school group as the R.A.M.s smash through the garden and onto the promenade. They don't discriminate when it comes to who or what they mow down as cherry trees are bashed over and Drones are flattened into the ground.

Gazelle slides to a halt a safe distance from the horror that's unfolding in the garden, and I drop from her back. Suddenly there's a huge explosion, and both of us look back in the direction of the transport.

"Zero! Kestrel!" shouts Gazelle.

Fire and smoke seem to be spreading everywhere, and as I look her in the eyes, I can tell that we're both thinking the same thing. "Go," I whisper. "If they're still alive, get them the hell out of there."

She gives me a solemn nod, then turns and takes off at top speed back toward the fire. I scan the area for Otto and see her in the distance. She's still running, and Brody is still beside her as they make their way across the wide path of the promenade. Jack, Bulldog, and Mantis, having successfully avoided two of the R.A.M.s' deadly descents, are swerving toward the garden as the third R.A.M. rolls at blinding speed down the bottom of the hill. Suddenly it slams into a stone statue and bounces high in the air, catapulting over the three members of Zero's team. It slams to the ground, and deflected from its original course, it barrels across the smooth paving of the path and plows straight into a silver support tower.

All three R.A.M.s have come to a stop, and I watch in horror as all three begin to unfold. Soon their weapons will begin destroying everything in sight, and there's absolutely nothing I can do. I feel so weak and utterly useless, but I can't just stand here. I know I can't help the Professor or Zero and his team, not when I'm this weak and broken, but I have to do *something*. I have to find a place to hide, a place to rest and get my strength back. All I can do is hope that they survive. I decide to make my way back along the promenade and meet up with Otto and Brody when they reach the other side. If there truly is a sanctuary beneath that pond, then it makes sense that we all try and get there. Forget fighting; this has become a matter of survival. I look up at the line of buildings and think I can see the top of something that resembles a Japanese pagoda. The man who sent the message said the hatch is by the pond, and the pond is somewhere near a pagoda. With my mind made up—and hoping I'm heading in the right direction—I start limping, keeping my eye on the upturned edge of the building over the top of the monorail track.

As I go, I look down toward the survivors. Most of the Drones have been either shot down or crushed, their artificial corpses littering the ground all around the sand garden. But the danger is far from over as the three fully unfolded mechanoids begin swaying their weapons and opening fire. Missiles launch and curve from their shoulders at people running toward the line of buildings. The air is filled with the haunting scream of rail guns, cries of pain and terror, the brutal thuds of detonations, and the rolling rumble of disintegrating walls—but through all of that noise, I hear something else.

It's the grinding squeal of metal straining to breaking point. Up ahead, I see the silver tower that the R.A.M. crashed into lean and then topple. A tangle of cables and wires and concrete comes thundering to the ground as another whole section of monorail track collapses onto the promenade. In a crumbling chain reaction, the next section falls, then the next, then the next, and as I look above my head, I'm suddenly filled with a terrifying realization. The track splits off in a three-way junction, and that junction crosses over the promenade . . . directly above me.

I try to break into a run, but my injured leg won't support me; I stumble and fall as the next section of track loudly slams and breaks apart on the ground. A wave of dust engulfs me. I cough and sputter; I can't see anything. I hear the next section hit the promenade, and then the next. I panic and stagger to my feet as huge chunks of concrete pound the top of my head and my arms and my body, every impact like a blow from a hammer. The breaking, grating, roaring all around me is deafening, terrifying, overwhelming.

I can't hear my own thoughts.

I can't see a way out.

My fear becomes dread.

And that dread becomes my desperate, bloodcurdling scream.

CHAPTER NINETEEN

"AAAAAAAAAAAH!"

Heaving at the air, I wake up lying in pitch-black darkness. I thrash my head from side to side, seeing absolutely nothing as my heart drums in my chest. I can feel a mattress beneath my body. I sit bolt upright and jerk my arms, but my wrists are bound and jolt to a stop. A door flies open, and I wince with pain in the bright flood of light.

All I can see is the silhouette of a man in the doorway. He's tall and wide—so big, he fills the entire frame. He speaks, and when I hear his voice, a rising panic courses through every inch of my body and grips my very soul.

"It's alright, sweetheart. You're safe now . . . Jonah is here."

ABOUT THE AUTHOR

S. Harrison is from New Zealand, where he often indulges in his love of watching superhero movies and art house films. He frequently escapes to some of the many islands of the South Pacific to focus on his writing. He is the author of *Infinity Lost* and *Infinity Rises*, books one and two in the Infinity Trilogy.